"We'll be seeing quite a bit of each other for the next little while," Slade told Hayley

In your dreams, she said silently.

"I've got to tell you something that will frighten you. But try not to panic, because it isn't nearly as bad as it sounds."

He hesitated, eyeing her, then continued. "We have your son. He was picked up just a few minutes ago, while he was out riding his bike."

The world froze around her, and her heart froze inside her chest.

"Max is perfectly safe," he added quickly. "I swear he is. And I promise he'll stay that way as long as you cooperate."

She almost couldn't hear him over the thunder in her head. She'd never felt such terror before, and when she tried to speak, the words caught in her throat.

"I want my son back," she whispered fiercely. "Right now... Get him back for me!"

"I can't. Not—"

"What kind of man are you?" Her entire body trembling, she pushed herself out of her chair and stood glaring across the desk at him. "You're trying to help a convicted felon plan a prison break? You let his men kidnap an innocent child? Are you a monster?"

Dear Reader,

Have you ever found yourself falling madly and passionately in love with a man you knew was totally wrong for you?

That's what happens to Hayley Morgan in *Falling for the Enemy*. New Orleans lawyer Slade Reeves has a certain *je ne sais quoi* that starts her heart beating faster the moment she gazes into the deep blue depths of his eyes.

But once she discovers the truth about him, feeling even a twinge of attraction is out of the question.

Still, have you ever tried to stop yourself from falling in love? Especially when you're constantly thrown together with the man in question? If so, you know it would be easier to stop a tide from turning.

Hayley and Slade's story is truly one of love against all odds. I hope you enjoy reading about how they manage to find happiness together.

Warmest wishes,

Dawn Stewardson

P.S. I invite you to visit my web site at www.superauthors.com

FALLING FOR THE ENEMY
Dawn Stewardson

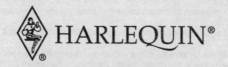

HARLEQUIN®

TORONTO • NEW YORK • LONDON
AMSTERDAM • PARIS • SYDNEY • HAMBURG
STOCKHOLM • ATHENS • TOKYO • MILAN • MADRID
PRAGUE • WARSAW • BUDAPEST • AUCKLAND

ISBN 0-373-70861-0

FALLING FOR THE ENEMY

Visit us at www.romance.net

Printed in U.S.A.

To John, always.

ACKNOWLEDGMENT

With special thanks to fellow authors Anne Logan
and Linda Kay West for generously sharing their
knowledge of rural Louisiana

PROLOGUE

MR. WILLIAM FITZGERALD, "Billy Fitz" to his friends, rated one of the "executive suites" at the Poquette Correctional Center in Plaquemines Parish, Louisiana. That meant he didn't have to share. He was the sole occupant of a six-by-eight-foot windowless cell.

Despite his privileged status, every morning when Billy woke up he wished he were anywhere else on earth.

The cell walls were cinder-block gray. The sink and seatless toilet, which occupied one open corner, white. At least, he assumed it was the color they'd been before becoming permanently stained putrid yellowish brown.

The bed was concrete, the mattress a slab of foam. The cell door had a slot where a battered food tray was pushed through at mealtimes.

Inmates from the executive suites didn't eat in the communal dining room. Prisons like Poquette were filled with meltdowns who figured they could make their reputation by killing someone with a big name. That meant living like a hermit was conducive to Billy's continued good health.

Five days a week, he was allowed to take a

shower while a guard stood outside the shower room. Mondays, Wednesdays and Fridays he had an hour in a fenced-off section of the exercise yard. Weather permitting.

He'd been in Poquette for three weeks that seemed like three years. The place was intolerable. Worse for him than for most because of what he was accustomed to—an old mansion in the elegant Garden District of New Orleans, where dinner was served on bone china in his enormous dining room.

In his cell at Poquette, he ate off a dented tin plate with a plastic spoon. No forks allowed.

Billy was fifty-eight years old, and came from long-lived Irish stock. With any luck, he'd see the far side of ninety. He had no intention, though, of seeing it from a prison cell. In fact, he had no intention of seeing fifty-nine from behind bars.

After being convicted on three separate counts of manslaughter, he didn't have a hope in hell of his appeal going anywhere. But there were other ways for him to regain his freedom, and as head of New Orleans' "Irish Mafia," he had both the money and connections to get what he wanted.

All he needed was a little help from his friends. And from Dr. Hayley Morgan.

Until now, he'd never had much use for psychologists. But he certainly had use for her. She was the key. The weak link. A woman with something valuable to lose.

One way or another, she was going to get him out of here. "We're better off to take things slowly and try the most obvious route first," his lawyer had advised. "With any luck, she'll cooperate. Then there'll be one less problem to worry about."

Billy didn't like the prospect of taking things slowly. It meant spending longer in this rat hole. But although he'd never admit it to a living soul, if he'd listened to Sloan Reeves more often he might not have ended up in prison. So he'd listen now and see where it got him.

If Dr. Morgan didn't cooperate, then they'd use their ace in the hole. Her son.

CHAPTER ONE

HAYLEY MORGAN HEARD Max coming long before he reached the kitchen—hardly surprising when he was doing his imitation of a jet plane breaking the sound barrier.

Satchmo switched his tail a couple of times, then scurried into the sheltered space beside the fridge. He was a smart-enough cat to avoid the paths of small boys in motion.

A second later, Max zoomed into the room, skidded to a stop in front of Hayley and focused on the shorts she was wearing.

"Not goin' to jail today, huh, Mom?" he said with a grin.

She couldn't help smiling. He thought his "goin' to jail" line was hilarious and used it regularly— which was all right as long as he said it to people who knew what her job was. Last fall, though, he'd told his first-grade teacher that his mom was goin' to jail and for weeks the woman had believed Hayley was incarcerated.

"It's Saturday," she reminded him, turning to get the orange juice from the fridge. With school over for the summer, he was finding that the days blended into one another.

As she poured the juice, he sat contemplating the three different cereal boxes she'd put on the table. "Jimmy's mom got him some real good cereal," he informed her at last. "It tastes like candy."

She set the glass of juice in front of him. "Well, call me old-fashioned, but—"

"You're old-fashioned," he interrupted, bursting into a fit of giggles.

"Which is why," she said, ruffling his hair, "I think cereal should taste like cereal."

Once he'd decided on corn flakes and began shaking some into his bowl, she wandered over to the window.

This early in the morning a cool mist still hung in the air, but by noon the city would be ninety degrees and steamy, reminding residents and tourists alike that much of it was built on reclaimed swampland and lay below sea level.

Yet even in the scorching heat of the summer New Orleans had an appeal she'd never felt anywhere else.

Three years ago, when she and Max had moved here from Pennsylvania, the Crescent City had quickly lulled them with a gentle sense of belonging. And even though New Orleans was far from the safest city for raising a child, this section of the Bayou St. John District had a secure, friendly atmosphere. Children played outside without their parents feeling they had to be watching every minute. And there were enough stay-at-home moms right on their own street that Hayley never had a problem finding someone to look after Max.

She glanced at him, making sure he wasn't mushing his cereal instead of eating it, then looked out again, this time focusing on the way the sunshine filtered through the branches of the ancient oak in their side yard, backlighting the gray beards of Spanish moss that hung from its branches and dappling the street below in light and shadow.

That century-old tree, perfect for a boy to climb, was part of the reason she'd bought this place. That and the house itself, of course. A scaled-down version of a French-Colonial plantation house, with cypress woodwork and beautiful columned room dividers, it had murmured it was the one for her the first time she'd walked into it.

She turned from the window and, for a few moments, stood watching Max eat his corn flakes. Fair-haired and blue-eyed, he looked like his father. Personality-wise, though, he was completely different—as happy and easygoing a child as any parent could hope for.

He was the single good thing that had come from her failed marriage. She loved him more than she sometimes believed possible.

MONDAY MORNING, SLOAN REEVES was a man on a mission. He had to convince Dr. Hayley Morgan not to make the wrong decision. And he had to do it without telling her even one of the reasons why.

After striding across the lobby of the Orleans Parish state government building, he walked into a waiting elevator and pushed the button for the sixth floor. That was where the regional office of the

State Department of Corrections was located, and where he'd find Dr. Morgan, regional director of Mental Health Services for the three state prisons closest to New Orleans—among them, the Poquette Correctional Center.

As the elevator carried him upward, he reviewed what he'd learned about the woman. Her job was partly administrative, partly clinical. She normally spent two days a week in her office and three in the field, giving the prisons' staff psychologists whatever support or direction they needed. And she'd been known to personally evaluate prisoners who, for one reason or another, warranted special attention.

She was thirty-four, which struck him as young for someone in her position of authority. But having worked closely with the previous regional director, she'd been the logical choice to replace him when he'd retired five months ago.

The elevator reached six; the doors opened. Sloan stepped off, straightened his tie and started down the hallway to his right, not even glancing in the receptionist's direction.

He knew exactly where Hayley Morgan's office was located and that, as of late Friday afternoon, she'd had no appointments until ten-thirty this morning. In his line of work, it was wise to check those sorts of things out beforehand and leave as little as possible to chance.

When he stopped outside her doorway, she didn't immediately realize he was there. She was engrossed in an open file on her desk, so he took the opportunity to appraise her, surprised his source hadn't mentioned how good-looking she was.

Her plainly styled blue suit was the only plain thing about her. She had smooth, lightly tanned skin, full sensuous lips and hair the color of rich cognac. It was long enough that she was wearing it pulled back into some sort of knot—an attempt, he suspected, to make herself appear both older and less attractive. Being young and good-looking would *not* be an advantage to a woman working with incarcerated men.

But if she didn't want them to notice her, she needed to do a whole lot more than just pull back her hair. And even the effectiveness of that was spoiled by the tendrils escaping the knot. If they could speak, he knew that right this minute they'd be whispering "Sexy" to him.

His visual inspection completed, he said, "Excuse me? Dr. Morgan?"

She glanced up then, her large brown eyes meeting his gaze. They were decidedly sexy, as well.

"Yes?" Hayley said, doing a three-second once-over of the man with the lazy Louisiana drawl.

In his mid-to-late thirties, he was well dressed, tall and attractive, with dark hair, an easy smile and eyes a deeper blue than Gulf waters on a sunny day. As he stepped into her office, she couldn't help thinking they were the kind of eyes women found themselves drowning in if they weren't careful. And sometimes, she suspected, even if they were.

"I'm Sloan Reeves," he said, extending his hand

across the desk. "May I have a few minutes of your time?"

His hand was warm, his handshake firm but not crushing, and she was absurdly aware of his touch.

When that realization skittered through her mind, she told herself it meant nothing. Her hormones were simply reminding her she was a woman.

That wasn't something she exactly forgot, but between her job and Max, she seldom had time to notice men.

Checking her desk clock, she said, "I have a meeting in twenty minutes, but if you don't need any longer than that…"

"I doubt I'll need even that." He took a business card from his wallet and handed it to her as he sat down.

Sloan Reeves, Attorney at Law, it informed her.

"I'll come straight to the point," he said. "I'm here on behalf of William Fitzgerald."

"Oh?" And what, she wondered, did the newest executive-suite prisoner at Poquette want from her?

When she asked, Reeves flashed her another easy smile, then said, "Well, first off, I hope you won't take any personal offense, but he isn't happy he was sent to Poquette."

"Really."

She did her best to conceal her amusement. Fitzgerald should be grateful one of the smaller prisons had had space available for an inmate requiring protective custody. Otherwise he'd have ended up in Angola.

"What, specifically, does he find wrong with Po-quette?"

Sloan Reeves leaned forward in his chair. "He's being kept in virtual isolation."

Reeves had to be aware of the reason for that, but since he was apparently waiting for an explanation, she said, "Surely he realizes it's for his own safety. The prison staff can't assign…celebrity prisoners, for lack of a better term, to the general-population cell blocks."

"No, of course not. But we both know isolation is brutal. That it almost always leads to deterioration—mental or physical or both."

"You're right, it's far from ideal. I'm afraid there's no magic solution, though. Even if Mr. Fitzgerald qualified for a minimum-security facility, we don't have country-club prisons in Louisiana. He'd be segregated no matter where he was."

Reeves nodded slowly. "I guess the basic problem is that he's a very sociable man. He finds the lack of human interaction difficult to cope with."

Rather than respond to that, Hayley merely gazed across her desk at Reeves. He was falling short on his promise to come straight to the point, because he couldn't possibly be suggesting that Fitzgerald wanted to be moved into general pop. Not unless he'd like to end up graveyard dead, courtesy of some inmate with a shiv.

After a few seconds, she checked her clock again, assuming Reeves would get the message. He did.

"Here's the bottom line. Mr. Fitzgerald wants to be transferred to a prison with a rehabilitation program. Being in one of them would give him both human contact and something to occupy his mind. And inmates in a rehab program shouldn't be a threat to his safety.''

"I see," she said again, still trying to figure out the game. Reeves wasn't being straight with her, she knew that much.

The prison psychologists did a psych assessment on each new prisoner, and she'd read her copy of the one on Fitzgerald. He didn't believe he belonged locked up with a bunch of low-lifes. So even if he did want more human contact, she wasn't buying that he'd want it with his fellow prisoners.

As for a rehab program to occupy his mind, it would more likely bore him to death. Besides which, he wasn't an even remotely viable candidate. The programs were strictly for prisoners nearing the end of their sentences, and she'd bet Reeves knew that. All of which added up to a hidden agenda of some sort.

Since she had a meeting to get to, she didn't probe Fitzgerald's motivations further but simply said, "You know, I rarely have anything to do with transfers. The person you should talk to is Warden Armstrong, at Poquette.''

"Yes—in fact I have an appointment with him this afternoon to file the request forms. But I wanted to let you know I'll be asking him to have *you* do the mental-health assessment.''

"Oh?" That news made her more concerned about what the hidden agenda might be.

"It *is* something you occasionally do, isn't it?

Some of the mandatory evaluations? In this case, give your opinion about whether a transfer might benefit Mr. Fitzgerald?''

She nodded. Obviously Reeves had done his homework, and it had included checking into her job description. The realization unsettled her. She didn't like having a stranger poke around for information about her.

''The staff psychologists at Poquette are more than competent,'' she told him. ''Why would you request that I assess Mr. Fitzgerald?''

''Because of your position. Because your signature on a transfer recommendation would carry more weight.''

''You're assuming I'd recommend it.''

''I'm hoping you will.''

''Well… Look, there's a fundamental problem here. The rehab programs are solely for prisoners close to their release dates, and with Mr. Fitzgerald not meeting that criterion…''

Reeves gave her a slow shrug. ''I think I'll be able to get around that by emphasizing his need for more human contact. You see, the way I look at it, there's an Eighth Amendment violation involved.''

''A what?''

''I feel that his being kept in isolation constitutes cruel and unusual punishment.''

Hayley almost groaned. Sloan Reeves had things figured upside down and inside out.

''After you've talked with Mr. Fitzgerald,'' he said, ''I'm sure you'll recommend a change of scenery to improve his mental health. If you don't... Well, I'm sure you will.'' With that, he leaned back and smiled at her once more.

It was a warm smile that reached his eyes and turned them an impossibly deeper shade of blue, a smile that under different circumstances she knew she'd have found both engaging and appealing. Under these circumstances, she found it neither.

Maybe her overdeveloped sense of fair play was coming to the fore, but she didn't want to be involved in any attempt to manipulate the system.

And there was something else, of course. She was annoyed as hell at the way this man had walked in unannounced and told her what she was going to recommend.

THERE WASN'T a law firm's name on Sloan Reeves's business card, and several times during her ten-thirty meeting Hayley caught herself wondering whether he had a one-man practice. And whether he specialized in representing clients who were unquestionably guilty. The minute she got back to her office she phoned Peggy Fournier, a detective with the New Orleans Police Department, to find out.

A couple of years ago, Hayley had helped Peggy talk a jumper in off a ledge. During the aftermath, the two women had established that they were both single mothers with young boys. In no time, their sons were buddies, while she and Peggy became the sort of friends who were always trading favors.

If Peggy didn't recognize Sloan Reeves's name, locating someone who did wouldn't take much effort. Since he was representing Billy Fitzgerald, three-quarters of the cops in the city could probably fill her in about him.

When Peggy proved to be on duty but not in the station, Hayley left a message. Then she grabbed a salad from the cafeteria downstairs, took it back to her office and spent the next hour reviewing every last detail in the Poquette psychologist's intake assessment of Billy Fitzgerald.

He and his wife had divorced long ago, and she'd given him custody of their sole child, a son named Brendan, without an argument. According to Billy, at least. The wife's version of the story would probably be very different. Something like, if she hadn't given Billy custody he would have killed her.

His psychological profile, as Hayley had noted during her first reading of it, showed him to be a charming, highly intelligent, extremely manipulative psychopath.

Deciding she had as accurate a read on him as she could get from the file, she set it aside and started in on some backed-up paperwork while she waited for Peggy to return her call. It was close to four o'clock before she did.

"Sloan Reeves?" Peggy said when Hayley asked about him. "Good-looking? Smart enough to win on *Jeopardy?* Sets the ladies' hearts aflutter with his smile? That Sloan Reeves?"

"Well, he hardly set my heart aflutter."

Even as Hayley said the words, an imaginary voice reminded her that the touch of his hand on hers had sent a definite tingle through her. But that was before she'd known anything about him.

"It was more like he set my teeth on edge," she told Peggy. "But yes, I'd say we're talking about the same man."

"Where did you meet him?"

"He walked into my office this morning and informed me that Billy Fitzgerald didn't like his accommodations."

Peggy laughed. "Well, Reeves should know. He's the only lawyer in town with a client list of one. Or I guess it's two at this point. We might have put Billy away, but so far it hasn't stopped him from running the Irish Mafia. He's just doing it through his son, Brendan, now. And I guess that means Reeves is acting as legal adviser to both of them."

"Wait a minute, are you serious?"

"Hey, the world changes and the wise guys keep up. They've got legal advisers, financial advisers, certified public accountants—you name it."

"Reeves works exclusively for Billy Fitzgerald?"

"I take it he didn't mention this."

"No, he didn't." And the fact that he was so close to Fitzgerald's organized crime family—more like part of it, really, than close—made Hayley uneasier still about his visit.

She did her best to force the uneasiness away as Peggy continued.

"What a waste, huh? If he really did set your teeth on edge, you're one of the few women in the city with that reaction. He'd probably get voted Most Eligible Bachelor in New Orleans if he wasn't in bed with the bad guys. What exactly did he want?''

The question made Hayley hesitate. Sometimes, in her job, there was a fine line between what was confidential and what wasn't. Still, she trusted Peggy, and she definitely wanted her take on the situation.

"He came to tell me," she finally said, "that Fitzgerald is looking to transfer to a different prison."

"Why?"

"The story is so that he can be in a rehab program."

"What? They aren't for lifers, are they?"

"No, and it gets better. Fitzgerald supposedly wants into one for the social contact."

"Oh, puh-leeze. Like he *wants* to socialize with his fellow cons?"

Hayley almost smiled. Thus far, Peggy's take was exactly the same as her own.

"I'm sure the real story is that, for some reason or other, Fitzgerald's determined to get out of Poquette."

"And you don't know why?"

"No, but they had to come up with *some* explanation for a transfer request."

"They came up with a pretty lame one. I wonder what Fitzgerald's problem with the place is."

"Me, too. But *my* problem is that they're involving me in their game. A psychologist has to evaluate a prisoner's mental health when he requests a transfer, and—"

"It's going to be you, right?"

"Exactly. And Reeves is expecting me to recommend the transfer."

"He said that?"

"He didn't come right out and say 'expecting,' but there was no missing the message."

Peggy was silent for a few seconds, then she said, "Does that have you worried?"

"I...yes, a little, now that you tell me he has friends in low places. But the final decision is the warden's, not mine. I only give him my recommendation. And neither Fitzgerald nor Reeves will know what it is. So if the request's turned down, which I'm certain it will be, they'll have no way of knowing whether I—"

"Oh, Hayley, don't play naive with me. Guys like those two can find out anything they want and you know it."

"Maybe. But this isn't the first time I've faced a little...subtle intimidation, shall we call it?"

"I could think of better terms," Peggy muttered.

"Well, when you work with criminals this kind of thing comes with the territory, right? As a cop, you must see that all the time. I've never let anyone frighten me out of doing my job yet, however, and I'd like to keep it that way."

"Yes, of course. I only... Well, this is a red-tape sort of thing, anyway, isn't it. It'll be forever before you have to assess Fitzgerald, so we can talk about it the next time we get together. But..."

"But what?" Hayley said uneasily.

"Look, I don't think Reeves would get physical himself. Billy Fitz, on the other hand, has more than enough boys who play as rough as it takes. So if the good counselor pays you another visit I want you to call me."

Once Hayley had promised that if Reeves showed up again Peggy would be the first to know, they chatted about their sons for a few minutes before hanging up.

It wasn't ten seconds later that the phone rang again.

"Dr. Morgan," Hayley said, answering it.

"Dr. Morgan, it's Warden Armstrong at Poquette."

"Yes, Warden?" A dryness settled in her throat. She had absolutely no doubt what he was calling about.

"You'll be here in the morning, won't you?"

"Yes. Tuesday's my regular day."

"Good, because Billy Fitzgerald's filed an application for a transfer and he's asked that you do the psych assessment. I want to give him a quick decision, so I'd like you to work the evaluation into your schedule tomorrow."

CHAPTER TWO

HAYLEY HADN'T SLEPT WELL. Monsters wearing
Sloan Reeves's handsomely chiseled face had
chased her through a series of nightmares, making
it a relief when morning stole into her bedroom.

The first thing she did when she got up was
phone Poquette and arrange to have Billy brought
to the psych area at nine o'clock sharp. She might
not know why Armstrong wanted to make a quick
decision, but her job was to cooperate with him.

Naturally, Max picked this morning to dawdle.
He usually ignored Satchmo's game of always being on the wrong side of the door, but today he let
the cat out and in three times before reluctantly sitting down at the table. Then he played a seemingly
endless round of eenie-meenie before he decided
which cereal he'd have.

Finally, she managed to get him to finish his
breakfast and collect what he wanted for his day at
the sitter's.

After walking him and his pint-size two-wheeler
the few houses down the street to Anne Kelly's,
she headed back to her car.

Despite Max's delaying tactics she made it to the
highway by 8:00 a.m. Once she started down the

peninsula toward Poquette she was able to drive on automatic pilot.

The surrounding terrain was flat and wet—not completely barren but close to it—so the area wasn't highly populated. That made for little traffic on the road, which gave her a chance to think through how she felt about this situation Sloan Reeves had dragged her into.

Peggy had been right in saying that prisons dealt with most requests from inmates at a snail's pace. Armstrong's asking for an immediate evaluation was highly unusual, and Hayley couldn't help but wonder what leverage Reeves had used.

Regardless of how he'd done it, she was annoyed that he had Armstrong jumping through hoops. She didn't like the idea of any prisoner, or his lawyer, having the power to force a warden into giving preferential treatment.

Force.

As the word repeated itself in her mind, she realized she shouldn't assume Armstrong was jumping through hoops at all. She'd had enough contact with him to know that, like most wardens, he was hardly the type of man who'd let himself be intimidated.

Of course, bribery was always a possibility, although she seriously doubted Armstrong could be bought. In fact, she could readily imagine him throwing Reeves out on his ear if he tried either intimidation or bribery. So why this big rush?

Quite possibly, she'd never know. Armstrong wasn't obliged to give her any explanations. When it came to things at Poquette, he was in complete charge. Which, in this case, was definitely a good thing.

As Peggy had said, if Reeves or Fitzgerald wanted to find out what Hayley recommended, they could. So it was just as well they were aware that the ultimate decision on a transfer wasn't hers. Because, at least based on what she knew to this point, there was no way she could recommend one. Not with a clear conscience.

When she turned her attention back to her driving she was nearing the tall bridge that lay partway between Port Sulphur and Buras. The structure always struck her as spooky, although she wasn't quite sure why.

Possibly it was the weirdness of there being freshwater on one side and saltwater on the other. Or maybe there was just too little land and too much ocean along this stretch.

Whatever, she was always glad to leave the bridge behind and drive the remaining few miles to the gravel road leading from the highway to the prison.

A couple of minutes later she could see it in the distance, a tired-looking big brick quadrangle in the middle of nowhere. Surrounded by a heavy link fence topped with razor ribbon, it always struck her as utterly depressing—the sight of it frequently reminding her she could have specialized in other areas of psychology.

But with a mother who taught criminology at Penn State and a father who was a district attorney, her interest in the correctional treatment of psycho-pathology was hardly surprising.

And even though the vast majority of prisoners were damaged beyond repair, there were enough she *could* help to make her work rewarding. In fact, one of her most treasured possessions was a little box containing cards and letters from ex-cons who'd made it on the outside.

Reaching her destination, she stopped at the concrete post in front of the gate and pressed the button.

"Yes?" a guard asked through the speaker.

"Dr. Hayley Morgan."

The gate slowly swung open. She drove through, parked and headed for the staff entrance—where she stepped reluctantly from the cheery daylight into the dim interior of the prison.

After signing in, she passed through the metal detector and started down the hall. At the end of it, a correctional officer unlocked the heavy door and let her into another world. One in which an eerie sense of pent-up danger hung in the air like static before an electrical storm.

In contrast to the Orleans Parish state government building, with Muzak whispering in the elevators and sunlight streaming through the windows on every floor, Poquette was stark and harsh—the epitome of uninviting.

It felt…*hollow* was a good word. The clicking of her heels on the stone floor echoed far too loudly. And even though sounds from the cell blocks didn't actually reach the admin wing, she couldn't keep from imagining steel doors clanging and voices calling out from behind bars.

At Records she picked up Billy Fitzgerald's file, then proceeded to the psych area. She barely reached her little Tuesdays office before nine o'clock. Minutes later, as prearranged, a C.O. delivered Billy Fitzgerald.

He was a few inches taller than she was, five foot nine or ten, and somewhat overweight, although not sloppily so. His eyes were blue, his thinning hair mostly gray, with just enough traces of red to tell her that was its original color.

In media shots she'd seen of him he'd been a dapper and confident-looking man. Not surprisingly, he was far less imposing in drab, prison-issue cotton. His bearing, however, said he was a man used to issuing orders and having them followed.

The C.O. caught Hayley's glance and said, "I'll be right outside if you need me."

After nodding to him, she looked at Fitzgerald again. "I'm Dr. Morgan, Mr. Fitzgerald."

"Billy," he said, giving her a smile. "Call me Billy."

She returned his smile and gestured for him to sit, thinking that even though he'd lived in the Garden District before he landed in Poquette it wasn't where his roots lay.

He spoke with a slight accent that was almost Brooklynese, almost movie gangster—typical of the Irish Channel part of New Orleans, where, generations earlier, a rough, tough collection of Irish immigrants had settled.

As he sat down across the desk from her, she opened his folder. The top document was a photocopy of his request for a transfer.

"Wishes to enter a rehabilitation program" was all that was typed as the Reason for Request.

She flipped through the routine incarceration documents until she located the original of the intake evaluation she'd studied yesterday.

"I have your initial psychological assessment records here," she told him. "You've been at Poquette so briefly I don't think we need to spend time going over the same things again. Why don't we just talk about why you want a transfer."

"Sloan Reeves spoke to you about that, didn't he?" Fitzgerald's tone was carefully nonconfrontational. He sounded like a man simply seeking information, nothing more.

"Yes, he came by my office yesterday. There was one question I didn't think to ask him though. Is there any particular prison you'd prefer to be transferred to?"

"Not really. Any one with a rehab program would be fine."

"I see." It had occurred to her that there might be some way he could arrange for special treatment at a specific prison, but his answer shot down that theory.

"Why don't you tell me, in your own words," she suggested, "the reasons you'd like to be in one of the programs."

He nodded, the picture of cooperation, then proceeded to recite from the same script Reeves had used. He had a problem with the isolation; he wanted more human interaction; he needed something to occupy his mind.

Fitzgerald's explanation was pat and polished. Hayley didn't buy it from him any more than she'd bought it from Reeves.

She'd spent years in classrooms studying human nature, followed by more years in the real world doing the same. And she was absolutely certain Fitzgerald had no more desire to get into a rehab program than she did.

He obviously figured he had something to gain from a transfer, but the longer they talked, the more apparent it became that he wasn't going to tell her what it was. Finally, she concluded the interview and opened the door to tell the correctional officer they were finished.

"Thank you," Fitzgerald said when he rose to leave.

He gave her another of his charming smiles and extended his hand with an uncertainty she doubted was real.

"I'm not up on prison etiquette yet, Dr. Morgan, but on the outside..."

She reached over and shook hands with him, guessing that his was damp because he was far more anxious than he'd let on.

After the C.O. escorted him out and their footsteps had faded into silence, she sat staring at the blank evaluation form in front of her for a few minutes. Then she picked up her pen and began to write.

Once she was done, she tucked the form into her briefcase. Then, after gathering up the file on Fitzgerald, she returned it to Records and headed for Armstrong's office.

The instant she arrived, his assistant buzzed the warden and ushered her in.

"Dr. Morgan." Armstrong half rose behind his desk and gestured for her to sit. He was a large, beefy man with a ruddy complexion that made her assume he liked his bourbon.

"I understand you arranged to see Fitzgerald first thing."

"Yes. I've just come from the interview."

"And what are you recommending?"

She handed him the form. He skimmed what she'd written, then jotted down something on a different form, scrawled his signature and looked at her once more.

"That's it," he said. "Mr. Fitzgerald stays where he is."

"May I ask a question?" Hayley said before he had a chance to dismiss her.

"Sure."

"Why did you want to get this done so quickly?"

He shrugged. "Fitzgerald's like a lot of executive-suite prisoners. They're used to wielding power on the outside, and they come in here expecting to do the same. I like to give them a dose of reality as fast as I can."

"Ah."

"Anything else?"

When she shook her head, he picked up the two forms and escorted her out of the office.

His assistant looked up expectantly as the door opened.

Armstrong handed him the papers, saying, "Make sure Fitzgerald's advised of my decision."

SLOAN REEVES ANSWERED his phone on the first ring. It was the call he'd been waiting for.

"She recommended against a transfer," Armstrong's assistant said quietly. "And the warden's turned down the application."

Sloan swore under his breath. "Thanks for letting me know."

"No problem."

Right. Few people had a problem dispensing information if enough money changed hands.

Hanging up, he slowly shook his head. Why the hell couldn't she have just gone along with them? Done what he'd asked and said a change of scenery would benefit Billy's mental health?

It wouldn't have made Armstrong approve the application. They'd known he wouldn't do that. But if Hayley Morgan had simply said what they'd wanted her to, she'd have given them the perfect ammunition to go straight to the governor's office and make a case there about getting Billy out of Poquette on the cruel-and-unusual-punishment angle. Since this was an election year and the governor counted on the support, or at least the non-interference, of the Irish Mafia, Billy would have been on his way to another prison in no time.

Now, though… Sloan knew only too well what Billy would say now.

It would take a while to arrange everything, probably till the start of next week, but he'd want the wheels set in motion as soon as possible.

Sloan glanced at his watch, aware that he had to talk to Billy just as soon as he could. Maybe he could convince him to try another tack. But if he couldn't…

If the man was determined to proceed with plan B, with or without Sloan's help, then Sloan's only option would be to stay closely involved. Give Billy suggestions and hope to hell he took them. Otherwise, things could get awfully bad. For Morgan and for her son.

"DON'T FORGET THE RULES," Mrs. Kelly reminded Max from behind the screen door.

"I won't," he told her.

She was nice, 'cept that every Monday she always talked about the rules. He'd told his mom he didn't like that, but she said Mrs. Kelly was just afraid he'd forgotten them over the weekend.

He never did, though. So she didn't have to keep tellin' him over and over. And she always had the same look his mom did, the look that warned if he broke them he'd be in big, big trouble.

"Only ride on the sidewalk," she said. "And don't go off the block."

"I know. I'm just goin' to see if any kids are out playin'."

Pushing off, wobbling a little until he got going,

he headed toward the end of the street, watching real good while he passed the house where King lived. Sometimes he was out on the porch, and Jimmy's mom said that dog was born to chase bikes.

He was born to chase cats, too.

His own mom said that Satchmo probably only had about three of his nine lives left 'cuz of King.

"Yes!" he whispered as he reached the far side of the yard. Now he was into what he and Jimmy called "the safe zone." There were no more big dogs for the rest of the block.

But there were no kids out playing, either. Disappointed, Max stopped in front of the last house, wishing that Jimmy and his family hadn't gone on their car trip. The summer wasn't half as much fun when your best friend was away.

But Mom had circled on the calendar when he'd be back, and Max was marking off the days, so he knew Jimmy would be home soon. Then—

"Max? Max Morgan?"

Startled, he looked toward the curb. The man who'd called his name was in a car with another man. He didn't think he'd ever seen either of them before.

Never talk to strangers. That was one of the serious rules.

"You are Max, aren't you?"

He nodded. That wasn't talking.

"Good, because your mother asked us to pick you up for her. But when we went to Mrs. Kelly's and she told us you were out riding your bike, we didn't know if we'd be able to find you.''

Max looked back the way he'd come, surprised they'd had enough time to talk to Mrs. Kelly.

The man who wasn't driving got out and opened the back door. "Hop in. I'll put your bike in the trunk."

"I can't," Max said, feeling kinda scared.

The men hadn't said the secret word, and if Mom wanted him to go with them she'd have told them it. She always said he should never go anywhere with anyone he didn't know unless they told him the secret word.

"Max, it's okay. Your mom's getting off work early and she wants to take you someplace straight from her office. We're not supposed to tell you where 'cuz it's a surprise, but it's a place you really like."

He scratched his arm, thinking it might be the zoo. That was his favorite place, and the white alligators were his favorite things to see.

"Come on," the man who'd gotten out of the car said with a smile.

Maybe they just forgot. "You have to say the secret word first," he told them. "I can't go unless you do."

The man standing outside looked at the one driving. "Uh…Max," he said. "We didn't want to frighten you by telling you this, but your mom fell on some stairs and hurt her leg. She's okay," he added quickly. "But she had to go to a hospital and get checked over, so I guess in all the excitement she just wasn't thinking about the secret word.

"She wanted us to drive you to the hospital, though. 'Cuz she's going to take you out for dinner after she's done there. And it's really okay to come with us. We're cops."

"Detectives," the other one said. "That's why we aren't wearing uniforms."

He didn't want to cry, but his eyes started to sting and tears began rolling down his cheeks. What if his mom was hurt worse than they were telling him?

"Come on, Max. When we get to the hospital you'll see for yourself that she's just fine."

SLOAN STOOD in the lobby of the Orleans Parish state government building, waiting for O'Rourke's call and assuring himself that nothing could have gone wrong.

Watching the sitter's house for a few days last week had told them Max Morgan was a child of habit. Every day right after lunch he hit the street on his bike. So it was merely a matter of picking him up without anyone noticing.

But what if something *had* gone wrong? Despite the air-conditioning, that possibility was enough to start him sweating.

Both O'Rourke and Sammy were family men, though. And he'd suggested that Billy choose them for the job because he'd figured neither would ever harm a six-year-old. Just as he was reminding himself of that, his cell phone rang.

"Sloan Reeves," he answered.

"Got him," O'Rourke said. "No problems."

"And he's okay?"

"Yeah. Fine. But he ain't a happy camper."

Sloan exhaled slowly, not wanting to even think about how frightened the boy must be. "Do your best to reassure him, huh? And tell him his mom's going to phone him soon."

"Sure."

He just hoped that Hayley Morgan was in her office. Otherwise, soon might not be possible. "You're being careful not to use your real names?"

"Yeah, of course. Sammy's 'Tom' and I'm 'Dick.' Like the Smothers Brothers. How're we gonna forget that?"

He hadn't figured either O'Rourke or Sammy was old enough to remember the sixties folk-song duo. He barely was himself. But since they did, it should help them keep from slipping up.

Once they'd finished their conversation, Sloan headed for the elevators. He waited until a car arrived, then stepped in and pressed the button for six, wishing to hell this hadn't played out the way it had.

But there'd simply been no talking to Billy Fitz. He wasn't a patient man and he wanted out of prison yesterday. So after Morgan had recommended against a transfer...

The elevator slowed, nearing the sixth floor. As the doors opened, Sloan squared his shoulders.

The last thing he wanted to do was tell Hayley Morgan her son had been kidnapped. When you worked for Billy, though, you followed orders. Otherwise, you ended up floating in Lake Pontchartrain.

He strode down the hall, reminding himself his work had its rewards. But this session sure wouldn't be one of them.

When he reached Hayley's office she was sitting behind her desk again, every bit as appealing as she'd been the first time he'd seen her. He barely had time to think that a woman in her line of work just shouldn't look the way she did before she glanced through the doorway and met his gaze—making him wish, once more, that he didn't have to do this.

Without taking her dark eyes from him, she slowly sat back in her chair. She obviously wasn't pleased to see him, even without knowing why he'd come.

"I have to talk to you," he told her.

Hayley glanced at her desk clock, wishing she had a legitimate reason for telling Sloan Reeves she had no time to talk. She didn't like him. Didn't like what he stood for.

And she particularly didn't like the fact that she was so aware of his animal magnetism.

Just looking at him did funny things to her, which made her very uncomfortable. She couldn't recall her brain and her body ever being completely out of sync before, and the sense that they were when it came to him was most disconcerting.

"It's urgent," he said. "And personal," he added, stepping into the office.

When he closed her door, isolating the two of them from her co-workers, her sense of discomfort grew.

"I prefer that open," she told him.

"As I said, this is personal." Leaving the door shut, he sat down in the visitor's chair.

Her anxiety level began edging higher, even though there was no logical reason it should. Her brain was in charge, not her body. And being alone with him didn't represent any actual danger.

Lord, how many times had she been alone in interview rooms with prisoners? Too many to remember. So being in her own office with Sloan Reeves, attorney at law, shouldn't faze her in the slightest.

The problem, she decided, was simply that he was Billy Fitzgerald's lawyer. She could certainly live without some lawyer to the mob walking into her office—on two consecutive Mondays yet—and taking charge.

Leaning forward in his chair, he said, "Billy was disappointed you didn't support his transfer request."

She let that pass, although it struck her as strange that he was still working at intimidating her after the fact.

"You see, applying for it was part of an escape plan. He intended to make a break while he was being transported from Poquette."

For a moment she was so stunned she couldn't speak. Then she said, "And you were helping him try to get the transfer? Mr. Reeves, does the word *disbarred* mean anything to you?''

Never mind disbarred, he'd probably go to prison. Sloan Reeves was nothing but a criminal in lawyer's clothing.

But why in the world had he confided in her? He must realize she'd tell Warden Armstrong. Along with a few other people.

''Just hear me out,'' he said. ''Unfortunately, when you deep-sixed that transfer—''

''Look, I don't want to hear you out.'' Her opinion of Sloan Reeves, not high to begin with, sank lower each time he opened his mouth. ''In fact, I don't want to listen to anything more at all. I'd like you to leave.'' She had better things to do than waste another minute with him.

''Not until I'm finished. Trust me, you need to hear the rest.''

She didn't trust him any more than she respected him, but something in his expression made her decide against calling Security.

''All right,'' she said, slowly sitting back in her chair. ''What's the rest?''

''Billy wants you to help him. As you know, breaking out from inside Poquette is practically impossible. He'd likely end up dead if he tried it.''

''He wants me to help him escape.'' She could scarcely believe that was what Reeves was saying, even though it clearly was.

''Yes. We had a solid plan, but you screwed it up. So he wants you to help figure out some other way of getting him on the outside.''

"Are you insane? Why on earth would I?"

When he didn't reply, she just sat watching him. If he seriously thought she'd—

"Hayley...is it okay if I call you that?"

She nodded. For all she cared he could call her Lady Godiva—just as long as he finished what he was obviously determined to say and left.

"Good. And please call me Sloan, because we'll be seeing quite a bit of each other for the next little while."

In your dreams, she said silently. She intended to blow the whistle as soon as he left.

"I've got to tell you something that will frighten you. But try not to panic, because it isn't nearly as bad as it sounds."

He hesitated, eyeing her, then continued. "A couple of Billy's men have your son. They picked him up just a few minutes ago, while he was out riding his bike."

The world froze around her and her heart froze inside her chest.

"Max is perfectly safe," he added quickly. "I swear he is. And I promise he'll stay that way as long as you cooperate."

She almost couldn't hear his words over the thunder in her head. A couple of Billy Fitzgerald's men had Max! She'd never felt such utter terror before, and when she tried to speak the words caught in her throat.

"Look...I can't tell you how sorry I am this has happened," Sloan said. "But—"

"I want my son back," she whispered fiercely. "Right now."

"I know."

"Then get him back for me!"

"I can't. Not—"

"What kind of man are you!" Her entire body trembling, she pushed herself out of her chair and stood glaring across the desk at him. "You're trying to help Fitzgerald plan a prison break? You let his men kidnap an innocent child? Are you a monster?"

He shook his head. "I don't 'let' either Billy or the people who work for him do anything. Sometimes he tells me what he's thinking about and asks my opinion. But even then my advice doesn't always carry much weight with him.

"Your son's going to be fine, though. I'll ensure you get him back safely. I just can't do it until Billy gives the okay. And that won't be until he gets what he wants."

"Oh, God," she murmured, choking back a sob.

"Hayley, all you have to do is help him out. And as long as he can count on your silence, no harm will come to either you or Max."

She ordered herself to calm down. As frantic as she felt, it was essential she think straight.

All she had to do was help Billy out. Enter into a conspiracy to help a convicted felon escape from prison. Betray the trust the State of Louisiana had placed in her. Knowing that if anyone ever learned what she'd done, the career that meant so much to her would be over.

Her career would be over? How about she'd end up in prison herself if she got caught? After all, she'd be breaking a hundred different laws.

But what would happen to her didn't matter. All that mattered was what would happen to Max. And if by agreeing to go along with this...

"No one will ever know you played any part," Sloan said. "I guarantee that. However it gets set up, Billy will arrange things so it doesn't look like an insider was involved."

She took a slow, deep breath. Helping with a prison break wasn't something she'd ever in a million years have thought she'd consider. But right this minute that was exactly what she was doing. Because if she didn't agree...

"Just help him out and you'll get Max back safe and sound," Sloan was saying. "That's the deal he's offering you, and even his enemies admit he's a man of his word."

Was that true? Was it something she could believe, something to give herself a ray of hope? If she did conspire with the devil, would it really save her son? Or would they simply kill both Max and her in the end anyway?

Was William Fitzgerald actually a man of his word or not? Think. What was the likelihood?

Most psychopaths were consummate liars, yet that didn't mean they were compulsive liars. And she'd run across a few who'd actually taken pride in keeping their word. They'd just been careful not to give it very often.

Staring down at her desk, telling herself she

wasn't going to cry, she tried to stop her fears from tumbling all over one another. She simply couldn't fall apart.

"Hayley," Sloan said, "I tried my darnedest to convince Billy that taking Max was a bad idea. But when I couldn't, I volunteered to act as go-between. You'll be better off dealing with me than with some of the others he might have chosen."

"I see." She took a deep breath, still not looking up. Before she met Sloan's gaze again, she had to recover enough control to keep from telling him that she'd like to see him hung by his thumbs and flayed. If he was the go-between, angering him would be a very bad move.

What would be a good move, though? Calling the police the minute he left? Or the FBI?

No. How could she do that when Max's life was at stake? How could she do anything other than what Fitzgerald wanted?

For the moment, at least until she pulled herself back from the edge of hysteria, the only smart thing to do was say she'd try to help. Then, when she was thinking more rationally, she could figure out if there was any other realistic course of action. One that wouldn't end up with her and Max dead. In the meantime, she had to see if she could make what was happening less traumatic for him.

Desperately wishing she had more bargaining power than she did, she focused on her visitor once more.

When Hayley finally looked at Sloan again, her

eyes were filled with foreboding. And pure, unadulterated hatred.

Even though it was exactly what he'd been expecting, it made him feel hollow inside. There were aspects of his job he downright loathed.

"All right," she murmured. "I'll do what I can."

"Good." He breathed a sigh of relief, even though he'd been certain she'd agree. "The men who have Max, who'll be looking after him, have kids of their own," he offered. "He'll be just fine with them. But would you like to talk to him? Assure yourself that he really is all right?"

"Of course I would!"

"Then we'll call him. I want you to phone your sitter first, though. So she doesn't start worrying. And before you do, we've got to agree on a story. One that'll explains why Max will be gone from home for a while."

"A while," she repeated. "How long is a while? How long is this going to take?"

"That'll depend. The sooner Billy's out, the sooner—"

"But there's no guarantee he *will* get out, no guarantee I'll be able to help him."

Her voice was shaky, as if she were hanging on to her self-control by nothing more than her fingernails. Sloan tried to ignore the pang of sympathy he felt.

"Even if it turns out I can help, it won't happen overnight. And I can't go indefinitely without seeing Max. At the very least, I want to spend a couple of hours with him every evening."

"Billy'd never agree to that."

"Dammit, the man's sitting in a prison cell and he wants me to help get him out of it. He wants me to risk my job. Maybe risk my life, depending on what happens. And I might do that. But I don't want Max suffering any more trauma than he has to. And being separated from his mother for any length of time... Sloan, you just have to make Fitzgerald understand I won't try to help him unless I get to see my son. That simply isn't negotiable."

He knew she was bluffing. Now that she'd said she'd go along with them, she'd do whatever she had to. And if that included not seeing Max for the duration, she'd accept it.

She was right about nothing happening overnight, though. It could be weeks, possibly months, before they managed to spring Billy. And hell, it wasn't hard to imagine how tough having no contact would be on both her and the boy.

He tried telling himself that was just the way kidnappings worked, but it didn't do any good. He might have to help Billy but he didn't have to like what the man was doing. And if he could make this nightmare easier for Hayley and her son to get through, why shouldn't he?

If he couldn't, at least he'd feel better knowing that he'd tried. "All right," he said at last. "I'll speak to Billy and see what I can do."

CHAPTER THREE

STILL SHAKEN TO THE CORE, Hayley dialed Anne Kelly's number, not at all sure she'd get through the conversation without breaking down.

But she had to. If Anne realized something terrible had happened to Max, she might call the cops. And if that happened, Lord only knew what would become of him.

As Anne's phone began to ring, Hayley looked across her desk at Sloan, thinking she'd never despised a man more. And that included every single murderer and rapist she'd encountered in the course of her work.

Almost without exception, they'd had everything going against them from birth, whereas Sloan Reeves had everything anyone could ask for—brains, looks, an easy manner and a good education. So how could he be warped enough to be part of Billy Fitzgerald's sordid scheme?

"Hello?" Anne answered.

She took a deep breath, then said, "Hi, it's Hayley."

"Oh, hi."

"Anne, I did something so absentminded I just can't believe it. I forgot to tell you I asked a couple of friends to pick up Max from your place this afternoon.''

"Well, that's all right, you're telling me now. He's out riding his bike but—''

"No, what I mean is my friends already got him. They saw him down the block so they didn't bother going to your house. Max is here with me now, and it wasn't until they walked into my office that I realized I'd forgotten to call you.

"I guess things have just been in such a turmoil that I wasn't thinking straight. You see, my custody agreement gives Max's father the right to have him for part of the summer. And...well, it's a long involved story, but the bottom line is that his father phoned late last night and I'm putting Max on a plane to Pittsburgh at four o'clock. So he'll be away for a while. Exactly how long's still kind of up in the air. But as soon as we decide when he'll be coming home I'll let you know.''

"Hayley? Your ex isn't trying to get custody, is he?'' Anne asked, her voice filled with concern.

"No, no, it's nothing like that. What happened is his parents suddenly announced they were coming to visit him. And they wanted to see their grandson. So there's no real problem, it's just that everything happened awfully fast.''

"Oh. Okay. Well, tell Max I hope he has a good time.''

"I will. And thanks. Bye.'' She hung up, then looked at Sloan.

"Good,'' he said. "That was perfect.''

"Now, let me talk to my son,'' she demanded.

He nodded, dug a cell phone from his pocket and punched in a number.

She watched him, unable to keep from thinking that something awful had happened and he was going to hear about it right now.

"It's Sloan," he said when someone answered. "Put the boy on. His mother's waiting to talk to him."

After listening for a few seconds, he passed her the phone. Her hands were shaking so badly she almost dropped it.

"Max'll be a minute or two," he said. "He was watching TV in another room."

She exhaled slowly. He was all right, then.

He's all right so far, a voice inside her head whispered.

"Don't ask him any questions about where he is or the men he's with," Sloan warned her.

A moment later, Max's reedy little voice said, "Mommy?"

Her eyes filled with tears. "Yes, I'm here, darling."

"Is your leg okay?"

Her leg? Oh, Lord, what did they tell him? "My leg's fine, Max. Did someone say something was wrong with it?"

"Uh-huh. The policemen you sent to get me. I said I couldn't go with them 'cuz they didn't know the secret word. But they said you forgot to tell them 'cuz you fell and hurt your leg. And they were gonna take me to the hospital. But then they said it would be better to come here and wait for you. So when are you comin' to get me?"

"Well...I can't come just yet. But you're okay? The...policemen are being nice to you?"

"I guess. They gave me ice cream. Chocolate. And one of them said he'll play catch with me after. But I want to go home. So when are you gonna come?"

She closed her eyes against more tears. "Darling, I'm going to come just as soon as I can. But I have something very important to do and—"

"More important than me?"

"No," she said, wiping her eyes. "No, nothing's more important than you. But it's something I just have to do. So I really need you to stay where you are for a little while."

"With the policemen?"

"Yes."

"For how long?"

"Well...at least until tomorrow."

There was a silence. Then, his voice quavering, Max said, "You mean sleep here? Without you?"

"Yes."

"But I don't want to. Why can't I stay at Mrs. Kelly's?"

"Because she's going out tonight."

"But I don't have my jammies," he whined. "And Satchmo won't have me to sleep with."

"Max...darling, I know it's scary to stay in a strange place, but you've done it before, remember? When I went to that conference a few months ago? And you stayed with Peggy and Pace?"

"Yeah," he admitted slowly. "But that was different."

"Well, it was kind of different but kind of the same. And I need you to be brave and do this for me. Okay?"

There was another silence before he said unhappily, "I guess."

"Good. And I'll phone you again just as soon as I can."

"In the morning?"

She looked at Sloan, blinking back tears, and said, "Can I call him in the morning?"

"I'll have them phone you at home. Early. Before you leave for work."

Leave for work. It suddenly struck her that they expected her to carry on as if everything were normal. But she'd have to, of course, if she was going to help Billy Fitzgerald. The question was, would she be able to function even seminormally?

"Max?" she managed to say. "The policemen will let you phone me in the morning, okay?"

"And then you'll come get me?"

"As soon as I can, darling. I love you. Bye."

"Bye, Mommy."

Her heart feeling as though it were in a vice, she handed the phone back to Sloan.

"He's fine?" he asked.

"Fine? He's a six-year-old child. He's in a strange place with two men he doesn't know and he isn't sure when his mother's coming to get him. How fine do you think he can be?"

Sloan raked his fingers through his dark hair.

"I've arranged to visit Billy first thing in the morning."

So he could give a play-by-play account of today's events, she thought bitterly.

"I'll do my level best to convince him to let you see your son," he added.

But he hadn't been able to convince Fitzgerald not to kidnap Max in the first place! If he'd actually tried to.

He pushed back his chair and rose. "Tuesday's your regular day at Poquette, right?"

She nodded, knowing he didn't really have to ask.

"Then I'll stop by the psych area after I've seen Billy. Let you know where things stand. Oh, and I probably don't have to warn you to keep quiet about what's happening, but I'm mentioning it because of your detective friend."

Lord, they even knew who her friends were!

"I'm sure it'll be tempting to ask her for advice, but don't. Being a cop, she's liable to steer you wrong. Or, worse yet, take the matter into her own hands. And if Billy learns you've been talking out of turn…well, I'm sure you know how this would end up if you made him unhappy."

With a brief nod, Sloan opened her door, stepped out into the corridor and disappeared. That left her staring at the blank wall in the hallway. And thinking that if he was lying to her about trying to convince Billy, or if his level best wasn't good enough, she might never see Max again.

Doing her damnedest not to cry, she tried to decide which she hated more—the fact that Sloan Reeves represented her only potential source of help, or the man himself.

HAYLEY DIDN'T SLEEP a wink all night, and seven-thirty the next morning found her sitting at the kitchen table—numb with fear that the kidnappers hadn't called yet because something had gone wrong. Because her son was dead.

Fiercely, she told herself that couldn't be. Billy Fitzgerald needed Max alive to make her cooperate, so his men would be taking good care of him. For the time being, at any rate. Until Billy Fitz got what he wanted. But after that...

Even though she'd already cried a river of tears, fresh ones started spilling over. She didn't even try to stop them until Satchmo began winding himself around her ankles, loudly reminding her she'd forgotten to feed him.

She pushed herself up and poured some dry food into his bowl, then went back to waiting for the phone to ring, focusing her thoughts on having to help Fitzgerald.

The prospect ran counter to every principle she'd been raised believing in. And to her professional integrity, as well. But as important as her work was to her, Max was her world. If she didn't go along with Fitzgerald, if she went to the authorities, instead, would they be able to find her son and get him back alive?

She doubted the odds on that were very high. Far more likely, they'd barely start working on the case before Billy's boys would learn what she'd done. And then...

Wiping her eyes, she turned her thoughts to her other option. She'd promised Sloan Reeves she'd do what she could to help. But if she actually did that, would Billy live up to his side of the bargain?

Sloan had assured her he would. "All you have to do is help him out," he'd said. "And even his enemies admit he's a man of his word."

The problem was that she didn't know whether she could believe Sloan any more than she could believe Fitzgerald. So even though Sloan had told her to not to say a word about what was happening, she had to find out if she could trust Billy. And since she didn't have any friends who were members of the New Orleans organized crime establishment, the obvious person to ask was Peggy. Regardless of what Sloan had said.

It would have to wait, though. She couldn't call from home when Billy's people might have her phone bugged.

Glancing over at it, she wondered whether she should take it apart and have a look. Just as she was deciding that was a good idea, it rang.

She jumped a foot, then rose so quickly her chair toppled behind her. After racing the few steps to the counter, she picked up and said hello.

"Hi, Mommy," Max said.

"Hi, Max." She closed her eyes and offered up a tiny prayer of thanks. Then, reminding herself that if he could tell she was worried it would only upset him, she said, "How are you doing?"

"Okay."

"Are the...men being nice to you?"

"The policemen?"

So they were going to continue that ruse. "Yes, the policemen."

"Their names are Tom and Dick."

"Oh." And if there was a third one, she knew his name would be Harry.

But their not telling him their real names was a good sign. If they had, it might mean they figured it didn't matter—because they knew he was going to end up dead.

That thought sent a shiver through her. Doing her best to ignore it, she said, "And do you like them all right? Now that you've gotten to know them better?"

Please say yes, she added silently. *Please don't tell me they're mean, or that you're scared of them.*

"Uh-huh. You know what?"

"What, darling?"

"They got me that good cereal Jimmy's mom buys. The one that tastes like candy. 'Member I told you?"

"Yes, I remember." And she didn't care if they fed him pure sugar for breakfast, just as long as they didn't harm him.

"So are you comin' to get me this morning?"

The question made her feel as if someone had reached inside her chest and was pulling out her heart.

"No, I can't come this morning, darling. This is a workday."

"Then after work?"

"Well, I'll try. I'll try my very best, but I can't promise yet."

Lord, somehow she had to make him understand what was going on. But she didn't want to even attempt explaining until after Sloan had talked to Fitzgerald this morning. Until after she knew if there was even a chance he'd go along with her demand.

"Tom said you might not be able to come for a while," Max told her. "'Cuz if your leg was still sore you'd have to go to the doctor. But if you're goin' to work it's not sore, right?"

"Well…actually, Tom's right. I might have to get it looked at. And that just might keep me from coming as soon as I'd like to. But…Max, I'll be there as soon as I can. And in the meantime, you be a good boy today, huh? And do what the policemen tell you."

"And you'll come after work? If you can?"

"Yes, darling. But don't be too disappointed if I can't."

"But I want you to," he insisted, his voice quavering.

"I know, Max. And…honey, I've got to say bye now. I love you, darling."

"If you love me then you should come."

"As soon as I can," she told him once more, blinking back tears this time. "Bye, darling." Difficult as it was, she made herself click off then, before her emotions completely wasted her.

After taking a few deep breaths, in a futile effort

to make herself feel better, she grabbed her car keys and headed out. The burger place she and Max usually went to had a pay phone; she'd stop there and call Peggy.

Getting into her car, she tried to figure out exactly how she should explain why she was asking her question. It would be tricky, because Detective Peggy Fournier was no dummy. And since she knew about Sloan's initial visit, she'd be suspicious as hell.

There had to be a way of sounding casual, though, and she spent the drive trying to come up with one.

At the restaurant, she parked and hurried inside, ignoring the people catching breakfast on their way to work and making her way straight to the phone. She wasn't sure what shift Peggy was on, but with any luck she'd be able to reach her either at home or at the Ninth Division.

She tried the home number first, her pulse leaping when her friend answered. "Hi, it's Hayley," she said, making an effort to sound normal.

"Hi, how's it going?"

"Good. Terrific. Except that Max's father decided he wanted him for part of the summer, so I had to send him to Pennsylvania and I'm feeling a little lonely."

"Oh? I thought you said his father wasn't interested in maintaining contact. They've never had a summer visit before, have they?"

"No, but..." Taking a calming breath, she launched into the explanation Anne Kelly had bought—about Max's grandparents wanting to see him.

Then, without giving Peggy a chance to ask any more questions, she said, "But Max has nothing to do with why I'm calling." Not exactly a lie. He had *everything* to do with it. "Remember I mentioned I'd be doing an assessment on Billy Fitzgerald?"

"Of course. We said we'd talk about it the next time we got together."

"Right. In the meantime, I had another look at his intake evaluation. And could you check on something for me?"

"What?"

She swallowed anxiously. "Well, he made a big point of talking about being a man of his word. He claimed even his enemies give him credit for that. Apparently it was very important to him that the assessing psychologist believe him, which got me wondering. You know what I mean?"

"He doth protest too much, and all that jazz?"

"Exactly. I couldn't help thinking it might not be true at all."

"And you want to know whether it is because…?"

For a moment, she almost gave in to the urge to tell Peggy everything and ask her advice. If Billy's people had grabbed her son rather than Max, what would Peggy do? Would she trust the scandal-plagued New Orleans police force enough to report the kidnapping? Trust it with *her* son's life? Or trust the FBI?

Hayley couldn't ask, though. She was too terrified that, as Sloan had intimated, Peggy might take the matter into her own hands.

There couldn't really be much chance of it. Still, *any* chance was too much, so she simply said, "Knowing would make my assessment easier."

When only silence followed that, her skin began to feel clammy.

"Why?" Peggy finally asked. "You think Billy Fitz might give you his word about something while you're assessing him?"

"Well...sort of. I mean, if he swears he has no ulterior motive, that he really does only want a transfer so he can get into a rehab program..."

"I thought we agreed that was a crock?"

"Yes, but I've been thinking more about it and... Oh, Lord, am I out of line here? Maybe I shouldn't ask you to do this. I didn't figure it would be a big deal, but if it is I can—"

"No," Peggy said slowly. "No, it's not a big deal. I'll talk to a couple of informers, see what they say. You just surprised me. The question seemed strange."

"It did?"

"Yeah. But I guess that was just the cop in me. Once a perp's in for life, nobody on the job cares whether his word's worth two cents. Actually, at that point nobody cares *anything* about him. But I guess my mind-set's not quite the same as yours."

Hayley forced a laugh. "Right. Your job's putting them behind bars. Mine's keeping an eye on their mental health once they're there. And I don't want to make any mistakes when it comes to Fitzgerald. Don't want to see my name in the *Times-Picayune*, in some article on how the head of the Irish Mafia is getting special privileges. Or in one saying we're treating him unfairly, either.''

"Yeah…I see your point. Well it shouldn't take me long to ask around. I'll give you a call when I've got something."

"Do you think it might be today?"

Peggy didn't answer for a couple of beats. That started Hayley sweating even harder.

"I thought the assessment on Fitz wasn't going to happen for ages,'' her friend said at last.

"Oh, it probably won't. I'd just like to finish my notes for the file. So I can get it off my desk.''

"Ah. Okay. I'll see what I can do today. But it might be tomorrow or Thursday before I get back to you."

"Whenever you can. And thanks, I owe you one. Bye.''

"Bye, Hayley.''

She hung up, her hands trembling. She wasn't used to lying and she didn't like the way it made her feel. But at least she'd learn what she needed to know.

SLOAN PRESSED THE BUTTON on the post, then identified himself to the disembodied voice that responded. When the gate opened, he reluctantly drove into the Poquette Correctional Center compound, really not looking forward to this visit with Billy.

Hayley Morgan had done anything but endear

herself to him by not recommending a transfer, so predicting how he'd react to the idea of letting her see her son wasn't tough.

After parking his Cherokee in a visitor's space, Sloan climbed out into the gathering morning heat and checked the staff section of the lot for Hayley's car. One of Billy's boys had told him it was a silver Taurus and given him the plate number, which made it easy to establish that she was already here. Here and expecting him to stop by after he'd seen Billy.

And if he had to report that Billy had said "No way she can see her kid…" Hell, that was undoubtedly what he would say, regardless of how hard Sloan argued.

Telling himself he'd just have to hope the luck of the Irish was on *his* side today, and that his powers of persuasion were in top form, he started across the dusty parking lot toward the dirty brick quadrangle that was Poquette.

When he opened the front door, stale air wafted out toward him. Wishing for the tenth time that he didn't have to be here, he stepped inside and walked the few feet to the metal detector, sticking his keys and loose change on a tray before stepping through.

Once the correctional officer on door duty nodded for him to proceed, he retrieved his things and headed for the reception counter, trying to stop remembering the way Hayley had looked yesterday when he'd told her Billy's men had snatched Max.

He couldn't force the image from his mind's eye,

though. Hadn't been able to, in fact, since he'd woken up this morning. In mere seconds, she'd gone from a picture of calm composure to a portrait of anguish.

Seeing her face grow pale and her dark eyes fill with terror had made him feel lower than an alligator's belly. He hated being a part of what was happening to her and her son, and if he could, he'd simply deliver the boy back to her.

But that just wasn't an option.

Exhaling slowly, he reminded himself he was only doing his job. That usually helped.

It didn't this time, though. Probably, he knew, because Hayley Morgan wasn't like most of the other women he'd had dealings with while working for Billy.

Actually, unless his memory was failing, she wasn't like a single one of them. She was intelligent and cultured and...

And dammit, she appealed to him in a way he couldn't let any woman appeal to him. A way that was physical, yet dangerously more than that.

There was something about her, some substance or inner strength, that had reached out and grabbed him. As upset and frightened as she'd been, as close to dissolving into tears as he'd known she was, she'd pulled herself together and coped with the situation as best she could.

He liked that strength, liked the way... But hell, there was no point in defining what touched him about her. Since she had to figure he was the scum of the earth, thinking about that was nothing except a waste of time.

At the reception counter, he gave his name and identified himself as William Fitzgerald's lawyer. The correctional officer checked the appointment log, then buzzed the door unlocked. It led to a small room where another C.O. had him empty his pockets.

"What's that for?" the officer asked as Sloan set his minirecorder on the table.

"I use it to tape conversations with clients."

The C.O. picked up the recorder and examined it, removing and then reinserting the cassette before checking that the space for the batteries contained nothing it shouldn't.

As he put the unit back down, Sloan began to breathe more easily again. It hadn't happened yet, but there was always the risk that one of these guys would notice the extra switch.

"Face the table and place your hands on it," the C.O. ordered.

When he did, the man treated him to a thorough pat-down—one of the joys of visiting someone in protective custody.

"I'll call ahead and have the prisoner brought from his cell," the C.O. said when he'd finished. "Then I'll get someone to escort you to the visiting room."

CHAPTER FOUR

BEYOND THE PUBLIC AREA of the Poquette complex, the stale air was heavy with disinfectant. But even an industrial-strength cleaner couldn't quite mask the smells of urine, vomit, smoke and body odor. By the time the guard escorted Sloan all the way to the small room used for visits with segregated prisoners, he felt as though he hadn't showered in a month. Billy was already there, waiting with another guard. The man retreated into the hall when Sloan arrived, ostensibly assuring them of privacy by closing the door, but they were easily visible through its chicken wire window. Plus, Sloan suspected prison officials often listened in to what was being said in the room—despite the fact it would contravene prisoners' rights. That, of course, was the real reason for his tape recorder.

After setting it on the small table between Billy and him, he pushed both the switch that started the cassette recording and the one to activate the bug-detecting gizmo in the secret compartment.

Billy sat gazing at the unit, a look in his eyes that told Sloan he was smiling to himself. But why wouldn't he be? He loved beating the establishment. Any aspect of it. And the tiny detector was state-of-the-art. There wasn't an electronic listening device in existence it couldn't pick up on, and if it sensed one within a hundred feet its warning light would start blinking.

They waited a few seconds, but the light didn't come on. Even so, they'd watch their words and speak mostly in whispers—just in case the guard outside the door had supersensitive hearing.

"Mission accomplished," Sloan said once he was satisfied that nobody was eavesdropping electronically.

"I know. Brendan phoned last night."

Sloan nodded, not surprised. Most prisoners weren't allowed unrestricted access to a phone, but Billy had more than enough money to buy whatever privileges the guards were willing to sell.

He also had enough smarts to carry on conversations that, although they'd sound perfectly innocuous to anyone listening in, were actually full of messages and orders. That was what enabled him to be pretty much still running the Irish Mafia.

His son was the heir apparent, and no dummy himself. But at the moment Brendan's main job was simply to keep Billy informed and relay his orders to the boys.

Leaning across the table, Billy quietly said, "Does our friend have any good ideas?"

He was referring to Hayley, of course. And asking if, since she'd screwed up their plan, she'd suggested an alternative way of getting him outside the prison.

Other ways certainly existed. They all knew that.

But someone like her, on the inside, would know which ones were most likely to succeed at this particular prison. And which one she could be the most help with.

"We haven't really gotten into that yet," Sloan said. "Our friend wants something first."

"Oh?" Billy's expression suggested that nobody had invited her to negotiate.

"Wants…visiting privileges with her son," he whispered. "An hour or two an evening."

For a moment, Billy merely stared across the table. Then he sat back and said, "Fat chance."

Sloan swore under his breath. He'd known that would be the reaction.

"Getting what you want's going to take time," he said. "And our friend's concerned about the…item's emotional well-being. And…"

He paused when he saw that Billy was already growing impatient. The man didn't give a damn about why Hayley wanted to see her son. Or about Max's mental health. Hell, he never really gave a damn about anyone except himself. So the only thing to do was convince him it would be to *his* benefit to let Hayley have what she wanted.

"Look, Billy, I've given this a lot of thought, and the way I see it, agreeing would be a good idea."

Billy shook his head. "As long as we've got the item, I don't have to agree to anything."

"No, you don't *have* to."

"But you think I should? Why?"

"Because as things stand, if our friend cooperates it sure won't be willingly."

"If?" Billy repeated with a mean grin. "Like I said, as long as we've got the item…"

"You're right. We can take the cooperation as a given. But say our friend goes along with us, then sees an opportunity, or creates an opportunity, to double-cross us."

"Not a chance. She'd have too much to lose."

Sloan told himself he had to do better. "Okay, here's what's really worrying me. You know everything we learned about our friend as well as I do. We're talking someone who takes job responsibilities seriously. Plus, being part of the system, doesn't look at things the same way most people might. And if you and I are making assumptions that might not exactly apply in these particular circumstances…"

After a glance at the guard, Sloan looked back at Billy and whispered, "Aside from anything else, for all she knows she'll never see the item again even if she does cooperate. That just might make her try something we're not expecting."

Billy hesitated, then said, "You did promise the item would be returned safely, didn't you?"

"Of course."

"But you weren't convincing enough?"

"I did my best. The problem is that we're not talking about someone naive. We're talking someone who knows how often this sort of thing ends badly. So I can't see why we shouldn't give a little.

It wouldn't hurt us, and there might be a major benefit.''

''What?''

''It would show you've got a heart. And it would be taken as a sign that you sincerely intend to return the item. If our friend is convinced you really will, that'll practically guarantee cooperation.''

When Sloan stopped speaking, Billy resisted the impulse to say that no way was he letting that bitch anywhere near her kid. Even though he hated the thought of giving in to her, if Sloan figured the idea had merit then he'd better not dismiss it too fast.

Sloan was paid help, not part of the family, so he wasn't always worrying about his place in the pecking order. That meant he didn't always say what the boss wanted to hear. What he said usually made sense, though. So if he figured Hayley Morgan really might try to cross them...

Maybe it *was* a possibility. She was smart. And as Sloan said, she knew the system. So maybe she *would* be arrogant enough to figure she could...

But, dammit, they had her kid. Didn't that outweigh everything else?

''Billy?'' Sloan said quietly.

He continued to stare at the table, not done thinking his way through this. He wanted his freedom back so badly he could taste it, and he'd get only one shot at escaping. If he tried and failed, the guards wouldn't take their eyes off him until he was so old he couldn't walk.

But how great was the risk that Morgan really might throw him a curve? He figured it was damned unlikely. Still, damned unlikely was no guarantee that she wouldn't.

"Billy?" Sloan said again.

Billy looked across the table this time, reminding himself that Sloan was both a smart guy and a good judge of people. So if he thought that tossing Morgan this bone would convince her she'd get the kid back safe in the end, that it would keep her from trying anything funny...

The boys wouldn't like it, though. They'd read it as a sign of weakness.

But what if he put Sloan in charge of the game plan? Then letting her see the kid would be viewed as *his* weakness.

That's good, he silently congratulated himself. He hadn't lost his touch yet.

"All right," he muttered. "I'll talk to Brendan and tell him you're calling the shots as far as the kid goes. He'll let the boys know, and you make the arrangements. Be careful, though. You'll have to be sure our friend doesn't... But hell, I don't have to tell you how to handle the details. You've never let me down before."

"And I won't this time."

Billy nodded. His people almost never let him down. They knew that anyone who did it once wouldn't be around to do it again.

EVERY TIME SHE HEARD footsteps in the hallway outside the office, Hayley froze. Thus far, though, none of them had belonged to Sloan Reeves.

She was starting to wonder if he'd actually bother

"stopping by," as he'd so casually put it. Maybe he'd just call, avoid having to deliver the bad news face-to-face.

She told herself not to assume the worst. But promising he'd try to convince Fitzgerald and actually doing it were two different things. Even if he honestly did his "level best," believing she at least had a chance of getting what she wanted was probably just a pipe dream.

It was all she had to cling to, though. And thinking about going day after day without seeing Max, about how the ordeal would be even harder on him if—

"Dr. Morgan? Gentleman would like to see you."

When she looked up her throat went dry. Sloan Reeves was standing beside the correctional officer.

"Thank you," she managed to say. "I...there's no need to wait. I'll see Mr. Reeves out of the secure area when we're done."

The officer nodded, then headed off, while Sloan stepped into the office and closed the door.

As he turned back toward her, she searched his chiseled face for a clue to Billy's decision. She saw none.

"Mind if I switch this on?" he asked, taking a tiny tape recorder from his suit pocket and setting it on her desk.

"No." But why would he want to tape their conversation?

Because he intended to raise the subject of her helping Fitzgerald? Because if she agreed to do it the tape would be incriminating evidence, something the police could hold over her head?

She considered that possibility for a moment, then rejected it as senseless. Sloan's voice would be on the tape, too. And regardless of anything she said—or anything she did, for that matter—she was under extreme duress.

Not that she had any illusions about that being enough to get her off if she was caught. Not in a Louisiana courtroom, where "tough justice" was the bible most judges swore by.

Sloan would be in a far worse position, though. Aiding a convicted felon in escaping lawful custody was conspiracy to obstruct justice. Add that to being a willing accessory to a kidnapping and they'd lock him up for two hundred years.

Barely breathing, she watched him sit down, dying to ask what Fitzgerald had said but afraid to hear the answer.

"I've just come from seeing Billy," he began.

"And?" she made herself say.

"And I convinced him that letting you spend some time with Max was a good idea."

For the first few seconds, she couldn't believe she'd heard right. For the next few, she was terrified that Sloan was playing a cruel hoax, that any instant he'd say, "Ha! Gotcha!"

But all he did was eye her, an almost imperceptible smile playing at the corners of his mouth.

When she finally decided he was telling the truth, such a strong rush of gratitude swept her that she felt like hugging him. Despite knowing what an utterly despicable man he was.

Stockholming, she silently warned herself, pulling a summary of the syndrome from a mental filing cabinet. The term had been coined following a bank robbery in Stockholm in the 1970s. Female employees, held hostage, had fallen in love with their captors and become convinced the cops were the bad guys.

But bonding with one's captors had undoubtedly been going on for centuries, and she was as much a hostage to Sloan Reeves as those bank employees had been to the robbers.

Exhaling slowly, she reminded herself the Stockholm syndrome was so powerful that even being aware of it didn't make people immune to it. She, however, intended to keep firmly in mind that Sloan Reeves was one of the bad guys.

Looking at him again, she said, "Thank you for getting Billy to agree."

"You're welcome. I told you I'd do my best."

"Yes. I was afraid to get my hopes up, though. I..." She managed to swallow over the lump in her throat, but she just couldn't force any more words out.

"With any luck, we'll be able to set up a meeting with him for tonight," he told her. "Otherwise, you can see him tomorrow for sure."

"That's wonderful," she said, finding her voice again.

"I'm glad I could help."

He paused for a couple of beats, still watching

her, his expression almost…*sad* was the word fluttering in her mind, although she couldn't think why it was the right one. Not when he had her exactly where he wanted her.

"Now," he continued, "I guess we should talk about how you're going to help Billy."

Her mouth went dry. She didn't want to discuss that yet, didn't want to suggest even one possible way until after she'd heard from Peggy.

If it turned out that Fitzgerald wasn't a man of his word, if she couldn't count on getting Max back safely no matter what she did, then she'd have to carefully consider exactly how to proceed.

Of course, if he *was* a man of his word, her decision would be made for her. She'd do anything if it truly ensured Max's safety.

"I'll need some time to think," she said. "I've been so worried about Max that… Well, helping your boss won't—"

"He's not my boss. He's simply my client."

"Yes. Of course," she said uneasily. The last thing she wanted was to annoy Sloan. Despicable or not, he was her link to her son, so if he wanted to delude himself with semantics that was fine by her.

"What I started to say," she began again, "is that helping Billy won't be easy."

"Hayley, we both know that transferring a prisoner isn't the only way to get him outside the walls. All we're asking you to do is figure out which way we should go, how you can give us the most help."

"Yes…I know. It's just…"

She stopped speaking once more, this time her eyes full of tears. She still couldn't really convince herself Max would be all right in the end. Too many things might go wrong.

"Why don't you spend the rest of the day giving the situation some thought," Sloan said. "I'll call you after you get home. And…nothing's going to happen to Max. I promise."

Nodding again, she wished she'd asked Peggy to find out if Sloan Reeves, too, was known as a man of his word.

DRIVING HOME FROM POQUETTE, Hayley found herself constantly checking the rearview mirror. She spotted no one on her tail, but she didn't have the slightest doubt somebody was back there.

Maybe Billy's people had put a transponder on her car so they could follow at a healthy distance. Whatever, they'd be aware of what she was up to.

If she made any side trips, Fitzgerald would want to hear about them. He'd have his boys doing everything it took to ensure that if she tried to cross him he'd know. And if she did, it would be game over.

As she left the highway behind and headed into her own neighborhood of Bayou St. John, she forced her thoughts from what Fitzgerald was doing to what she intended to do. Like it or not, assuming she didn't learn the man had a reputation for breaking his word, she'd do her best to help him escape. Because when it came to her son's life…

Telling herself not to go there, she turned onto

her street. The moment she did, her emotions threatened to swamp her.

Normally, no matter how hot the day, Max would be waiting outside for her, sitting on Anne's front porch or riding his bike up and down the block as he kept one eye out for his mom's car. Today the street was deserted. In her mind's eye, though, she could see Max's little face break into a grin when he spotted her. The image tore at her heart.

After pulling into the driveway, she climbed out of her car and walked toward the house. Even though she sensed eyes boring into her back, she resisted the urge to look around.

If she was going to be a goldfish in a bowl she might as well just try to ignore the fact. The same way she'd done her best to ignore the terror that had relentlessly been gnawing at her ever since Sloan had dropped his bombshell.

Her heart heavy, she unlocked the front door. Cool air greeted her, as did Satchmo, who began meowing tales about his cat day before she even closed the door.

She picked him up and hugged him, wishing with all her heart that Max were there to hug, as well. Then she carried the cat into the kitchen. Her pulse skipped a beat when she saw that the light on her answering machine was blinking.

Had Sloan called already? Left word that she could see Max tonight?

She put Satchmo down, pressed Play and waited anxiously while the tape rewound. The message wasn't from Sloan, but it was one she was eager to hear. She held her breath and listened.

"Hi, Hayley, it's Peggy. I talked to a few people about Billy Fitz, and the stain on the street is that when he gives his word he generally keeps it. Hope that's enough to let you get his file off your desk. If not, give me a call.

"Actually, give me a call anyway. If we don't get together before Max is back from Pennsylvania, as soon as he's home we should take the boys out somewhere. Pace has been asking when we're going to do something together. Bye for now."

Billy Fitz *generally* kept his word. Hayley let the words echo inside her head, wishing she could phone and ask Peggy exactly what that meant but knowing she couldn't. Peggy had been suspicious enough the first time around.

Generally kept his word.

Generally wasn't as good as *always,* but it was a whole lot better than *generally didn't.*

She pressed Rewind, thinking that if her phone really *was* bugged, then whoever was listening in would have heard the message. That meant Billy would know she'd asked Peggy to check up on his reputation.

The realization almost sent her into panic mode. But surely he wouldn't object to her satisfying herself that his word actually meant something. Or would he?

He well might, she decided. In fact, odds were that he would. An egomaniac like Billy Fitz wouldn't like her having the audacity to suspect he was a liar.

Making an effort to ignore that unsettling thought, she told herself she'd have to be careful not to do anything more he might not like. Not even in the privacy of her home.

Quite possibly, the entire house was bugged. And her office. And her car. For all she knew, Billy would hear about anything and everything she said or did.

Satchmo was rubbing against her legs and loudly trying to convince her he was the hungriest cat in the entire universe, so she opened a can of food and spooned it into his bowl. Just as she was setting it on his mat, someone rang the doorbell.

When she checked the peephole and saw it was Sloan, every muscle in her body tensed.

He was wearing casual clothes now, jeans and a short-sleeved shirt the same blue as his eyes. She doubted he was off duty, though. Working for a man like Billy Fitz, he'd never be off duty. But he'd said he'd phone, not drop by. So why was he here? Because something had gone wrong? Because Billy had changed his mind about letting her see Max?

Apprehension wrapping itself around her like a shroud, she unlocked the door and made herself open it.

"Hi," Sloan said. Then he smiled and added, "Why don't you change into something cooler and we'll go visit your son."

CHAPTER FIVE

WHEN HAYLEY CAME down from upstairs, a single
glance told Sloan that at least one of his assumptions about her had been bang on. Without the tai-
lored suit and school-marm hairstyle, she was absolutely gorgeous.

She'd changed into a white cotton shirt and
denim shorts—revealing legs that were going to
start him drooling if he wasn't careful. As for her
hair, he had an unsettling feeling that an image of
her with it spilling down onto her shoulders the way
it was now would haunt his dreams tonight.

Pretending he was totally oblivious to her looks,
he simply gestured her ahead of him when she
reached the bottom of the stairs.

Outside, he stood waiting while she locked up,
not quite able to keep his eyes off her. Or keep from
thinking that in casual clothes she seemed far more
approachable.

Not approachable by him, though, he reflected as
they started for his Jeep. Not by a long shot. He
was playing a role in holding Max hostage. If he
tried to ''approach'' her she'd gouge his eyes out.

But that was neither here nor there, because even

under entirely different circumstances he'd steer clear of her.

His relationships with women were always casual, with few expectations on either side. That was simply the way things had to be. And since Hayley Morgan set off alarm bells in his head, warning him that if he got involved with her there'd be nothing casual about it, she'd be off limits no matter what the situation.

Once they were under way he headed south from New Orleans, down into fishing-and-crabbing swampland in Jefferson Parish. His destination was a cove on Lost Lake where he sometimes fished with a buddy. They'd never seen another soul there, which made it an ideal place for Hayley and Max to get together. Even if she was entertaining any crazy thoughts about grabbing the little boy and running, she wouldn't try it in the middle of nowhere.

He drove for another mile or so, then glanced across the Cherokee at her. Her entire body looked tense, which probably meant she was afraid he wasn't actually taking her to see Max at all. Or was thinking that, in the end, her son might not come through this alive.

He wished he could reassure her, but he'd be one of the last people on earth who could do that. He was on Billy's team, which meant she'd suspect every single thing he said.

With that in mind, he just kept quiet while she continued to stare out at the trees that lined the two-lane road—old live oaks, loose-limbed willows and cypresses draped with gray Spanish moss. Finally, he told himself that her retreating into silence was just as well. Figuring out how they were going to spring Billy could wait until after she'd had some time with her son. As for the rest of what they had to discuss, he'd be better off watching her expression while they talked.

Less than an hour out of the city, they reached the narrow dirt road that would take them to the cove. As soon as he turned onto it the stagnant swamp waters closed in around them. On either side the willows towered over everything, doing their best to obliterate the light and reducing all the colors of nature to a murky shade of greenish-brownish gray.

He stopped the Jeep where the road ended and cut the engine. To their left was a thick stand of canebrakes that looked as if it had been there forever. Before them lay the lake, eerily still and covered near the shoreline by a motionless blanket of lily pads.

The egrets and herons that would have been active on a fishing morning were nowhere to be seen; the only movement came from long-legged bugs scurrying across the surface of the water.

"It's positively primordial," Hayley murmured.

He nodded, thinking that was precisely the right word.

"And Max...?"

"They'll be here soon."

"'They' being my son and the policemen?" she asked, giving him a wry glance.

He shrugged. "They figured he'd be less frightened if he thought they were cops. But only one of them will bring him."

"I...I guess I should ask about a few things before they get here—so I don't say anything that will mislead him. Billy *did* agree to let me see him for a little while every day? I can tell him that?"

"Yeah, you can tell him that."

The look of relief that crossed her face said she'd been afraid he'd answer no.

"And he'll probably ask if it's always going to be here."

"Tell him it'll be different places."

"All right," she said slowly.

"Anything else?" he prompted when she said nothing more.

"I don't really know what other questions he'll have."

"Well, if anything else occurs to you, just ask."

Reaching across in front of her, he opened the glove compartment and took out his gun. That few inches closer to her, he was very aware of the faint scent of her perfume. It was a sultry, sexy scent that went straight to his groin.

"The gun is for...?" she said uneasily.

"Just in case a snake gets too close. There are a lot of copperheads and water snakes around here."

"You're not kidding, are you," she said nervously.

"Uh-uh. They generally steer clear, though. Unless they're provoked."

He considered mentioning the alligators but

didn't. He'd already decided she'd never try to take off with Max in the middle of a swamp. And as long as she'd be staying near the cars, he saw little point in frightening her half to death.

When he opened the door and climbed out of the Jeep, the smells of the swamp greeted him—the earthy aroma of vegetation rooted in water, of wet moss covering the exposed roots of the cypresses.

Tucking the gun into his belt, he started forward. The ground was soft and so oozing with moisture that the Jeep's wheels had sunk into it a couple of inches. The mud sucked at his shoes with each step he took.

They stopped a few feet from the edge of the lake and he scanned the cove before speaking again, more out of habit than necessity. He'd checked en route that no one was tailing them, even though he was almost certain that Hayley wouldn't have said a word to anyone about the kidnapping, let alone said that she was going to see Max.

Satisfied they were entirely alone, he said, "You had your detective friend ask around about Billy."

She looked at him. "You've got my phone bugged."

"No. *I* don't. But Billy does. And he won't like your checking up on him."

"I know," she murmured, biting her lower lip.

Sloan swore to himself. Her distress was so obvious it stung his heart.

"Before I agreed to help," she explained, "I had to be sure Billy would likely keep his end of the bargain. Will you be able to make him understand that?''

He hesitated, not wanting her to start figuring that he had more power over Billy than he did. "I think," he finally said, "that he'll understand as long as he knows you're really going to help him. Whatever you do, though, don't cross him."

"I'm not intending to."

"Good. And don't do anything that could even start him wondering if you might. No matter where you are or who you're with, don't say anything or do anything or—"

"I know. I've already figured things out." She glanced along the shoreline. "Is somebody watching me right now?"

I am, he said silently.

I'll be the one telling Billy about this visit.

Aloud, he said, "No. Nobody's watching us. But getting back to your detective friend, it would be best if you don't talk to her again until after this is over."

"I...she expects me to call. She'll think something's funny if I don't."

"And Billy will think something's funny if you do. Hayley... Look, I told you before that I was against this kidnapping. But now that Billy's gone ahead with it, I just want to see it end right."

"'Right' being that he escapes."

Sloan's eyes met hers. He saw disgust in her gaze and he could almost hear her thinking he was a real piece of work. That didn't surprise him, but it made him feel like two cents.

"'Right' being that nothing happens to your son," he said quietly.

Then he looked away and stood staring out over the water, wondering why he was letting her get to him. She was hardly the first person to think he was completely immoral. When you were Billy Fitz's lawyer, a lot of people didn't exactly hold you in high esteem. So he'd long ago developed a tough skin and learned not to give a damn about anyone's opinion.

This would be one hell of a time to start caring. And one hell of a person to do it with.

FOR A SECOND, Hayley was afraid to let herself believe the sound was a car engine. Then Sloan said, "That'll be them," and her heart began to race.

A moment later the car appeared and pulled to a stop behind the Jeep. And there in the front seat was her son, alive and looking just fine.

Seeing him made her feel like laughing and crying at the same time, and she started running for the car before the driver had even cut the ignition.

Max fumbled with his seat belt, then opened the door and raced into her arms.

"Oh, darling," she whispered, sweeping him up as if he weighed nothing at all.

He wrapped his arms tightly around her neck and buried his face in her shoulder.

"Oh, Max, are you okay?"

She felt him nodding against her, not uttering a word. That meant he was on the verge of crying. She didn't know what to say to reassure him, though. She couldn't tell him she was taking him home, which was what he wanted to hear. And as hard as she'd tried, she hadn't come up with a good way to explain what was going on without frightening him even more. So she merely held him and murmured sweet nothings about how glad she was to see him.

"Mommy?" he finally said. "How come we hadda come here?"

"Well...they just thought it would be a good place."

"But we're gonna go home after, aren't we?"

Hot tears filled her eyes. Blinking hard, she looked over at Sloan.

The driver was standing next to him, wearing a jacket despite the muggy heat. She just knew it was to conceal a gun, and that sent a shiver through her.

She could have done without a reminder that until she got her son back his life would be in constant jeopardy.

Telling herself that as long as Max believed his kidnappers were cops, their having guns wouldn't frighten him, she focused on Sloan again.

"Is it okay if we take a little walk? Just by the water's edge?"

"Sure. Be careful, though."

"Right. Snakes."

"Snakes?" Max repeated.

"There might be one or two," Hayley told him. "But we'll watch out for them. So how about if I put you down and we can talk about what's happening while we walk?"

With obvious reluctance he loosened his hold and slid down her body to the ground, then reached for her hand and held on with all his might as they started off.

They'd taken only a few steps before Sloan called, "Hayley?"

When she looked back, he said, "I guess I should have mentioned it before, but keep an eye out for alligators, too."

"Alligators? Real ones?" Max asked, his eyes big and round.

Sloan nodded.

"That's okay. I like alligators. The white ones at the zoo are my favorite things."

"Yeah?" Sloan grinned at him. "Well, the ones here aren't behind a fence, so if you see any, you just bring your mom straight to me."

Max gave him a solemn nod, then carefully looked around before they began walking again.

"Is that Tom or Dick who drove you?" she asked once they had.

"Dick."

"Ah. And one of them bought you some new clothes, I see."

"Yeah. Tom. But he didn't take me to the store with him. He said he's got a son just my age, so he knew what I'd like."

"He got the size right, too. And how are you making out with the two of them? You still like them okay?"

While Max gave an exaggerated shrug, she continued searching for words to lead into what she had to tell him. They still wouldn't come.

"Let's sit for a minute," she suggested as they neared an old log.

Max stopped dead and eyed it. "You're sure it's not an alligator, huh?" he whispered.

"I'm sure."

Once they were sitting, he pressed up against her as if afraid she'd vanish any second. She gave him a good, hard hug. Then, shifting so she could see him, she brushed his hair back from his eyes.

"You know I always do my best to explain things to you," she said, making herself begin.

He nodded.

"Well...every now and then there's something I just can't explain very well. And this is one of those times. You see...darling, you're going to have to stay with Tom and Dick for a little while longer."

When the blue of his eyes darkened with tears, she hurried on.

"I know you don't want to, but it just has to be that way."

"Why?" he demanded, his voice quavering.

"Because...it just has to. That's the part I can't really explain."

"You don't love me!" he cried. "I love you, but you don't love me!"

"Oh, Max," she murmured, wrapping her arms around him. "Oh, darling, I love you more than anything in the world." She simply held him for a minute, unable to go on.

"Max, you know that even grown-ups can't always do what they want," she finally managed to say. "I'd give anything to take you home right now, but I can't."

"Why?" he sobbed.

"Because there's something I have to do. Part of my job. It means I'll have to work in the evenings a lot and get home really late. And there'd be nobody to look after you."

"What about Mrs. Kelly? Or one of my nighttime baby-sitters could come."

"I just couldn't set it up with any of them, Max. I—"

"But I don't wanna stay with Tom and Dick. Why can't I go stay with Pace and Peggy? Like when you went to your conferns?"

Hayley shook her head, feeling her control slipping and desperately trying to hold on to it.

"You can't stay with them this time, darling. They've got other plans. But you and I will see each other every day. It's just that until I'm home in the evenings again you've got to stay with Tom and Dick."

"But I don't want to! I want to be with you! And Satchmo."

"I know," she said softly. "I know. That's what I want too. And as soon as I finish what I have to do that's where you'll be."

"When are you gonna finish?"

"Just as soon as I can, darling."

Pulling him to her once more, she shut her eyes and lightly rested her chin on his head. With him so close and warm, smelling of a soapy-little-boy smell, it was hard to believe this nightmare was actually happening. It was, though, and the only way to end it was to do something she'd never have imagined herself doing.

So just as quickly as she could, she was going to help a convicted felon escape from prison—then pray that he lived up to his side of their bargain. And that she didn't get thrown in prison for the rest of her life.

WHILE HAYLEY AND SLOAN sped back toward New Orleans, she kept trying to stop picturing Max, tears streaming down his cheeks, waving goodbye to her as he drove off with Dick. But she couldn't erase the image from her mind any more than she could banish the pain from her heart.

Telling herself she'd see her son again tomorrow—assuming Sloan hadn't lied to her, that was, she glanced across the Jeep at him. He was watching the road ahead, still every bit as quiet as he'd been since they'd left the cove.

She'd expected that once they got under way he'd press her about how they were going to get Billy out of Poquette. It surprised her that he hadn't, and if she didn't know better she'd think he was being sensitive, intentionally giving her time to pull herself together.

But no man with even a drop of sensitivity would keep a terrified little boy from his mother, and if Sloan Reeves was a decent human being he'd... He'd what?

She realized she wasn't sure. Would he go

against Billy Fitz's orders? When odds were that he'd end up dead for his trouble?

No, she silently answered herself. Even a decent man would have self-preservation instincts. But no decent man would represent the head of the Irish Mafia. So, if that was what Sloan was, he wouldn't be involved in this. Someone else would be acting on Billy's behalf.

Her gaze flickering across the Jeep once more, she wondered where she'd be if that was the case.

As much as she hated to admit it, she knew she'd probably be worse off. Quite possibly, a lot worse. After all, Sloan had convinced Billy to let her see her son. She doubted that many of Billy's boys would even have agreed to try.

And Sloan had let her spend far longer with Max tonight than she'd expected. Long enough that Dick had grown fidgety and clearly anxious to leave.

Looking out into the gathering twilight, she reminded herself about the Stockholm syndrome. But was it *really* relevant here? Sloan had gone out of his way to be kind. She wasn't simply imagining that. And since she hadn't expected kindness from him, she couldn't make him add up quite right in her mind.

Finally, she decided the problem was that she'd been thinking about him in terms of evil and good, black and white, whereas he was actually a shade of gray.

Dark gray, though. He might have shown her some kindness, but that hardly wiped out his involvement in how Max's kidnapping would play out.

She felt panic rising inside her and told herself that everything would turn out fine—just as long as she helped Billy escape.

That was what she had to hang on to, the thing that would keep her from falling apart. But the sooner they got Billy out of Poquette, the better.

"Hayley?"

Sloan's voice startled her. As she looked over, he shifted his gaze from the road to her.

"I'm sorry that was so hard on you and Max. When I thought about your seeing each other, it didn't occur to me how tough it would be when he had to leave again."

"I...if my choice is between tough goodbyes and not seeing him at all... Sloan, I appreciate your convincing Billy to let me. I really do."

He nodded. "How did you explain things to Max?"

"I said I needed him to stay with Tom and Dick because I'd be late getting home at night for a while—on account of my job."

"And he was okay with that?"

"He wasn't happy. I guess he was as okay as possible, though."

Sloan lapsed back into silence. But a minute later he said, "I want you to know you can count on nothing happening to him. Billy's told his people I'm calling the shots as far as Max goes, and I've made it damned clear he's to be treated well."

"I...appreciate that, too. More than I can say,"

she added, her throat tight. Something in his tone made her believe she really could count on him.

But was that only wishful thinking? Was she deluding herself because she so badly wanted to believe Sloan Reeves had a decent side? Believe her son's fate didn't lie in the hands of a monster?

He'd turned his attention to the road again and she sat watching him, remembering the first time he'd shown up at her office. Before she'd known anything about him.

The moment she'd laid eyes on him she'd felt an instant attraction, a warm glow of interest. But learning who he represented and why he'd come to see her had extinguished it quickly.

For a moment, she let herself imagine what might have happened if he'd walked into her life under completely different circumstances. If he'd come to see her about some sort of legitimate business.

Then, knowing that kind of speculation was only an exercise in futility, she closed her eyes to his handsome profile and tried to remember which old song had called some man "a walking contradiction."

Whichever, the term certainly fit Sloan. Only a man without a conscience would work for Billy Fitz. Yet a man without a conscience wouldn't be concerned about her son—assuming he wasn't putting on an act for some reason, that he really *was* concerned. And if he was...

Despite being on Billy's team, was he actually a far lighter shade of gray than she'd realized?

She didn't know. All she knew was that he was

her sole link to Max. And the man she had to work with to get Billy out of Poquette.

Turning to that subject, she said, "I took your suggestion this morning and spent a lot of the day considering the best way to get Billy on the outside."

"Oh?"

"Actually, I did more than consider. I spent some time in the prison's staff library, doing research on the Internet. And I came up with something that might be good."

Sloan looked over at her, then back at the road. "Which is?"

"I could tell Warden Armstrong that when I did my assessment of Billy last week, some of the things he said made me think he'd developed a neurological disorder."

This time Sloan's glance was dubious. "He'd believe a psychologist would pick up on that?"

"Maybe not most psychologists. But I took some neurology courses as part of my degree. If I mention that, it should give me enough credibility. I could claim that based on what Billy told me I'm pretty well convinced he's been having TIAs."

"TIAs," Sloan repeated slowly. He looked as if he thought he knew what they were but wouldn't mind her refreshing his memory.

"Transient ischemic attacks," she elaborated. "They're caused when a blood clot temporarily clogs an artery and creates a shortage in the blood supply to the brain. They're actually small strokes, with obvious symptoms when they occur but no residual effects afterward.''

"So you tell Armstrong you think Billy's been having them and...?''

"Well, I couldn't go directly to Armstrong. First, I'd get Jack Kolodny, the prison doctor, on side.''

"Would that be tough?''

"It shouldn't be. A doctor can't just ignore TIAs. He'll take my concern seriously enough to examine Billy. But before he does, I'll see Billy again myself.'' Pausing, she began to imagine being one-on-one with the man for a second time.

The moment she'd learned he'd had Max kidnapped, she'd started hating him with a passion she hadn't known she possessed. If she had any choice in the matter, she'd never be in the same room with him again. Unfortunately, for her plan to work she'd have to coach him on his part in it.

"If I have another session with him,'' she continued, "nobody will wonder why I waited before voicing my concern. I can tell Jack that I didn't want to bother him unduly but that I'd been worrying about what I suspected, so I did a follow-up. And it was only then that I decided I had to tell him what I thought.''

"But you aren't at Poquette again till next Tuesday. You're talking about not getting started on this for a week?''

She shook her head. She'd be a total basket case if she couldn't get things moving for an entire week. "I'll go back to Poquette tomorrow.''

"Hayley, it's important you don't arouse any

suspicions. If you vary your routine and somebody starts wondering whether you're up to something, it—"

"No, going there when I'm not scheduled to will actually be good. It'll look as if I really *have* been worrying. And I can spend the session with Billy coaching him on the symptoms he supposedly has."

"This session. You'd do it in the office you use there? Not in an interview room?"

"Yes. Why?"

"Because it's less likely anyone would be listening in."

"There's not a chance anyone would be. Not when we're talking a staff office. Even in prisons, some rules are never broken."

Sloan nodded, then reached down beside the seat and produced the little tape recorder he'd used that morning. "Would you mind recording you and Billy? Just turn these two switches on when he gets there and tell him I asked you to tape the session."

"Why?"

"Oh, I'd like to listen to it afterward."

"But—"

"Just humor me on this, okay?"

Shrugging, she reached for the recorder, then turned her thoughts back to the plan. "So, I tell Billy everything he's supposed to say when Jack Kolodny sees him. And as long as Billy can be convincing enough..."

"He can. You don't have to worry about that."

"Good. Then Jack and I would simply have to

convince Warden Armstrong that a specialist should be involved. That would get Billy a trip to New Orleans.''

"You're sure? Wouldn't it be easier to have a specialist come to Poquette?''

"Easier for us, but doctors have busy schedules. They won't waste half a day visiting a prisoner, so we've got an arrangement with the New Orleans Medical Center. When we have a problem our people need help with, we transport the prisoner to the med center. They know he's coming, and if it's an emergency he gets attention right away. Otherwise, he waits until one of their staff has time to fit him in.''

"Billy wouldn't be an emergency," Sloan pointed out. "So assuming Armstrong okayed sending him, how long would it be before he went?''

"He'd go pretty well right away. You know how bureaucracies work. Once a procedure's established, it's always followed. Since our procedure is to transfer a prisoner as soon as we identify a serious medical problem, Billy would be on his way in short order.''

Sloan was silent for a few seconds. "It's a good plan," he said at last. "I like it.''

She smiled. Then she realized why she had and felt utterly appalled. For a tiny moment she'd been pleased by Sloan's approval. And she didn't want to be.

He was on the wrong team, a member of the enemy forces. She didn't want his opinion of her, or of what she did, to mean anything at all to her.

"Open the glove compartment," he told her. "There's something in it for you."

She clicked it open. Inside were a couple of maps. Resting on top of them was a cell phone and the dull black automatic he'd put back before they'd left the cove.

For a split second, the thought that she could grab the gun and shoot him skittered through her mind. But it was a crazy thought. Shooting him would only mean she'd never see Max again.

"You know how to use one of those?" he asked.

"The basics," she said, nervously wondering if he'd been reading her mind. "Why?"

"Just curious. But it's the phone that's for you, not the gun. Now that we've got a plan, I want you to keep me up-to-date on your progress. Let me know what's happening every step of the way—just as quickly as you can.

"Only use that phone, though, and only call me on my cellular. It'll be safer than land lines. To get me, just press the 'memory one' button."

"And the number for this phone?" she asked, reaching for it.

"It'll light up when you turn on the power. But don't give it out. I don't want anyone using it except me. Now, getting back to the plan, how soon after you've seen Billy can you talk to this Jack Kolodny?"

"Probably right away, unless he's got some kind of medical emergency with a prisoner."

"Let's hope he doesn't. What about the warden? Is getting to see him a major problem?"

"No. He's pretty accessible to staff."

"Good. And you don't figure on any problem with him? He'll go along with Billy's seeing a specialist if you and the doctor recommend it?"

Closing her eyes, she tried not to think that Max's life could depend on whether Armstrong went along with them. But it might.

If she requested something that involved taking Billy out of Poquette, and Armstrong vetoed the idea, he'd be suspicious as hell if she requested anything else. Which meant that if this idea didn't pan out...

"The warden will probably give his approval," she said.

"Probably," Sloan repeated. "We need better than that, so let's figure out how we can *ensure* he does."

"All right, let's." She put the cell phone into her purse, waiting for him to begin. He'd made it sound as if ensuring Armstrong would cooperate would be a piece of cake, but she knew it wouldn't.

Closing her purse, she gazed unseeingly out into the evening, still waiting for him to start—and unable to keep from thinking that every day this dragged on would be another day on her roller coaster of fear.

CHAPTER SIX

BILLY FITZ DIDN'T SAY a word while Hayley outlined the plan. He simply sat on the other side of the desk in the little office and listened intently.

"Did I make everything clear?" she asked when she'd finished.

"Uh-huh."

"No questions before I go over the symptoms you'll tell Dr. Kolodny about?"

"No. You explained things exactly the way Sloan did."

It took a second for that to register.

"I see," she said once it had. "You've already talked to him this morning." Even though she'd gotten to Poquette first thing.

"Of course. He's my lawyer. I talk to him all the time. I like to be kept in the picture."

She nodded, uncomfortably recalling how last night, while she and Sloan had been fine-tuning the plan, she'd had the sense that they were working together, two people with a common goal. She hadn't really been thinking that even though they were working toward the same end, they had entirely different reasons for doing so.

But Billy had just reminded her of it. Any sense

that she'd been working with Sloan had been utterly sense*less*. They hadn't been working together at all. Not in any true meaning of the word.

Sloan worked for Billy. Period. And she had to keep in mind that he couldn't possibly be on Billy's side and hers at the same time.

"There's something you and Sloan didn't think of," Billy said. "I told him I'd mention it to you."

"Oh? What's that?"

"You have to come with me."

She looked at him blankly. "I have to come with you where?"

"When they take me to the medical center. You have to come along."

"What? Oh, no! No way! That wasn't part of the deal."

Billy shrugged. "It is now."

"But why?"

"You really have to ask?"

Nodding numbly, she prayed that his reason was silly. One she could logically argue against.

"Because prison breaks are dangerous," he said. "Especially if someone's tipped off the guards beforehand."

"Billy, I won't tip anyone off. I wouldn't do anything that might mean Max getting hurt. I—"

"Uh-uh. I'd rather have you worried about *you* getting hurt. So when my people intercept that van, there's no way I'll be sitting in it with only a bunch of guards. I want you right there in back with me.

"Otherwise, someone might just accidentally shoot me in the excitement. Especially if they were expecting the excitement. But if you know you're going to be in the line of fire…''

"No, Billy," she said again, her heart pounding. Helping plan a prison break was bad enough. Being in the midst of the action would be more than she could handle. "Look, I'm doing everything I can for you, but as I said, that wasn't part of our deal.''

He gave her a cold smile. "And as *I* said, it is now. You came up with a good idea, but it needed an added ingredient. And Sloan tells me your job description gives you leeway when it comes to doing things for prisoners.''

"Billy, aside from anything else, the warden would never let me go with you.''

"Never? Oh, I think you could convince him you should. And that you should ride right beside me, too. After all, you do still want your little boy back safely, don't you?''

"Of course I do!''

"I thought so. Now, I've got Sloan looking into the regulations for transporting prisoners. I'm sure he'll come up with something that we can interpret in our favor if it becomes necessary.

"But if I ask that you go with me and you say you think that makes sense… Well, before you start telling me about those symptoms, let's figure out the best way of working this.''

JACK KOLODNY HAD HIRED on with the Louisiana prison system straight out of med school. After ten-plus years, he projected a hard-as-steel image to the prisoners. But it concealed a kind heart and an easy sense of humor.

Hayley liked him, and they'd developed a good professional relationship. Even so, right this minute his skeptical expression was scaring the hell out of her.

Things had gone from bad to worse when Billy had added his wrinkle to the plan. The thought of being in the van when his men stopped it still had her shaking inside. But the thought of not *having* a plan frightened her even more. And if Jack refused to get involved, their plan would be dead in the water.

"You know how many neurological disorders there are?" he asked.

"Not exactly."

Clasping his hands behind his head, he pushed his chair back from his desk, almost banging it into the wall of his cramped office.

"Well, they've probably diagnosed a lot more since I graduated, but the number I recall is something over six hundred. So the odds on your pulling an accurate diagnosis out of the air based solely on a few symptoms Fitzgerald told you he's been having—"

"Jack, I know you're the medical doctor here, but I didn't simply listen to what Billy told me and come running to you. I've been digging through the literature, and I wouldn't have made a special trip to see him a second time if—"

"Why the special trip, anyway? Why didn't you

see him again yesterday, when you were already here?''

She swore under her breath. She'd known he'd ask that, and the best answer she and Sloan had come up with was pretty lame.

''I'd intended to,'' she said. ''My day turned out to be one crisis after another, though.'' She'd just have to hope he wouldn't check up on that. If he did, he might learn she'd spent half the day on the Internet.

''I simply couldn't find the time to see him,'' she went on. ''But I lay awake all last night thinking that I should have made time. And now that I have seen him again, I want you to. Because what really scares me is that the literature basically says TIAs are warning signs. And if we ignore them, Billy Fitzgerald might have a major stroke.''

When Jack didn't respond to that, she said, ''Look, regardless of what we think about him as a person, he's a very high-profile prisoner. And if anything happens to him, his people won't just let it slide. I documented my suspicions about his condition, and I've got a feeling they can find out just about anything they want to.''

She paused, thinking it was far more than a feeling. She knew that Sloan had somehow gotten access to her own job description and employment records. And he'd learned that she'd recommended against Billy's transfer.

''What I'm saying,'' she continued, ''is that if Billy *does* have a stroke, his son or his lawyer or whoever will raise such a stink about the inadequate health care here that the governor will be on the phone to the warden and—''

"All right," Jack said wearily. "I'll check him over. But I'm hardly an expert when it comes to this sort of thing. I'd be a lot happier if you were asking me to stitch up a knife wound or set a broken bone."

"Thanks," she said, trying not to let the full extent of her relief show. "Can we do it now?"

"We?"

"If you don't mind, I'd like to sit in. See what you ask him that I didn't think to."

He grinned. "Just remember I'm not a neurologist, and I'll be bloody embarrassed if you tell me afterward that I only repeated questions you already asked."

With a brief phone call, Jack arranged for William Fitzgerald to be brought to his office. Then he took a fat medical text from his shelves and started flipping through it.

"I'm just going to skim the neurology section," he explained. "Refresh my memory."

While he pored over the book, Hayley sat trying every trick she knew to make herself relax. She needed them all, because if Jack Kolodny picked up on the fact that she'd enjoy seeing Billy boiled in oil, he'd wonder why the hell she was going to such effort on the man's behalf.

Jack had barely finished his reading before a correctional officer arrived with their prisoner.

As they made their way to an examining room, Hayley was careful not to let Billy catch her eye.

He was just cocky enough to give her a nod or a wink.

"I'll be right outside," the C.O. said as Jack led the way into the room.

"Hayley, why don't you sit." He gestured to the chair in the corner, then turned to Billy. "All right, Mr. Fitzgerald, take off your shirt and—"

"In front of this pretty lady?" Billy smiled over at her.

She gritted her teeth. He was so damned pleased with himself because his plot had succeeded, because she was helping him, that she could happily wipe that smile off his face with an electric sander.

"Remove your shirt and get on the examining table," Jack ordered, ignoring Billy's remark.

After he'd taken off the top of his uniform and hoisted himself onto the table, Jack began checking him over—blood pressure, heart, lungs, ears, eyes and reflexes.

That done, he leaned back against the counter and said, "Dr. Morgan tells me she has some concerns about you."

Billy nodded, glancing at her again. "She told me, too. That's why she wanted me to see you. Just how serious is it?"

"I didn't notice anything wrong at all. You seem perfectly fine. But why don't you tell me what you told her. About the problems you've been having."

"Sure. For the past couple of weeks, I've been feeling kinda dizzy sometimes."

"Any particular times?"

When Billy hesitated, Hayley's heart leaped to

her throat. If he got anything wrong they'd be screwed.

"It mostly happens when I'm walking."

"I see. And have you noticed anything else unusual?"

"Yeah, I get a funny tingling sensation now and then. And a couple of times my leg suddenly went so weak I almost fell."

"And how long do these things last?"

"Usually just a few minutes, but once I'm not sure how long it was. I lay down as soon as I felt dizzy, and I think I passed out."

"Has there been anything else? Any other symptoms?"

"Well..."

Hayley was dying to prompt him, but she couldn't.

"Every so often," he continued at last, "I go to say something and it doesn't come out right. It sounds slurred, as if I've been drinking. But there's not a chance in hell I've been doing that in here."

"I see."

Billy watched Jack make some notes. "You think those things mean there *is* something serious?" he asked at last.

"Not necessarily. It isn't uncommon for people to start suffering from dizzy spells as they get older—for various reasons. And you're..." Jack paused, checking Billy's chart.

"You're almost fifty-nine. Everything's just not going to work as well as it did when you were twenty-nine."

"But something could really be wrong."

Jack nodded slowly. "There's always that possibility."

"Then I should be seeing a specialist."

When Jack glanced at Hayley she met his gaze, assuring herself he had no reason to suspect that she'd told Billy to demand a specialist. After all, the head of the Irish Mafia was used to the best of everything—including medical treatment.

"I should be getting tests," Billy added. "What kind of tests do they do for symptoms like mine?"

"It depends," Jack told him.

"But not ones you can do here, right?

"I know I'm right," he continued when neither Hayley nor Jack replied. "So where do they do them?"

"New Orleans," she said.

Jack shot her a glance that told her not to volunteer anything more.

"Well, I want them," Billy demanded. "I want whatever tests the friggin' governor of Louisiana would get. And I want them just as fast as he'd get them, too.

"And you," he added, looking at Hayley. "I want you to go with me when I'm having them."

"Nobody said you'll be having as much as your temperature taken," Jack snapped. "And if you do go anywhere, Dr. Morgan sure as hell won't be going along."

"Why not? She's the only one I trust in this rat hole. The only one who gives a damn about me. Nobody would even have realized something was wrong with me if not for her. Or if they had, they would have ignored it.

"So you'll come with me, won't you?" he said, looking at her. "Make sure I get treated right?"

"No, Billy, that really wouldn't be appropriate."

"Appropriate? Listen, my lawyer had a look at your job description. And you can use discretion when it comes to what you do for prisoners. Plus, we know you've gone out on a limb for other guys. But with me, first you recommend against my transfer and now you say you won't even take a little ride with me? When I don't trust anyone else? When having you along would do my mental health the world of good?"

Hayley stared at the floor, not letting herself look at Jack. Billy seemed to have remembered every single thing she'd told him to say, but would that be enough?

"You know, Dr. Morgan," he muttered, "you and the warden can't just go around denying requests because you feel like it. You, neither," he added to Jack. "And you can't discriminate against me. I might be behind bars, but I've still got my rights. So unless the three of you want me suing the pants off you—"

"That's enough!" Jack roared.

The door flew open and the correctional officer burst into the room. "Everything all right in here?"

Jack nodded, then turned toward Hayley.

Before he could catch her eye, she looked away. If she met his gaze this time, he might see something in it that she didn't want him to see.

Billy's performance had been flawless, and as much as she despised the man, she wanted to applaud it. She'd want to applaud anything that made it more likely she'd get her son back.

THEY'D BEEN SITTING in Warden Armstrong's office for almost ten minutes as Jack progressed slowly through his account of their session with William Fitzgerald. When he reached the part about Billy threatening to sue all three of them if he didn't get what he wanted, Armstrong's face flushed with anger. He didn't say a word, though. He simply let Jack continue.

Hayley, too, kept perfectly quiet. That had to be the wisest thing she could do—at least until she had a sense of which way Armstrong was leaning. With luck, he'd come to the "right" decision on his own. If he didn't, she'd do her best to ease him toward it. And if that wasn't enough to do the trick, Sloan would pay the warden a visit and try his routine about cruel and unusual punishment and denial of constitutional rights. Or he'd threaten to take the story to the media, or do anything else that might get Billy his trip out of Poquette.

Hopefully, though, it wouldn't come to that. Because she'd bet the farm that Armstrong would be just as likely to turn stubborn in the face of Sloan's threats as to give in to them.

"So that's about where we stand," Jack concluded.

Hayley's attention flashed back to the moment.

"And there's no way you can tell whether Fitzgerald's merely claiming he's been having these symptoms?'' Armstrong asked.

''No, I don't think even a neurologist could be certain without seeing test results. If we take Fitzgerald into the med center they'll do a CAT scan, some radiological procedures and who knows what else. Sophisticated testing's really the only way to determine exactly what's causing the problem.''

''If there is a problem,'' Armstrong muttered.

''You don't figure there is?''

The warden shrugged. ''Billy Fitz is a smart guy. And he's got to be bored as hell in here. My guess is that he's just looking for a little excitement. That he boned up on this TIA stuff in the hope of getting a vacation from Poquette.''

''It sure wouldn't be the first time one of them faked an illness,'' Jack said. ''But Hayley was right to bring this to my attention,'' he added.

She gave him a weak smile, feeling incredibly guilty. He was trying to protect her from the warden's anger, because Armstrong clearly wished that she'd simply kept her concerns to herself.

But if Jack knew the truth… Or, worse yet, if the warden did…

She suddenly realized that both men were looking at her and her anxiety level jumped.

''I take it you don't believe Fitzgerald's faking,'' Armstrong said. ''Otherwise, you wouldn't have asked Jack to have a look-see.''

She forced down the urge to say that she definitely didn't believe he was faking, that she thought they should be getting him to the med center just as soon as possible.

"Actually, I'm not sure whether he really has anything wrong with him or not," she said, instead. "But he makes me nervous enough that I think we should handle this carefully."

"Oh?" The warden gestured for her to elaborate.

This was her chance. Praying she didn't blow it, she said, "Well, as you pointed out, he's smart. And bored. He's also a man who, until recently, spent his entire adult life successfully beating the system. For decades, the authorities couldn't put him behind bars. And now that they finally have, *we've* become the system.

"When I assessed him, it was obvious his mindset hasn't changed, only his perception of who the enemy is. He no longer thinks in terms of how William Fitzgerald can beat the NOPD or how he can beat the feds. Now his goal is beating the Louisiana state prison system. Beating us."

"I hope you realize how much you're sounding like a psychologist," Jack told her.

She managed another smile. "That's what I get paid for."

"You've probably got him figured right," Armstrong said. "When he and his fancy lawyer filed that transfer request, he was just trying to push his weight around. And I'd say this is another example of that. He gets us to send him on a little trip and he's won."

"Exactly," Hayley agreed. "I'm just afraid that he's got things figured so he'll win either way. If we don't send him and he causes trouble for us, from his point of view that's winning, too.

"And I don't want us to end up wishing we'd simply taken the path of least resistance," she added hurriedly before either man could interrupt. "Because if Billy *is* faking, I think he's gotten himself into a win-win position. Either he gets his vacation from Poquette, or he and his fancy lawyer…" She glanced at Armstrong as she repeated his words, reminding herself that as far as he and Jack knew, she'd never laid eyes on Sloan Reeves.

"Even if they didn't try to sue us," she continued, "I'm sure they'd be screaming to the media and every politician who'd listen about how we're denying Billy his rights. And Billy would love every minute of it. He's used to a lot of attention, and now that he's out of the limelight he's got to be missing it."

"Damn," Armstrong muttered. "I'd hate to let the bastard win even one round. What do you think, Jack?"

"Well, I don't like the idea of his putting anything over on us, either. On the other hand, Hayley has a good point. He couldn't have made it clearer that he wants to be examined by a neurologist. So either we can quietly send him into the city or we can expect a whole lot of fallout for denying his request."

"And we can't forget that he might not be faking," Hayley put in.

Jack nodded. "If he really is having TIAs; and

we don't get him the appropriate attention after he's asked for it..."

Hayley tried her darnedest not to add anything more, but she just couldn't resist saying, "A third of untreated TIAs progress to CVAs.

"Cerebral vascular accidents. Strokes," she elaborated when the warden looked at her. "I did some research," she added, aware her face was growing warm.

"She's right," Jack said. "And if we do nothing, or even if we drag our feet and he has a major CVA, his lawyer would try to sue the pants off us. And the state of Louisiana to boot."

"Damn," Armstrong muttered again. He was silent for a minute, then slowly shook his head. "Is there anything else I should know?"

Jack looked at Hayley.

"What?" the warden demanded.

She cleared her throat. "Assuming you do approve sending him to the med center, Billy wants me to accompany him. Ride right in the back with him, in fact."

"What?" This time, Armstrong rose a foot out of his chair.

"He claims she's the only one he trusts," Jack explained. "And that's probably true. I think, because she brought his symptoms to my attention, he's deluding himself that she's his friend."

"Well, her going with him is out of the question," Armstrong snapped. Then he noticed Hayley's expression and said, "You don't think we should give him that too, do you?"

"I...it depends. My schedule's flexible enough that it wouldn't be any big deal for me. And the more I've been thinking about it... I guess where I'm at is that if you don't approve sending him we're going to get a lot of flack. So if you decide it's better to just send him and avoid that, then it seems to me we might as well avoid it entirely. I mean, if you say that no, I can't go with him, that would still leave him with something to scream about."

Jack nodded. "He was going on about how we're discriminating against him. Giving other inmates special treatment but withholding it from him."

"And if his lawyer's sharp," Hayley added, "he'll come up with a list of every example of special treatment in the past fifty years."

"Billy Fitz is a little weasel," Armstrong snapped. "Why the hell did they have to send him to my prison?"

Hayley held her breath, waiting for him to make his decision. But when he finally spoke again, he said, "Leave it with me. I want to think about it."

CHAPTER SEVEN

IT WAS PAST NOON when the meeting with Warden
Armstrong finished. Outside, the temperature had
already climbed into the low nineties. By the time
Hayley made it across the parking lot to her car she
was pouring sweat—which did nothing to improve
her state of mind. Feeling upset, infuriated and terrified about where things would go from here was
bad enough. Adding hotter than hell to the mix was
just too much.

When she opened the car door the heat was so
scorching there might as well have been a dragon
breathing flames at her, so she leaned in only long
enough to start the engine and turn on the air conditioner full blast. Then she dug the cell phone out
of her purse and pressed the "memory one" button.

She didn't even reply to Sloan's hello, simply
demanded, "Why didn't you tell me you were going to phone Billy this morning? And after you
talked to him, why didn't you call to warn me that
he wants me to go—"

"Were you straight with him?" Sloan asked.

His interrupting made her hotter yet.

"Did you tell him *exactly* how we had things

figured out?'' he continued. ''You didn't say anything that wasn't quite…right?''

''Of course not!''

''Good.''

''You haven't answered my questions,'' she
snapped, climbing into the rapidly cooling Taurus
and pulling the door shut behind her. She didn't put
the car into drive, though. This conversation re-
quired her complete attention.

In his office, Sloan leaned back and uneasily
shifted his cellular to his other ear.

''Dammit,'' Hayley was saying, ''the least you
could have done was warn me about what I was
walking into. Why didn't you?''

Hearing why would only make her more upset,
so he said, ''I'll explain in a second. But first tell
me what happened. Did the doctor examine Billy?
Have you talked to the warden?'' He counted to
twenty, imagining her trying to decide whether she
was still speaking to him.

At last she said, ''Yes, Jack examined him. And
Billy acted out his part perfectly. Then Jack and I
met with Warden Armstrong and replayed the ex-
amining-room scene for him.''

''And he said…?''

''He said he wanted time to think before he de-
cides.''

Damn, he silently muttered. He'd been expecting
the warden to make a decision right away. Then he
could have gotten going on his next step.

''Which way is he leaning?'' he asked.

''I don't know.''

Sloan told himself not to worry. Even if Armstrong didn't go along with things initially, he would in the end. There was absolutely no doubt about that.

"Sloan, you have no idea how angry I am right now! So let's get back to why you didn't call me after you talked to Billy. I mean, I walked him through the entire plan before he told me that you'd already gone over it with him. And I was still feeling like an idiot about that when he hit me with his new demand. Can you imagine how it made me feel? How much I do *not* want to be in that van with him?"

"Yeah, I can imagine." Easily. Because he didn't want her on the escape run with Billy any more than she wanted to go along.

But Billy had made up his mind, so that was how they'd have to play things. Still, they didn't have to play them exactly the way Billy expected. And whatever Sloan could do to protect her, he intended to do.

"You did agree to go, though?" he asked.

"Yes. I told him I would if Warden Armstrong said it was okay, but that's a big if."

Not really. It was just something else Armstrong would agree to—either right off the top or after a little persuasion.

"So?" she said. "You didn't let me know you'd talked to Billy because...?"

"Because I have no idea how good an actor you are. Look, Billy wanted to be sure you'd tell him the whole truth and nothing but. If you hadn't, he'd have been certain you had ideas about double-crossing him. So—"

"And you didn't think you should warn me? You didn't—"

"Hayley, if I had, you'd have been watching every word you said. And Billy would have realized it. He picks up on things like that." Sloan waited after he'd finished explaining, practically able to hear her seething in the silence that followed.

At last, she said icily, "You were testing me."

"*Billy* was testing you."

"But you let him. You didn't tell him it wasn't necessary. Does that mean you actually thought I'd be stupid enough to risk Max's life? Did you actually think…"

When he heard her dissolve into tears, he began wishing he'd never come within a hundred miles of Mr. William Fitzgerald.

"Hayley," he said quietly. "To answer that question, no, I didn't think you'd risk Max's life. In fact, I was absolutely certain you wouldn't, which meant there was no need to warn you. As for testing you, don't forget that I'm not running the show. Billy is. And he can't afford to take any chances."

Another silence followed, then she said, "What would you have done if I *had* lied to Billy? What would you have done if I'd tried to double-cross him? Would you have killed my son?"

He closed his eyes, not knowing how to answer.

"Would you?"

"It wouldn't have been up to me," he said, knowing that was a cop-out.

She didn't let him get away with it for a second.

"No? Then who would it have been up to? Last night, you said that Billy told his people you were calling the shots as far as Max was concerned. So what shot would you have called if I hadn't been straight with him this morning?"

"Hayley…if I'd thought for a minute you weren't going to be, I'd have…"

"You'd have what?"

The truth was on the tip of his tongue, yet he couldn't say it. Couldn't tell her that if he'd had the slightest fear she *would* try something he'd have warned her. Couldn't say that if he'd read her wrong and she *had* lied to Billy, he'd have protected her son's life with his own. That even though his job was to ensure Billy's escape went smoothly, he wouldn't do it at the expense of a child's life. Not any child's, and especially not hers.

But he couldn't tell her any of those things. She was only cooperating because of her fear for Max's safety, which meant there was no way he dared alleviate that fear.

"Hayley, I knew you wouldn't try anything," he said again. "So I didn't give a thought to the possibility you might—or to how I'd react if you did. But look, how long do you figure Armstrong will leave us hanging? Will he decide today?"

She didn't reply right away, making Sloan suspect she had more she wanted to get off her chest before she let him change the subject.

Finally, though, she simply said, "I think we'll get his answer either this afternoon or in the morning. Jack and I made it clear that Billy won't let this slide, so he knows he can't sit on the fence for long."

"Should I give him a call and apply a little pressure?"

"No. Save that in case he digs in his heels."

"Yeah. You're right. But what time does he leave for the day?"

"Five. On the dot. Jack always says that only a riot would keep him at Poquette any later."

"All right, as soon as Billy gets an answer he'll let me know. You'll probably hear before he does, though, so phone me when you do. If I don't hear from you before five, I'll just come by your place to take you to see Max."

"Yes. All right. Bye."

He kept the phone to his ear once she'd clicked off, letting the sound of her voice echo in his mind—even though he knew it was a bad idea.

He didn't want to be feeling anything for her, let alone the things he was. Didn't want something as basic as merely hearing her speak to send tiny ripples of desire through him.

But like it or not, he'd been attracted to her from the first moment he'd seen her. And the better he got to know her, the faster that attraction was growing into something far beyond a merely physical one. She was a gorgeous woman. More significantly, she was intelligent and brave. And when it came to how much she loved her son...

He'd mentioned seeing Max tonight and her tone had suddenly softened, her anger had dissipated. Try as he might, Sloan couldn't stop himself from wondering how he'd feel if she was looking forward to seeing *him* that much.

That's something you'll never know, he told himself. On a list of people she'd ever look forward to seeing, probably the only name below his would be Billy Fitzgerald's.

IF FRANK ARMSTRONG had arrived at his decision before he'd left Poquette for the day, he hadn't let Hayley know. That meant she was still worrying about him digging in his heels and refusing to let Billy go.

She glanced across the Jeep at Sloan, wishing she felt as certain about how things were going to unfold as he seemed to be.

He was sure that once the warden had considered all the angles he'd simply approve Billy's trip to the med center. That no matter how stubborn he was, logic had to tell him that Billy would get what he wanted in the end, so it only made sense to avoid any hassles.

In theory, she knew that should be true. When an inmate warranted special medical attention he was entitled to it. The rules were cut-and-dried. But if Armstrong was totally convinced that Billy was faking...

If that was the case, then considering how much the man hated being manipulated, he just might turn down the request—even knowing there'd be fallout.

And if he did, would Sloan have an easy time convincing him to change his mind or not?

She didn't know. But she knew that if they had to resort to a media campaign or some other ploy to force him into reversing his decision, things could drag on forever.

At least, it would seem that way. Every day between now and when she got Max back home would feel like an eternity.

Telling herself not to think about that, she focused on the passing scenery—and realized they were on the same road they'd taken the night before.

"We're going back to your fishing cove?" she asked.

"Uh-huh."

"But you said we'd be meeting at different places."

"Yeah…well, I got to thinking it might be better for Max if we went to the same place again. I don't know much about kids, but I remember someone once telling me that consistency makes them feel more secure."

"Yes, it does."

When Sloan said nothing more she simply sat gazing at him, thinking, as she had last night, that he was a walking contradiction. Sometimes he was so darned kind…

Stockholm syndrome, an imaginary voice reminded her.

Don't let yourself start believing he's a basically good man, when you know he isn't.

"You don't have nieces and nephews?" she asked, the question just sort of popping out.

He glanced over at her.

"I don't," she volunteered so he wouldn't figure she was being unduly nosy. "I'm an only child. And when you said you don't know much about kids I wondered if you were too."

"Uh-uh. I've got two younger sisters and a younger brother. And between them they have three boys and four girls. But I don't really see much of them."

"Oh?"

"Well, now and then," he said with a shrug. "And always at Christmas. My parents like the whole family there, so I go. And I get a kick out of 'spoiling the kids rotten,' as my mother puts it. But aside from that..."

"Your family's not in New Orleans, then."

Staring out at the road ahead, he didn't reply for so long that she thought he wasn't going to. Then he said, "No, I was born and raised in New Orleans. But...when I do see my family things are sometimes strained, so it's easier just to not see them very often."

"Strained," she repeated, knowing she was probably pushing harder than she should but unable to stop herself.

He hesitated once more. "They don't exactly approve of my client list," he said at last.

"Ah." His client list of one. Thinking that she and his family had something in common, she gazed out of the window once more.

It was only another few minutes before they reached the cove, and this time they didn't have to wait for Dick to arrive with Max. The two of them were already there. Max greeted her enthusiastically, then immediately began asking when she was taking him home.

It tore at her heart every bit as much as it had last night, but he didn't appear quite as upset as he had yesterday. Hopefully, that meant he was feeling more comfortable with Tom and Dick.

"Are we gonna go for a walk?" he asked.

She glanced at Sloan.

"Just be careful," he said.

Max's hand clutched in hers, they started for the shoreline.

Once again, the cove was a picture of tranquillity, its peacefulness disturbed only by an occasional fish breaking the surface of the lake. When that happened, the lingering sunlight filtering through the trees to snooze on the water would dance briefly before the surface stilled again.

"Dick likes fishing," Max informed her. "He told me."

"Oh?"

"Uh-huh. And Tom taught me a neat card game."

"So you're having fun staying with them?"

He shrugged. "It's okay, I guess. But I still wanna come home. And you still didn't say when I could."

She forced a smile. "Just as soon as I start getting home on time again. And I'm hoping that'll be really soon.''

"Yeah, Tom said it would be."

Her heart leaped. Did Tom know something she didn't? Had Billy heard he was getting his trip to New Orleans even though she hadn't?

"Oh?" she said as casually as she could.

"I was tellin' him I miss Satchmo. 'Cuz I woke up in the night and didn't 'member I wasn't home. And I was scared 'cuz Satch wasn't on the bed. I thought he was lost. But when I told Tom, he said I'd be back home real soon."

"Ah." So Tom didn't know anything. He'd only been reassuring Max.

Trying to ignore her disappointment, she told herself she should count her blessings. Somebody kidnapping your child had to be one of the worst things that could ever happen. And she was incredibly lucky this wasn't a standard kidnapping—that not only were Billy's men treating Max just fine, but she was getting to see him.

Thanks to Sloan, she thought, glancing back toward where the cars were parked.

He was standing talking to Dick, and she was struck by the contrast between them. They were roughly the same age; Dick might even be a little younger. But whereas he appeared world-weary and had a substantial beer belly, Sloan looked like the lead in a romantic movie. Tall and lean, with chiseled features and a commanding presence, he looked...

So desirable that you don't dare even let yourself think the thought? an imaginary voice asked.

She closed her eyes, her heart suddenly pounding. He *wasn't* desirable. At least, she didn't find him so. She couldn't. He was on Billy's team. That made him her enemy.

Yet there was something about him that… Something that, if she was being deep-down honest, she'd admit reached right inside and touched her.

Just as it had last night, her mind drifted back to the first moment she'd seen him. He'd been standing in her office doorway, her eyes had met his and she'd felt an undeniable pull. But once she'd learned—

"Mommy!"

Max's whisper was one of pure terror.

Her eyes flashed open and she looked down.

He was gazing straight ahead, his body rigid, his hand squeezing hers impossibly tightly.

She followed his gaze, then froze. "Don't move," she murmured. "Don't move."

Her heart pounding even harder, she stared at the snake.

It was lying a yard or so in front of them, curved around on itself, with its head across its tail. Maybe three feet long, it had a reddish head and light and dark brown bands on its body. And it was eyeing them, its tongue flickering.

Some of Louisiana's snakes were poisonous, but was this one? She no more knew that than she knew whether they should stand or run.

"Mommy?" Max whimpered.

"Max, please don't cry! Try your hardest not to."

The snake's tongue had vanished. The reptile was completely motionless now but still watching them, its eyes unblinking.

Hayley didn't breathe. She simply continued to stand motionless herself, willing Max not to cry and still trying to decide what to do.

"You're going to be all right," Sloan said, his voice coming from the direction the snake was looking, his words so quiet they were barely audible.

"Max, when I say now, you and your mom take a really slow step back, okay? Just one and then stop. Now."

She took a deep breath, then stepped backward with Max.

"Good," Sloan said softly. "Good. And another one—now."

They moved another step away from the snake, but this time it focused on them once more.

"Don't worry," Sloan murmured. "You're almost out of striking range. One more step...now. Good. That was terrific. Okay, just walk backward very slowly, all the way to the cars."

Still clutching Max's hand, her heart still racing, Hayley took a few more steps backward.

She could see Sloan, then, standing off to the side, his gun pointed at the snake. When she and Max were a good twenty feet from it, he began to ease backward himself, his gaze not leaving the reptile, his finger not leaving the trigger of the gun.

By the time he reached the cars, Hayley was holding Max in her arms and he was crying uncontrollably.

"Sorry," she whispered over his shoulder. "I guess the snake was the last…everything's just gotten too much for him. But thank you. If you hadn't realized something was wrong…"

Sloan simply nodded, not knowing what else to do. Seeing Max sobbing his heart out and Hayley looking so upset, and knowing he was involved in what had brought them to this, made him feel like total pond scum.

Kevin O'Rourke cleared his throat. *Dick,* Sloan reminded himself. If he used their names when Max or Hayley was around, Kevin O'Rourke was *Dick* and Sammy was *Tom.*

When he glanced at O'Rourke, the man gave him a look that said, *I told you letting her see him was a bad idea.*

Sloan shot him a glare in return. He didn't give a damn what Kevin O'Rourke thought.

"Could we go someplace else?" Hayley asked. "Max won't settle down as long as we're here."

"Sure. They can both ride with me," he added to O'Rourke.

"Sloan…"

Dick swallowed the rest of his words, but Sloan knew what he'd been about to say. *Billy wouldn't like that,* and *You're pushing your authority too far.*

Instead, all O'Rourke said was, "Where are we going?"

"I don't know," Sloan told him. "Just follow me."

He opened the Cherokee's front passenger door and Hayley climbed in, Max still clinging to her.

O'Rourke got into his own car, not bothering to even try concealing his disapproval.

There was no doubt that Brendan Fitzgerald would hear about this later tonight. Or that Billy would be informed just as soon as his son could get a call through to him.

And O'Rourke was right. Billy wouldn't like it.

"Screw Billy," Sloan muttered.

He started the Jeep and backed out onto the narrow dirt road that dead-ended at the cove. Then, the other car on his tail, he headed for the two-lane road that would take them to the highway. But once they got back to the city, where the hell would he go? Public places were too risky. Someone Hayley knew might see them. Yet they could hardly head for the house where Max was being held. Even though Sloan was convinced Hayley had no intention of crossing them, if she knew where Max was it might be just too tempting.

And Hayley's place was out of the question. Her neighbors thought Max was in Pennsylvania visiting his father. As for Sloan's apartment...

He glanced across at the two of them, not even wanting to imagine what Billy would think about his taking them there.

Max gradually calmed down as they drove. Eventually, he wiped his eyes, then untangled himself from his mother's arms and sat gazing out into the gathering evening.

"Does he like ice cream?" Sloan asked Hayley after they'd hit the highway. "Would a cone or a shake or something make him feel better?"

"Yeah!" Max said, looking over excitedly. "Yeah, ice cream would make me feel lots better."

Sloan nodded. That was the solution, then. They'd hit an ice-cream place, get something and just sit in the Jeep until Max was totally okay. The odds on someone Hayley knew seeing them sitting in a dark parking lot had to be one in a billion.

Once they'd driven a little farther, Max whispered loudly to Hayley, "What's his name?"

"Sloan," she told him. "Oh," she murmured when Sloan looked at her. "Maybe I shouldn't have...?"

He shrugged. She was right, of course; she shouldn't have. But he wasn't going to lie awake nights worrying about it. She knew it would be worth her life to talk about any of this even after it was over, and she'd do her best to explain to Max that he had to keep it all a secret, too. That could be a problem, but he didn't intend to worry about it at the moment, either.

"Sloan?" Max said after they'd gone a few more miles. "How come you didn't shoot the snake?"

"I would have if he'd tried to hurt you or your mom. But I think he was as scared as you were. When he saw you coming, I bet he was afraid you were going to step on him."

"Yeah?"

"Uh-huh." He half watched the road ahead, half watched the boy consider that.

"You think so, Mommy?" Max asked at last. "Do you think that snake was scared of me?"

"Well...I don't know much about snakes. But if Sloan says it was, then I guess it must have been."

"I wasn't really scared of it, you know."

"No?" Hayley said.

As Max firmly shook his head, she looked across at Sloan and smiled. For half a second, he felt a warm connection between them. Then he remembered who she was. Who he was. Why they were together. And his heart felt stone-cold dead.

CHAPTER EIGHT

SLOAN PULLED INTO the driveway behind Hayley's car, cut the engine, then glanced at her.

When she'd finally said goodbye to Max and watched O'Rourke drive off with him, she'd seemed awfully fragile, as if she'd pretty well reached the end of her emotional rope. Now, he was relieved to see, she seemed to be feeling better.

"I've got something for you," he told her, climbing out into the warm fragrance of the summer night.

Above, the black sky was filled with stars. All around him, moonlight dappled the yard with its pale glow. In another place and time, the gentle breeze rustling the leaves might well have been whispering, "Romance." But not here and now. Not to him and Hayley.

By the time he'd opened the tailgate she was standing in the driveway, watching him curiously. He took out the box and handed it to her, doing his best to ignore the sultry scent of her perfume. But ignoring it was impossible—as impossible as the thoughts it engendered.

Not here and now, he reminded himself. *And definitely not her.*

"It's... " She gazed at the gift, then looked at him, her expression uncertain.

He shrugged, thinking the vest was as far removed from anything romantic as it could possibly be.

"To wear on the trip with Billy," he told her. "Just in case anything goes wrong."

"You're really convinced the warden will let him go, aren't you? And let me go along."

"Uh-huh."

"Why?"

"If I told you I had a crystal ball, would you believe me?"

"Not unless you showed it to me."

"Then I'll do that sometime." Before she could pursue the subject of his fortune-telling skills, he focused on the vest again and said, "It's Kevlar. A state-of-the-art skinny model. If you wear it under a suit, nobody will even realize you've got it on."

"Ah. And I guess that's good. If Armstrong saw I was wearing a bulletproof vest, it just might make him wonder."

Sloan slowly smiled, surprised she was even trying to be humorous when she looked so nervous about needing a vest.

"It's pretty thin," she murmured, fingering it.

"I know, but it *will* keep you safe. There's a ceramic plate in the heart area. And the rest…well, even if you got shot, the worst you'd end up with is some bad bruising."

When she nodded, he couldn't help wondering if she was thinking, *Unless I got shot in the head.*

But dammit, he intended to do everything in his power to ensure the escape went off without a hitch, and without a shot being fired.

He'd had no trouble at all getting Billy onside as far as that detail went. The last thing the man wanted was to find himself in the middle of a shoot-out. So as long as Brendan put the fear of God into the escape team, as long as they believed it would be worth their lives if anyone ended up shot, the plan should go smoothly.

Telling himself that was enough worrying about the escape for the moment, he looked at Hayley again, saying, "I'll see you to the door."

He didn't want to leave her on her own just yet. She might feel better than she had earlier, but she was a long way from a hundred percent. So the least he could do…

Oh, hell, what was the point in kidding himself? He was seeing her to the door because it meant he'd have another minute or two of her company. Because, ludicrous as he knew it was, if he walked across the yard with her he could pretend they were a couple of ordinary people arriving home from a normal evening out.

You're losing it, Reeves, he told himself. *Regardless of what you feel for her, she thinks you're a sewer rat.*

"Keys," she said, fumbling in her purse as they reached the house.

He waited, gazing at her and deciding that in the faint porch light she looked even more beautiful than usual.

When she finally found her keys, he made himself stick his hands in his pockets and take a backward step. "I guess that with any luck, you'll hear from Armstrong in the morning."

She nodded.

"And he'll likely send Billy into the city tomorrow? Assuming he's decided not to be obstinate, I mean."

"That would be standard procedure."

"So, when he calls, he'll tell you what time the van will leave?"

"If he's going to let me go along, he'll have to."

"He'll let you. I'm sure he'll decide to just quietly give Billy whatever he wants this time around."

"You weren't there this morning," she said. "Didn't see how ambivalent he was."

"No, but I spent a fair bit of time with him the day we discussed Billy's transfer application. So I know what you mean. I could tell he hated the thought of anyone getting the better of him. But he knows he can't win this one in the long run, and I'd say he's smart enough to simply walk away from it.

"At any rate, phone me as soon as you hear from him. Things are pretty much arranged already. But if we're on for tomorrow, the sooner I let the appropriate people know what time you'll be leaving Poquette, the better."

The appropriate people, Hayley silently repeated. As in Billy's son, Brendan, or whoever would be orchestrating the escape. Whoever would be...

Merely thinking about what was coming made her shiver.

"You can't be cold," Sloan said quietly. "So what's the problem?"

She shook her head. She'd go along in the prison van with Billy because she had to. Because he'd made it a condition of ensuring Max's safety. But the escort guards would be armed, as would Billy's people. And even having the vest, she was terrified the escape might turn into a disaster.

Billy wouldn't be wearing any vest. If things went wrong, he could well end up dead. And if he did, what would happen to Max?

Looking at Sloan, she was tempted to ask him. To tell him how very frightened she was. But it would be absurd to get into that sort of conversation with the enemy. Besides, she wouldn't know how to start. And if she began, she might never be able to stop.

"Hayley..."

"Don't," she whispered, mentally searching for another topic before he could ask, again, what was wrong.

"I...Sloan, I didn't really say it properly before, but that snake... If you hadn't known what to do... If you hadn't... I didn't thank you properly."

She stopped there and simply stood gazing at him, her heart aching. Because of her son. Because she had no choice but to go along with Billy. Because the man involved in this mess with her, the man who right this minute looked so much as if he wanted to help her, was the wrong man.

He couldn't be more wrong. She knew that. Yet she couldn't stop wishing it wasn't so.

"I..." He took a step forward and tentatively rested his hand on her bare arm. "Hayley, is there anything I can do?"

What did he expect her to say? That yes, there were all kinds of things he could do? That he could go and collect her son from wherever they were keeping him, then take the two of them someplace where nobody would find them and kill them? That he could call Warden Armstrong and warn him about Billy's escape plan? That he could go to the police and volunteer everything he knew about the Irish Mafia's activities? Or that he could tell her he was finished working for Billy Fitz? Tell her he'd seen the error of his ways and was turning over a new leaf?

Oh, Lord, she was afraid even to imagine how she'd feel if he said that. Because despite knowing it was totally insane, she couldn't help thinking that if only he wasn't one of the bad guys, she'd...

Stop right there! she ordered herself. She didn't dare finish the thought.

He *was* one of the bad guys. And there was no way in the world she could be falling for the enemy.

"Let's get you inside," he said, taking the keys and opening the door.

She'd left the light on in the front hallway, and Satchmo was waiting there for her. He gave a quiet meow in greeting, then spotted Sloan and scurried off to hide.

As she put the box with the vest in it down on

the hall table, her gaze lingered on the framed picture of Max that sat on top—and her thoughts returned to what would happen if things went wrong
during the escape attempt.

Maybe she *should* talk to Sloan about it. Maybe,
regardless of which side he was on, she had to.
Because nobody else would know where to find
Max. And that meant Sloan could do something for
her that no one else could. That he was really her
only option.

"Sloan?" she made herself say.

"What?"

"If the warden does agree, and I go with
Billy..."

"Yes?"

"If anything happens to me, I want you to give
me your word that Max will be all right."

"Nothing's going to happen to you."

"But if something does," she persisted, her
throat tight. "If I do my best to help, if I live up
to my end of the deal..."

For a few seconds he merely stood looking at
her, then he moved closer and folded her into his
arms.

She tried to resist but couldn't. She was too
frightened and it felt too good to be held. Even by
the wrong man.

His chest was hard and warm against her, his
arms strong around her, and his clean, male scent
made her wish with all her heart that they were two
different people in an entirely different situation.

"It's going to be okay," he whispered against her hair. "I promise it's going to be okay."

Swallowing hard, she told herself to pull away—then didn't. Even though he was the wrong man, even though she'd never meant it to happen, she'd been touched by the things that were right about him.

That he'd let her see Max. That he'd protected them from the snake. That he cared enough to have gotten her the vest.

Maybe none of that outweighed his working for Billy Fitz. But right this instant, moving out of the reassuring circle of his embrace would simply take more willpower than she could muster.

"I just…I just need a minute," she said.

Sloan didn't speak, but he kissed the top of her head—so lightly that she barely realized he had.

She made herself draw away from him then, just an inch or two, and met his gaze. Slowly, he slid his hands down her back, pulling her close once more and lowering his mouth to hers.

Died and gone to heaven.

The words whispered in her brain as she lost herself in his kiss. It had been a long, long time since she'd been in a man's arms like this, since she'd felt the warmth of desire swirling inside her. And it felt so very, very good.

Tentatively, she grazed his ear with her fingertips and began moving them there in tiny, teasing circles.

"Oh, Hayley," he said against her lips. Then he deepened their kiss with a bone-melting passion.

She could feel his heart beating rapidly against her and the heat of his body seeping into her skin, sending hot little shivers of pleasure through her. Then, as he cupped her breasts, the words whispered again.

Died and gone to heaven.

She wanted him. Purely and simply wanted him. And when he began to brush her nipples with his thumbs, her need intensified a hundredfold.

But she couldn't have him! He was the wrong man.

"Sloan," she forced herself to say. "We can't do this. We just can't. I just can't."

He made a ragged sound in his throat, then slowly moved his hands from her breasts to her waist and took a single step backward.

"Maybe if things were different," she murmured, staring at the floor, knowing that looking at him would weaken her resolve. "Maybe, if you weren't you or I wasn't me..."

For a long moment, only the sound of their breathing filled the silence between them. Then Sloan quietly said, "I know."

Softly kissing her forehead, he dropped his hands to his sides—leaving her feeling desperately alone and lonely. She wanted his arms around her again. And she knew that if she moved forward even a fraction of an inch...

Instead, calling on every ounce of self-control she possessed, she made herself turn away from him.

Sloan watched Hayley walk over to the hall table,

his heart still racing. Holding her had felt so right, so good, that he'd wanted to hold her forever. But now…

Shaking his head, he wondered if it would have been better not to have kissed her at all than to be left with the aching, empty feeling that was filling his entire body.

He did his best to ignore the emptiness as she took a pen and a piece of paper from the drawer of the table.

"My parents live in Pennsylvania," she said. "I'll write down their phone number and address for you."

Her voice sounded so raw it started his throat aching.

"If anything *does* happen to me," she continued, "please get Max to them."

He swallowed hard. If she could act as though what had just happened meant nothing, that was what he'd do, too. "Not get him to his father?" he said.

"No. He doesn't want Max in his life any longer."

The empty feeling grew. How could anyone throw away a wife and son like worthless trash? A wife and son like Hayley and Max?

If there was any way Sloan could have a woman like her, a son like hers… But a man in his line of work simply shouldn't have a wife and children. That was an undisputable fact. One he'd resigned himself to long ago.

THE WARDEN CALLED HAYLEY at 7:00 a.m.—waking her from a nightmare in which she and Max were sitting amid a row of duck decoys, moving targets in a shooting gallery with faceless men firing enormous guns at them.

"Yes?" she said, half trying to struggle awake as Frank Armstrong identified himself, half wondering why on earth he was calling so early.

"I'm approving Billy Fitzgerald's trip to the med center," he snapped. "He'll go this morning and he still wants you along. So if you haven't changed your mind…"

"No. No, I haven't."

"Fine."

His tone made her cringe. He might be saying "fine," but he sounded mad as hell, as if his decision was totally against his better judgment and he already regretted it.

"I'll let the guards know to expect you. The van will leave at ten. You'll have to be here before that."

"Yes. All right. Exactly where should I go?"

He told her which wing and door, then abruptly hung up.

Her thoughts immediately turning to Sloan, she reached for her purse and dug out the cellular to call him—telling herself not to say a word about what had happened after he'd seen her into the house last night. Or about how she'd felt after he'd gone.

She certainly didn't want him to know she'd barely slept, that she'd lain awake until almost dawn. That when she hadn't been worrying about Max she'd been recalling how wonderful it had felt to be held by a certain man. How she'd wanted him to keep on kissing her. That if her guilt about who he was hadn't been so strong...

Closing her eyes, she listened to his phone begin to ring, and wondered if her nerves were so on edge that she'd lost the ability to think straight. She didn't want to believe that was true, but it certainly might be.

While she'd tossed and turned during the night, she must have warned herself a million times that she'd probably fallen victim to the Stockholm syndrome. Yet she just couldn't keep from thinking that wasn't it at all. Thinking that even though Sloan worked for Billy, he honestly cared about what happened to her and Max. And that he felt more for her than mere concern. So much more it frightened her.

Because he was who he was. There was no way she could change that. And she could never, ever allow a repeat of what had happened between them.

The best thing she could do was just keep her memories of how he'd made her feel locked tightly away in her subconscious.

As she was telling herself that, he answered his phone. She quickly filled him in about the warden's call, struggling, while she spoke, not to picture his strong, dark good looks—but failing miserably.

"Okay," he said once she'd finished. "I'll see you after it's over, then. And... Hayley, I wish I could be with you. If there was any way..."

Exhaling slowly, she did her darnedest not to wish the same thing. She failed miserably at that, too.

"Just do your best not to be frightened," he said.

"I will."

"And if by any chance somebody does start shooting…well, hit the floor if you even think anyone might. But the plan is to get Billy out of that van without anyone firing a shot."

"Right." Who was going to tell the guards not to start shooting, though? And if they did, wouldn't Billy's men fire back?

"Exactly where will they intercept us?" she asked.

"It'll be better if you don't know that."

His reply made her wonder why she'd bothered to ask, because she was certain it would be someplace along Highway 23, which had little traffic during the day.

Billy's people would simply block off a stretch of the highway while they stopped the van. Then they'd have as long as they needed to get Billy away from the guards, with no worries about any interruptions.

Freeing him would be so easy it made her wonder why there weren't far more escapes. But she knew why. Most prisoners had nothing like the resources Billy could call on.

"You really *are* going to be okay," Sloan was saying.

Forcing her thoughts from the imaginary road-

blocks, she said, "And once it's over you'll get
Max back to me?"

"Yes. Of course. Everything will end up just
fine."

She wanted to believe that so badly she could
taste her desire. But it was one thing for Sloan to
say everything would end up fine and another to
know she'd be right there when Billy's people appeared on the scene. All it would take was one itchy
trigger finger to...

Aware that the more upset she got the harder it
would be to make it through the next few hours,
she ordered herself to stop thinking of what might
happen later on and simply take things minute by
minute.

But even though she did her best to chill out,
getting ready to leave the house proved to be an
exercise in frustration.

First, when she phoned Cataouatche—the prison
she normally visited on Thursdays—to leave a message that she wouldn't be there today, her brain
went on pause. It took her three tries to reach the
right voice mail.

Next, she got entirely dressed before she remembered about the vest. Then, after she had it on and
thought she was ready to go, she checked the mirror
and discovered its outline showed beneath her linen
suit. That meant searching through her closet for
something else to put on and getting dressed again.

She ended up in a fall-weight suit, which would
have been too hot even without the damned vest.
And while the outfit was bearable in her air-

conditioned car, climbing out into the parking lot at Poquette felt like walking into a sauna.

She made her way to the staff entrance, then waited anxiously, checking her watch every few seconds, until a correctional officer found time to escort her to the secure wing the van would depart from.

When they reached the waiting area by the designated exit, four large uniformed guards were already there. She'd never seen any of them before, but that was hardly surprising if transporting prisoners was their regular assignment. In the three years she'd worked for the Louisiana Department of Corrections, this was the first time she'd ever accompanied a convict anywhere outside a prison.

"You're Dr. Morgan?" one of the guards asked.

"Yes."

He simply nodded, looking bored. But unlike her, he didn't know this wouldn't be a routine trip.

Uneasily, she checked out their weapons. They were all wearing holstered automatics. Two of them, undoubtedly the ones who'd ride with her and Billy, also held pump-action shotguns.

Her stomach began churning, harder and harder until she started praying she wouldn't throw up.

Then Billy was escorted into the area by a couple of correctional officers. Both his wrists and ankles were shackled, and the way he was shuffling along with his head down made him look utterly defeated. But she'd seen his performances before. She knew how deceiving they could be.

The C.O. carrying the paperwork that would accompany Billy gave it to one of the guards. Then the guard who was apparently in charge glanced at Hayley. "The warden said you'd ride in back with the prisoner? That right?"

When she nodded, his expression told her it wasn't exactly standard procedure. All he said, though, was, "Okay, let's hit the road."

Outside, the van was waiting. A white cargo type, identified on the side as belonging to the Louisiana Department of Corrections, it had a single window in the back compartment—a small chicken-wire one in the door. Far too small, she thought, following along behind the guards and Billy, for a prisoner to crawl through.

The two guards armed only with pistols got into the front, the one she'd decided was in charge climbing into the driver's seat. One of the two with shotguns motioned her to get into the back.

She set her purse and briefcase on the floor of the van, then hiked her skirt and managed the high step up, hoping her legs weren't shaking visibly.

The rear section of the van, completely partitioned off from the front by a metal panel, had benches along both sides. She scooted down to the far end of one, then sat there breathing as shallowly as she could. The van smelled as if it had been used for transporting livestock and given only a rudimentary cleaning afterward.

"I can't get up with these chains on my legs," Billy complained.

The guards grabbed him by either arm and half boosted, half heaved him inside, then climbed in after him. One attached the chain on his leg shackles to a steel doughnut in the floor, then sat down next to him, across from Hayley. The other pulled the door shut and locked it with a key chained to his belt. Once the door was closed, the interior was even darker and smellier.

You are not going to be sick, she told herself, although she sure wouldn't put any money on it.

As the engine roared to life and the van pulled away, Billy looked over through the gray light and gave her a wry smile. "Nice of you to come with me," he said.

CHAPTER NINE

THE LONGER THEY DROVE, the more nervous Hayley grew—and the total silence in the van didn't help. Not that she really wanted to strike up a conversation with either Billy or the guards, but she was tempted.

Without anything to distract her, she couldn't stop thinking that, any second now, their trip would be interrupted. And when that happened... Lord, those were the worst thoughts of all.

With only the one little window, she couldn't see where they were. But they'd gone over the bridge that lay between Buras and Port Sulphur about fifteen minutes ago. So by now they were probably somewhere between West Pointe à la Hache and Myrtle Grove.

That was a long, virtually unpopulated stretch, which made it an obvious place for Billy's people to intercept them. But would they go for the obvious or—

"BOOM!"

The blast of noise was earsplitting. The van rocked from side to side, its wheels crunching gravel on the shoulder, then grabbing pavement again and shooting crazily forward along the road, swerving and squealing as it went.

Hayley clung to the edge of the bench, certain that any second they'd explode into a million pieces.

"It was only a tire blowing," one of the guards in the front yelled, banging on the partition as they lurched to a stop.

Calm down, she told herself. *Breathe slowly.*

But her heart was racing a hundred miles a minute. Had they really blown a tire? Or had someone shot it out as step one in the escape plan?

She heard the doors opening and the guards getting out of the front. Most of what they were muttering was garbled, but it wasn't hard to imagine the gist of it.

"Open up," one of them called, banging on the rear door. "Let's just hope the spare's in good shape."

When the guard nearest the back door unlocked it and shoved it open, the bright sunlight that flooded in was momentarily blinding.

Shading her eyes, Hayley peered out—and saw nothing except deserted road behind them. She didn't know whether that made her feel better or worse.

She didn't want Billy to win, but he had to. And as much as she'd like to warn the guards that if this wasn't a setup one was coming soon, she couldn't. Max's life depended on Billy's escaping.

"Okay, everybody out," one of the guards ordered.

Another of them unchained Billy's leg shackles from the floor, telling him they didn't need to jack up his weight along with the van's.

Leaving her purse and briefcase on the bench, Hayley climbed out after the other three, perspiration beginning to trickle down beneath the Kevlar vest before she even reached the pavement.

As casually as she could, she surveyed the scene from this broader perspective. There was still nothing to see but a ribbon of empty highway.

And water, water, everywhere.

The old line of poetry drifted through her mind as she looked from one side of the road to the other.

To the east lay the mighty Mississippi. Between it and the highway was a mixture of marsh and swamp grass. At least, on her weekly trips to Poquette she'd always assumed it was swamp grass. Now, standing beside it, she wondered if it was actually *flauteau*—floating mud and grasses that she'd heard a person would simply sink into, before disappearing forever.

On the other side of the highway the land was just as wet and barren. It stretched, she knew, to a bay that reached up like a long finger from the Gulf of Mexico. She couldn't actually see Gulf water in the distance, but given the salty smell of the air she'd guess it wasn't too far.

After glancing along the still-deserted road once more, she turned her attention to what the guards were doing. One, casually holding his shotgun at his side, was keeping an eye on Billy. The others were busy changing the tire—two of them loosening the flat while the third lugged the jack and the spare out from under the floor in back.

They'd just started to jack up the van when a pickup truck appeared down the road. Scarcely breathing, Hayley watched it rapidly cover the distance between them. As it drew nearer, she realized it was slowing down. So did the guards. They were glancing at one another with silent warnings in their eyes.

She turned toward Billy just in time to see him look in the other direction. As she followed his gaze, a shiver of apprehension seized her. Barely visible in the distance, another vehicle was approaching from the north. When she looked at Billy once more, the tiny smile playing at the corners of his mouth assured her this was it.

She had a sudden impulse to run, to race into the swamp grass and take her chances with whatever snakes or alligators might be there. Instead, she forced herself to stay right where she was.

The truck pulled onto the shoulder about forty feet behind the van and coasted to a stop. All Hayley could see in the cab was the driver and one passenger, but if this really was it, others were probably hiding in the truck bed.

The truck doors opened. The driver and his passenger began climbing out, the driver asking, "Need a hand?"

"No, we're okay, thanks," the guard she'd pegged as being in charge told him. "Just move along."

"Got yourself a prisoner there, huh?" the passenger said.

The guard holding the shotgun nodded, his expression saying, brilliant deduction.

"That's right, so just move along," the head guard repeated. This time, his words were even more obviously an order. And as he added, "Now," the guard with the shotgun shifted it to a half-raised position.

"Hey," the driver said. "Hey, take it easy, fellows. We just thought you might like some help."

The vehicle coming from the other direction, a gray van, reached them now and pulled off onto the other shoulder.

"Everything under control?" the driver asked, sliding down his window.

"Yeah," the head guard told him. "Thanks for stopping. But like I was just telling this other fellow, we need for you to move along." He glanced from the van to the truck.

The truck driver nodded. "On our way. But you have a good day, hear?"

For an instant, as he started to climb back into the truck, Hayley thought she'd been mistaken. That these weren't Billy's people after all.

But in the blink of an eye, four men were standing in the truck bed. Each had an assault rifle trained on the guards.

"Don't move a muscle!" The man driving the van was out of it like a shot. He positioned himself in the middle of the road with a machine gun at the ready.

"Lay down those shotguns," he ordered the two guards holding them.

The moment they did, the passenger from the truck collected them.

"Get the keys, too," the van driver told him. "Knock the radio out of commission and check for cell phones.

"And you," he continued, turning to Hayley, "you go take those guns out of their holsters and put them over on the road. Nice and easy. Try anything funny and you're dead. That goes for all of you," he added, his machine gun still trained on the guards.

Her hands trembling, she managed to get each of the guns from the holsters and set them on the pavement.

"Okay," the driver said when she'd finished. "Get back over here."

She walked toward him, fear pounding so loudly in her head she could barely think.

"You four." He nodded at the guards. "Start heading for the river."

You *four?* What about her? She tried to ask—but he spoke right over her words.

"And watch out for *flauteau,* huh? We wouldn't want any of you drowning."

"Is she coming with us?" the head guard asked, drawing her gaze to him.

She looked back at the driver just in time to see him glance at Billy, who shook his head. The motion was almost imperceptible, but she caught it. What did it mean, though? Were they going to leave her here on the highway? Or shoot her dead where she stood?

That thought sent total panic racing through her. Then she realized that Sloan might be coming here to pick her up.

Hope nudged at her terror. Maybe Sloan would be here any moment. Maybe he'd even have Max with him.

"Don't worry about her," the driver was telling the guards. "And don't even think about looking back until you reach the river. Someone will be tailing you. You look back, he shoots."

Without another word, the guards headed into the marshy grass. For several fearful seconds, Hayley followed them with her gaze, half expecting Billy's boys to open fire and gun them down.

But nobody moved until the van driver turned to her, saying, "Get in my van. In the back. With Mr. Fitzgerald."

Get in his van? Sloan wasn't coming, then? Cold, raw terror began creeping up her spine.

Swallowing hard, she shook her head. She'd played her part. She'd done what she'd promised. And she didn't know what more they had in mind for her, but she shouldn't have to go one inch farther with *Mister* Fitzgerald.

"Do what he says," Billy snapped.

"That wasn't part of the deal!"

"It is now," he told her.

SLOAN FELT ANGRY ENOUGH to wring Billy's neck with his bare hands. Billy, however, seemed completely oblivious to the fact.

He stood beside the bed, sorting through the contents of several suitcases his housekeeper had packed and separating things he'd leave behind from those he planned on taking with him to his new life.

"I told the guys they could only take one case each," he said, glancing over. "So I figured I'd better not have half a dozen."

Sloan watched him for a few seconds after he went back to his sorting, then strode across the motel room and stood staring out the window, trying to regain his cool.

So far, the plan had gone *almost* without a hitch. It was barely one o'clock, yet the men who'd helped Billy escape were already back in New Orleans.

They'd dropped off the pickup and van they'd used at a chop shop and the vehicles were probably in a hundred pieces by now. And this motel—about twenty-five miles from Baton Rouge—was owned by a member of the "family," so Billy was welcome to use it for as long as he wanted.

It was a good hideout, Sloan thought, gazing past the front office. Since the construction of Interstate 10, Highway 61 was no longer the main route from New Orleans to Baton Rouge. That meant few tourists would be driving by with an eye out for a place to stay—and the No Vacancy sign would deter any who were.

He glanced along the row of cars parked outside

the units, thinking they were a smart touch. They made the place look full, even though very few people were actually staying here. Billy had just three of his most trusted men with him. The three he was taking along to South America, to keep him company in his upcoming retirement.

Two of them, Alex McIver and Jack Dunne, were camped out in the motel office. Their job was to keep watch on the surrounding area and make sure nothing suspicious was happening. Like, for example, a SWAT team creeping up on the motel.

In addition to Alex and Jack, Keith Marshall was here. Across the courtyard in unit five. With Hayley.

She, needless to say, was the hitch.

Sloan looked across the courtyard again. He desperately wanted to see her, but he was running out of time. So instead of going over and explaining where things stood, he had to stay right here and make Billy change his mind.

If he could do that before it was too late, he could drive her back to somewhere along Highway 23 and leave her there. Then she could claim that Billy's people had taken her only a few miles from the escape site before setting her free—that she'd simply been wandering in a daze ever since.

But square one was convincing Billy to let her go, which would mean *some* convincing. Still, he had to try.

"I just don't get it," he said, turning away from the window. "You didn't need her anymore, so why the change of plans? What happened to leaving her behind with the guards?''

Billy shrugged. "When have I ever had a plan that was carved in stone? You've gotta go with the flow, right? Do what your gut tells you. And on the side of the road there, my gut was telling me it wasn't safe to let her go yet.''

"Why not? She knows if she ever opens her mouth you'll have her killed. The boy, too. You don't figure she believes that?''

"Could be.''

"Billy, trust me, she believes. So why not let her go right now? If you don't, the cops will notify her next of kin. Then they'll discover that Max isn't with his father and realize you grabbed him to make her help you—which will change the entire scenario. She won't be the hostage, the victim. She'll be an accomplice. And when you eventually do let her go, the cops will question her about every detail. About who was involved and—''

"Dammit, Sloan, I know all that! I didn't go senile while I was locked up. I considered the repercussions before I brought her along.''

Sloan swore to himself. He'd lay odds that taking her along had been a totally impulsive act—that Billy hadn't given a thought to a single repercussion until afterward.

"You don't believe me?'' he was saying. "Well, you should, because I've already explained the new ground rules to her. If the cops wise up, she'll admit my people forced her to cooperate. But she'll say that she and I worked out the escape plan all on our own. She won't implicate you. And she'll claim she has no idea which of my guys took the kid. That she never saw them."

"Billy, the boy will talk! He's six years old. You think he'll keep anything back if a couple of cops start in on him?"

"What? Like with rubber hoses?"

"Very funny. But you know what I'm saying. He'll tell them what Sammy and O'Rourke look like, tell them he saw Hayley while they had him, that he saw me. He'll—"

"But like you said, he's six years old. And his mother would swear she never saw him after he was grabbed, that she was allowed to talk to him only on the phone. Period. As for him knowing your name…"

Billy paused, then shrugged. "I guess someone must have mentioned you when he was around. Could be as simple as that. 'Cuz what Hayley will claim is that the only thing you had to do with her was talking to her about getting me transferred out of Poquette.

"Hell, Sloan, there'll be you and her telling one story and a little kid telling another. Who are the cops going to believe? Whether they really do or not? And she'll say exactly what I told her to. I made it clear I've got a lot of friends. She knows what'll happen if she ever says the wrong thing."

"This is totally nuts, you know that?" Sloan stopped right there, telling himself to cool it. But he was too steamed to manage that.

"All you're doing is complicating the hell out of

everything," he continued. "So why don't you just let her go right now? I'll drive her back to—"

"What in blazes is wrong with you? You got the hots for her or something?"

"Of course not."

"Hell, I don't care if you do. But I sure as hell care if you're after anything more than a few pokes. You know how I feel about loyalty, and you're just sounding too damned concerned about her."

Sloan exhaled slowly. He knew only too well how Billy felt about loyalty. He demanded one hundred and ten percent of it from his people. And if he started to think that his legal adviser's loyalty was even slightly divided, it would be a serious problem.

"Billy," he said evenly, "my only concern is that you gave her your word, said if she helped—"

"And when did I say anything about not keeping my word? The deal was I wouldn't hurt either her or the kid if she helped me. And that's still the deal. But I can't be too careful.

"She knows the system, remember? Knows the witness protection people would be only too happy to help her if she gave me up. So what if I let her go right now and that's what she did? What if, the minute she got her kid back, she spilled her guts? If she weighed the odds on whether the witness people could keep her safe... Well, their record's not *that* bad. So she might figure it was worth the chance. And why would I risk her deciding to try that route?"

"But—"

"Look, aside from anything else, letting her go would mean we'd have to get out of here. If she told the cops this was where we'd come, they'd be all over the place. And if they picked up my trail…"

Sloan mentally shook his head. When Billy was really stressed he didn't always think straight, and this was a perfect example. One minute he was saying that Hayley knew what his friends would do to her if she ever opened her mouth, the next he was saying that he was afraid she might.

There was no getting through to him when he was like this. Even so…

"Billy, listen," he said as calmly as he could. "All I'm—"

"No! I don't want to hear any more. The safe way to play this is just to keep her with me for a day or so. Not give her the chance to talk to anyone until after the Pelican's come through."

"Fine. Okay. I give up. You're right and I'm wrong," he added when Billy looked at him suspiciously.

As much as he disliked this turn of events, there was absolutely nothing to be gained by arguing further, and no sense in bothering to point out that "a day or so," until the Pelican came through, might actually prove to be "a week or so." Or even longer.

Brendan Fitzgerald had given the escape team a cell phone to pass on to his father, and the Pelican had the number. But despite the fact that Billy was convinced he'd hear from the guy later today, they really had no way of knowing when he'd make contact.

It was partly his unpredictability that had prevented the authorities from catching up with him before now. That and the fact he was a mystery man, that nobody seemed to know his real identity.

Even Sloan, who'd been the one to set things up with him, hadn't so much as spoken to him on the phone. Everything had been arranged and agreed to through intermediaries.

But regardless of that, there was little doubt the Pelican could get Billy safely out of the country and established in one that had no extradition treaty with the United States. He'd already done it for so many other criminals that he was climbing fast on the FBI's Most Wanted list.

And Billy was his current client. In exchange for five million bucks, the Pelican had promised him the deed to a fully staffed mansion on a beach in South America, along with safe passage to it.

Billy didn't yet know exactly which country he'd end up in, but he didn't much care. Not surprisingly, he figured that any mansion on any beach would be paradise compared with a cell in Poquette.

"Here's another one," he said, interrupting Sloan's thoughts.

Sloan looked over at the TV as a news segment about the escape began.

"We've just received further information on that Louisiana prison break we've been covering," the announcer said. "Apparently, there is some question about whether Dr. Hayley Morgan, the psychologist taken hostage by the escapee's confederates—'' a photograph of Hayley filled the screen ''—was actually taken hostage at all. It now seems possible that she played a role in the escape.''

Sloan swore under his breath, even though he'd known it was only a matter of time before Hayley's involvement in the escape became evident.

''For that news, we go live to Louisiana.''

The image of a young woman holding a microphone replaced Hayley's photo on the screen. ''This is Jane Clemont,'' she said, ''reporting from outside the Poquette Correctional Center in Plaquemines Parish, Louisiana. This is the prison that, since his recent conviction on three counts of manslaughter, has been home to alleged Irish Mafia head, William Fitzgerald.''

The reporter proceeded to detail how Billy's escape had unfolded, then returned to the subject of Hayley's role in it.

''After Dr. Morgan's family was notified of the incident, authorities discovered that her six-year-old son is missing. Last Monday, Dr. Morgan told several people she was sending the child to visit his father in Pennsylvania. We have learned this was not true, and can only hypothesize that the child was kidnapped in order to force Dr. Morgan to assist in Mr. Fitzgerald's escape.

''This is a picture of the missing child, Max Morgan,'' the reporter continued as a photograph of Max appeared. ''Anyone with knowledge of the boy's whereabouts or with any other information that might help in this investigation is asked to call the FBI at the number on the screen.''

''Well, that's that,'' Sloan muttered.

Billy shrugged. ''So? She was forced to help because we took her kid. Who's going to hold that against her?''

Sloan didn't bother to reply. Billy couldn't care less whether anybody held it against her or not. But having helped a prisoner escape—regardless of the circumstances—sure wouldn't do her career any good. Assuming she still had a career. Assuming Billy wouldn't decide on another change of plans and...

He ordered himself not even to think about the possibility of her ending up dead. That wasn't going to happen. He'd do whatever it took to ensure it didn't. In the meantime, even if he hadn't been able to convince Billy to let her go, he might be able to win on another front.

Hayley had to be frantic with worry about Max. Hell, for all she knew, he was dead by now. But surely there was some way...

''What about the boy?'' he asked Billy.

''He stays where he is.''

''You think that's best?''

''You don't?''

Sloan raked his fingers through his hair, searching for the right argument. ''Well, the house they're in is certainly well secluded, but he's been out at least twice—when O'Rourke took him to see his mother. People would have seen him in the car.''

''Taking him to see her was *your* idea.''

"Yeah, well, if you'd stuck to the plan it wouldn't have mattered if a million people had seen him. He was just a kid with a man they'd have assumed was his father. It's only now that his picture's on the blasted television, because he isn't back with his mother the way—"

"Dammit, Sloan, I—"

"Look, wait, take it easy." He ordered himself to relax. The worst thing he could do was get Billy so mad he wouldn't listen.

"Let's both take it easy," he continued. "We don't want to be snapping at each other instead of figuring out what's best to do. And I think maybe that would be telling O'Rourke to bring the kid here."

"Oh, sure, a kid's exactly what I need."

"Billy, if somebody remembers seeing him in the vicinity of that house and the cops do a door-to-door…"

"O'Rourke and Sammy are good men."

"I know they are. But if they get nailed for kidnapping they'll be lucky to see the light of day again. So if the cops show up at that house, what will the two of them be thinking about? You on a beach and them in a cell—that's what."

"And?" Billy pressed.

"And isn't it just possible they'd cut a deal? Spill whatever they know about your plans?"

"They don't know much."

"Billy…your guys talk among themselves. That's only human nature. So you can't really believe that McIver and Dunne and Marshall all kept

absolutely quiet about the fact they're taking off to
South America with you. Which means you don't
know exactly how much Sammy and O'Rourke—''

''It doesn't matter what they know. They
wouldn't cross me.''

''No, they wouldn't. At least, not normally. But
you'll be out of the picture soon. Maybe you
haven't made an official announcement, but after
you're gone Brendan will be head of the family,
right?''

He shrugged. ''I wouldn't want to be trying to
run things from South America.''

That would have made Sloan laugh if he wasn't
so upset. If Billy figured there was any conceivable
way he could run things long-distance, he'd give it
his best shot.

''Billy, what I'm saying is that O'Rourke and
Sammy know they aren't two of Brendan's favor-
ites. So they've probably already been worrying
about what'll happen after you're gone. And if they
start thinking they might get left holding the bag
on kidnapping charges... Well, when you consider
things from that angle, who knows what they'll do
if the cops show up at the door. And as you said
only a minute ago, you can't be too careful.''

He let Billy consider that for a minute. Then, as
if to himself, he said, ''But wait a minute. If anyone
does remember seeing the boy with O'Rourke...''

''What?''

''I was just thinking that someone might already
have I.D.'d O'Rourke from a mug shot. If that's
happened, it wouldn't be safe for him to bring the

boy here. Every cop in Louisiana will be watching for a guy matching his description.''

And whether they were or not, if O'Rourke got nervous and started shooting because some cop looked at him sideways, Max would be in deadly danger.

''But I could go get the kid,'' Sloan continued. ''And tell O'Rourke and Sammy that you said they should just disappear for a while. Then everything would be cool.''

A frown furrowing his brow, Billy mulled that over. ''You think your going would be safe? I mean, you're my lawyer. Every cop in Louisiana might be watching for you, too.''

Sloan shrugged. ''I'll use one of the cars parked out there, not my Jeep. And if I stick on a baseball cap and dark glasses…I don't think there'll be much risk.''

''Yeah,'' Billy said after a few seconds. ''Yeah, okay, that's not a bad idea. You collect the kid, and tell Sammy and O'Rourke I said they'd probably enjoy a couple of weeks in Mexico.'' He picked up the cell phone Brendan had sent him and turned it on. ''Let me give you the number for this,'' he said, checking the display and jotting down the number. ''You can call me if they've got any questions,'' he added. ''Or they can.''

Sloan stuck the piece of paper in his pocket, wondering if Billy figured they'd want to check that the instructions were actually coming from him.

Sloan Reeves, attorney at law, was one of

them—yet he wasn't. He realized that few of Billy's boys trusted him completely.

But Billy did. That was really all that mattered. And after this was over… Well, there was no point in thinking much about that until it *was* over.

"Wait a minute," Billy said as Sloan turned toward the door. "I want you to take something along for them. And make sure you tell them it's a token of my appreciation."

CHAPTER TEN

BEFORE SLOAN LEFT for New Orleans, he headed across the courtyard to unit five. Billy had told him Hayley was just fine, but he wasn't going anywhere till he saw for himself.

"It's Sloan Reeves," he called, knocking.

The lock snapped and the door opened up a few inches. The gun tucked in Keith Marshall's belt made Sloan hope that Hayley wouldn't decide to try anything crazy.

When he looked across the room and saw her, though, she didn't look up to trying anything at all. Billy's "just fine" had hardly been an accurate description.

She was a picture of dejection, sitting in the center of the bed with her legs pulled up to her chest, her arms wrapped around her knees and her forehead resting against them—her face hidden by her hair.

Seeing her like that made him wish he could just gather her up in his arms and tell the rest of the world to go away. Of course, lately he seemed to be wishing for a lot of impossible things.

"I want to talk to her," he told Marshall.

"Sure. Come on in."

"Alone," he added, walking into the room.

"No problem." The other man stepped outside, closing the door behind him.

Sloan waited a couple of seconds, expecting Hayley to look at him. When she didn't, he quietly said, "Hayley? Are you all right?"

He got his look then, but he sure didn't like it. She was glaring at him.

Just as he'd feared, she clearly figured he'd known Billy was going to take her with him.

He wondered if there was even a chance he could make her believe he hadn't. Or if she was completely convinced he was evil incarnate.

When she simply continued to glare at him, he took the minirecorder from his pocket and switched it on. Billy hadn't said his men had brought any listening equipment with them, but you never knew.

The recorder didn't begin flashing a warning, so he shut it off and tucked it back into his pocket.

"What was the point of that?" she demanded.

"Just making sure nobody's listening in."

She eyed him suspiciously for a moment, then said, "You mean it's not really a tape recorder?"

"It is, but it has a few added features."

"Then…that's why you used it in my office at Poquette? And why you asked me to tape my session with Billy? You thought someone might have been bugging my conversations? Are you completely paranoid? Along with everything else?"

He merely shrugged. She looked so angry, so full of hatred, that he didn't even know how to begin.

Eventually, *she* broke the silence. "Why don't

you just say whatever you came to say and get out of here?''

Both her words and her tone stung. She sounded as though she felt like crying but was determined not to—because she didn't want to give him the satisfaction. As if he enjoyed seeing her like this.

The fact that she could think he did, hurt more than he'd ever have imagined.

"It was entirely Billy's idea to take you with him," he finally said. "And it was a spur-of-the-moment decision. The last I heard, he was going to leave you behind with the guards."

"Oh? And I should believe that? Just because you say so?"

"No, you should believe it because it's the truth. And I'm more sorry than I can say that he didn't stick with the original plan. That's the truth, too."

"Sure. Just like you were sorry he had Max kidnapped in the first place. You know, you seem to spend an awful lot of time being sorry. Maybe you should do some thinking about that."

"I…" He paused, desperately wishing he could tell her things he knew he couldn't. "I just wanted you to know," he said at last, "that Billy still intends to let you go. This is only temporary."

She gestured toward the door. "That man. He said his name's Keith Marshall. And that's his real name, isn't it. Not like 'Tom' and 'Dick.'"

"Right."

"So if he doesn't care whether I know who he is… Isn't that because he figures I'll never be able to tell anyone? Because…"

"No," Sloan said quietly. "It's because Billy's leaving the country and Marshall's going with him. So are the other two guys who are here. Which means it doesn't matter whether you know who they are or not. But you know my name, too. And you know what Dick looks like. And... Hayley, Billy said he talked to you. About what your story will have to be if the cops learn you helped him escape."

She nodded.

"Well, there's already speculation on the news that you must have. So...you do realize you'll have to play things his way, don't you? You know he's serious about what would happen if you ever named any names? If you ever tried to implicate any of his people? No matter how much time had passed? And no matter how far away he was?"

"Yes. Max and I would end up dead. But what's happening to Max right now?" she demanded. "Now that I'm here?"

"I'm just about to go get him. I convinced Billy it would be better if he were with you."

She bit her lower lip and simply continued to watch him—looking as if she wasn't at all convinced he was telling her the truth, as if any faith she might have had in him had been totally destroyed.

That hurt, too, yet how could he have hoped for anything else?

He'd promised her that all she had to do was help Billy escape, then her life would return to normal.

But being held here as Billy's prisoner was hardly normal.

"So," he said, deciding there was no point in prolonging this, "I'll be back in a while. With Max." He glanced at his watch. "Depending on the traffic and all, I should have him here between four and five."

Hayley swallowed hard. Until three minutes ago, she'd been certain that she despised Sloan with all her heart. But he'd only had to walk in here to make her start remembering how she'd felt about him last night—felt when she was in his arms, when he was kissing her.

He'd merely had to say he hadn't known that Billy intended to keep her with him and he almost had her believing him. But why, when logic said he was probably lying through his teeth?

Hadn't she realized, at the very beginning, that he was nothing but a criminal in lawyer's clothing? And she knew better than to believe any criminal. She'd been lied to by the best of them. Yet when it came to Sloan...

When it came to him, she knew precisely what the problem was. Like it or not, deep down she *wanted* to believe him. To believe that last night had meant something to him, that his concern for her was genuine, that he was at least a little on her side.

She felt so alone, so helpless, that knowing he cared what happened to her and Max...

And he must care, mustn't he? Because there was no way in the world that Billy would have let her see Max unless Sloan had intervened—with some serious convincing. And now he'd convinced Billy they should bring Max here. That simply wasn't something Billy would have come up with on his own. So, regardless of anything else, Sloan was doing the best he could for them.

She looked over at him again. Even though he'd said he was going, he was still standing by the door, watching her.

"Does Max have a favorite baseball team?" he asked.

"Pardon me?"

"Does he have a favorite baseball team?"

"The Yankees. Why?"

He shrugged. "Just wondered. So…we'll see you in a few hours. Max and me."

Would she? It was possible. But it was just as possible she'd never see either of them again. That thought made her throat ache.

She followed Sloan with her gaze as he walked out into the courtyard, leaving the door ajar for her guard to come back in.

"I'm just going into the bathroom," she told him when he did.

"Don't lock the door," Marshall warned, then slumped into the chair he'd vacated earlier.

Hayley pushed herself off the bed and headed into the other room. She closed the door, resisting the temptation to ignore his order and lock it. There was no point. If he wanted to, he could probably kick it down in three seconds flat.

After taking off the bulletproof vest, she stashed

it out of sight in a corner of the cabinet beneath the sink. That done, she put her suit jacket back on and took a bath towel from the rack.

Then she sat down on the edge of the tub, buried her face in the thick white terry cloth and began to silently cry her heart out.

ON HIS WAY into New Orleans, Sloan stopped at a mall and bought some baseball stuff for Max and a few things for Hayley. He had to guess about the sizes, but there was no way he could risk trying to get anything from her house. Likely, the police would be watching it. And even if they weren't, one of the neighbors might spot him if he broke in.

Pulling out of the mall parking lot, he once again found himself picturing the way Hayley had looked at him back at the motel—with pure hatred in her eyes. He couldn't help contrasting that with the way she'd looked at him last night.

Night and day. Love and hate.

Well, maybe not love. Although he hesitated to admit, even to himself, how close it had been getting to that for him.

Every time he recalled holding her, kissing her, her kissing him back… The word *incredible* came to mind, yet no word could really touch on how he'd felt.

But the feeling had ended all too soon. And the hollowness he'd been left with still hurt. A whole lot.

"Maybe if things were different," she'd said. "If you weren't you or I wasn't me."

Things *weren't* different, though. Which was exactly why he'd known, all along, that he had to be careful not to get emotionally involved with her.

Of course, given the way she was feeling today, he wouldn't have to worry about that from here on in. The only emotion she felt for him at this point was...

Hell, he really didn't want to dwell on that. Not when knowing she'd never again look at him with warmth in her eyes hurt even worse than the hollow ache.

He was nearing his destination, so he made a concerted effort to purge every last thought of her from his mind. He'd almost succeeded by the time he turned into the secluded drive of the house where Max was being held.

Waiting at the front door, he reminded himself that—as far as the boy was concerned—Sammy and O'Rourke were Tom and Dick. Once inside, he spent a few minutes with the two men, then headed down the hall to Max's room.

He'd had no idea what sort of reception he'd get, but the little boy seemed truly glad to see him. That made him feel good, which was nice, because it had been a while since he'd had much reason to feel good.

Except for last night, of course.

Reminding himself he was through thinking about Hayley, he said, "I got you a present," then handed over the bag he'd brought in.

When Max opened it his face lit up. "Wow! Yankees stuff!" He slapped the baseball cap on his head. "They're my favorite team! How'd you know?"

"Your mom told me." The cap was a perfect fit. And just as Sloan figured, it not only concealed Max's blond hair but also made him look less like the school photograph they were showing on TV.

"Why don't you put on the shirt, too," he suggested.

He waited until Max had tugged it on over his T-shirt and began to do up the buttons before he said, "Guess what?"

"What?"

"Your mom says it won't be long before she starts getting home right after work again. But in the meantime, you're both going to stay someplace else for a little while. I'll take you to her as soon as you're set."

"Really?" Max looked ready to burst with excitement.

Sloan nodded. "Really."

"Oh, boy! Let's go!"

"You'd better say goodbye to Tom and Dick first, huh? They said they'd get your things organized while I was talking to you."

His Yankees shirt flapping, Max raced for the door. He was halfway into the hall when he applied the brakes, did a one-eighty and smacked his palm to his mouth. "I forgot to say thanks for the stuff," he whispered loudly. "Don't tell my mom, huh?"

"Well, you could say thanks now."

"Yeah, okay. Thanks, Sloan. It's real neat." Grinning, he took off again.

As Sloan followed along, the sound of the afternoon Rangers game drifted down the hall from the living room. When he'd arrived, Sammy and O'Rourke had been switching back and forth between the game and CNN, but he'd told them to stay away from the news until after he and Max were gone. The last thing he wanted was the boy to see either his mother's picture or his own on television—and hear who knew what from some reporter.

He reached the living room in time to hear Max saying, "Maybe you can look after me some other time. My mom sometimes has to go away. To conferns."

"Yeah, sure. That'd be good, huh?" O'Rourke gave Max a friendly punch on the arm.

Sammy settled for patting the boy on the back.

"Okay, we're outta here," Sloan told the two of them. "Oh, and Billy asked me to give you this," he added, taking the envelope from his pocket and handing it to O'Rourke. "A token of his appreciation, he said. So you wouldn't run short while you're away."

O'Rourke riffled through the bills in the envelope, then shot Sammy a grin.

It made Sloan wonder if they really figured it was a token of Billy's appreciation. Or if they knew it was nothing but a payoff for keeping their mouths shut. Either way, they had enough money for a couple of months in Mexico, never mind a couple of weeks.

"Tell Billy thanks," O'Rourke said.

"And tell him to have a good trip," Sammy added.

"Will do." He picked up the bags with Max's things in them, then glanced down at him. "Ready to hit the road?"

"Yup!" Max took off for the front door at a dead run. Apparently, like Sloan's nephews, the only gears he had were neutral and overdrive.

"Where *is* my mom?" he asked as they were getting into the car.

"In a motel."

"And that's where I'm gonna be, too?"

"That's right." Sloan backed down the drive, then sat at the end of it for a minute, checking out the street.

"Aren't we going?"

"In a second."

As far as he could see, no one was sitting in any of the parked cars. And no one drove by while they waited. Both were good signs, but he'd still keep an eye out. After all the effort that had gone into this operation, he sure didn't want to be leading any of New Orleans' finest to Billy's hideout.

"For how long?" Max said as they finally started off.

"Sorry? For how long what?"

"For how long are we gonna be in a motel?"

Good question. Billy would play things by ear. Whether he stayed where he was or not would depend on what was happening in the world at large.

Between news reports and what his own people

learned, he'd know whether the authorities were concentrating their search for him in New Orleans.

If they weren't, if he didn't think he'd be safe as far away as the motel, he'd move on. But wherever he was he'd have that cell phone. And the Pelican had its number. Sooner or later, Billy would get the call telling him where and when he'd be boarding his plane for South America.

"Sloan? For how long are we gonna be in a motel?" Max asked again.

"I'm not really sure," he said, turning his thoughts back to the moment. "Maybe for a few days?"

"But what about Satchmo?"

"Satchmo?"

Max nodded. "My cat. If my mom and me aren't there, who's gonna feed him?"

"I guess one of the neighbors will." One of them would be sure to think about the cat—as soon as they got over the shock of learning that Billy Fitzgerald had taken Hayley hostage.

"Which one?"

"Well…I don't really know. Do any of them have a key to your house?"

"Uh-huh. Mrs. Kelly. She's who looks after me."

"Then she'll look after Satchmo, too."

"You're sure?"

"Positive."

"Absolutely positive?"

"Absolutely, definitely, there's-no-possible-way-I-could-be-wrong positive."

Max smiled.

Sloan smiled back, then focused on the street once more—wishing to hell this were over, and that Max and Hayley could just go home.

"Is THIS IT?" Max asked as Sloan pulled off Highway 61. "Is this the motel?"

"That's right."

When he spotted Alex McIver standing inside the door of the office, watching them approach, Sloan slowed to a crawl and nodded a greeting.

He was almost surprised when McIver didn't gesture for him to stop so he could come out and check over the car. Assure himself a dozen cops weren't hidden inside it. McIver was just like the rest of Billy's people—not entirely sure he could trust Sloan Reeves.

After turning into the courtyard, he pulled up outside the unit Hayley was in and looked at Max. "You wait here for one minute, okay?"

"'Cuz we're gonna s'prise my mom? 'Cuz she doesn't know 'zactly when I'm gonna get here, right?"

"Right. We're gonna surprise her." He glanced into the back, wondering if he should take the things he'd bought for Hayley. There wasn't anything she'd need right this minute, but she might feel a little more kindly toward him if he gave them to her now.

Bribery wasn't his style, though, so he decided to leave them where they were till later.

"Aren't you goin'?" Max prompted.

Nodding, he climbed out of the car and headed over to the door of unit five. When no one answered his knock, his anxiety level notched up a little. He knocked more loudly. Still nothing. What the hell was going on?

He tried the door. When it proved to be locked, his anxiety level rose further. He turned rapidly on his heel and scanned the courtyard, his heart beating hard.

"Sloan?" Max said, opening his car door.

"Wait there one more minute, okay? She must have gone for a walk or something. I'll just go ask someone."

Forcing himself not to move so fast that Max would realize something was wrong, he headed across the courtyard to Billy's unit and banged on the door.

There was no response but he had a feeling Billy was inside—probably peering through the peephole right this second.

"Billy, it's Sloan," he said, trying to sound a lot friendlier than he felt.

A moment later the door opened and Billy stood there grinning at him.

Grinning. Okay, good. Nothing awful had happened.

"Where's Hayley?" he asked as his heart began slowing to normal speed.

Billy eyed him for a moment, then his grin grew. "I saw you go to number five first. You *do* have the hots for her!"

Sloan swore under his breath. Billy was just joking, but it was only one small step from his thinking someone was interested in a woman for sex to his thinking there was more to it. And in this situation that would get him worrying about divided loyalties. Which was the last thing Sloan needed.

"Very funny," he said, manufacturing a smile. "But what I've actually got is her kid—sitting in the car all excited. So where is she?"

"I moved her to a unit with an adjoining door to the one beside it. So she and Marshall can have separate rooms."

"That was nice of you."

Billy shrugged. "Marshall said he didn't want a kid in his face, and I figured he could keep a close enough watch on them if he just left the door open.

"Oh, and you'll stick around, won't you, Sloan? I want you to keep an eye on the news with me," he added, gesturing toward the TV. It was still tuned to CNN. "And make some calls for me," he continued. "Check that what they're reporting is really what's happening. Until the Pelican's ready to make his move, we've got to keep on top of what the heat's up to."

"Sure I was planning on staying," Sloan said, although the truth was that he'd been ambivalent.

The more work he'd put into setting things up, the more he'd found himself wanting to be on the scene when the elusive Pelican made his move. There was a downside to that, though, so he hadn't really decided what he'd do.

But now, with Hayley and Max here, he didn't have much choice. Even though Billy was still saying he intended to let them go, sticking close and ensuring that really happened would be a good idea.

"So," he said. "Why don't I take the boy to his mother, then come back here. Which unit's she in?"

"Twelve. Marshall's in eleven. Oh, and just check that he doesn't have any news on. And that she doesn't, either. I told him I didn't want her knowing what was happening in the world at large."

Sloan nodded, then headed back to the car.

Max was standing outside it, playing some kind of tug-of-war game with the door handle. "You took way more than one minute," he announced.

"Yeah, sorry, buddy. But I found out where your mom is."

"Awright!"

Before Sloan even realized what was happening, Max gave him a high five. The boy was so little that the gesture almost made Sloan laugh.

"Come on," he said. "I've just got to stop and say something to someone, then you can surprise her."

With Max dancing along beside him, he walked down the string of units. "Tell you what," he said, stopping at number eleven. "The one next door is your mom's. You go on ahead to it, and knock when I give the sign."

"Okay." Max hurried off as Sloan tapped on number eleven.

"Uh-huh?" Marshall called.

"It's Sloan."

When Marshall opened up, Sloan glanced past him to the doorway that connected his room to Hayley's. He couldn't see her from where he was standing.

"Where's the kid?" Marshall asked.

His TV, Sloan noted, was tuned to a rerun of *Mad About You.*

"Waiting to knock on his mother's door. Keep your gun out of sight now that he's here, huh?"

The suggestion earned him a look of annoyance.

"What if she tries to make a run for it?"

"Marshall, she's not an idiot. Just because she can't see the gun, she isn't going to think you lost it."

"I doubt Billy'd care if the kid saw it," he muttered.

"Yeah, well, I do, so just keep it out of sight."

Reluctantly, Marshall tugged his shirt out of his pants to conceal the pistol.

"Thanks," Sloan said. "There's no point in scaring the kid," he added, looking over at Max and giving him a thumbs-up.

Max shot him a huge grin, then knocked on Hayley's door.

"Answer that," Marshall called into the other room.

Sloan caught a glimpse of Hayley as she headed past the doorway, then he looked back at Max. When the door opened, the boy launched himself forward.

Hayley started excitedly saying something, and

Sloan could easily imagine her wrapping her arms around Max and holding him tightly to her.

Fleetingly, he recalled her holding him. It had only been last night, yet already it seemed long ago and far away.

Forcing himself to focus on Marshall once more, he said, "Why don't you take a break. I'll stay with them for a few minutes."

He'd have to get back over to Billy pretty soon, but he wanted another chance to talk to Hayley. He'd been trying to convince himself that once this was over they'd never see each other again, so it didn't really matter what she thought of him. But it *did* matter.

Like it or not, he knew he'd be a long time forgetting her. And when he thought about her in the months to come, he just didn't want to be thinking that she believed the absolute worst about him.

"I'm not sure Billy'd like that," Marshall was saying. "He told me to stay here."

"It'll be okay. I want to ask her a few things about the escape."

"Oh?"

"Make sure none of our people used a name or dropped any other clues those guards might have picked up on."

"Billy said they didn't."

"Well, maybe she noticed something he missed."

"He doesn't miss much."

"No, not usually. But you know how it is in a situation like that. Tensions run high and nobody ever catches everything. At any rate, right after I've brought her the kid has to be a good time to talk to her.''

Marshall considered that, then shrugged. ''Yeah, I guess she'll figure she owes you.''

''Exactly. But she'd probably talk more freely if there were only the two of us.''

''Yeah, could be. She hasn't been saying much to me.''

''Then why don't you go tell Billy what I'm doing. So he doesn't wonder why I'm not over there.''

Nodding, Marshall headed out of the room and started across the courtyard.

Sloan closed the door and slid the bolt. Marshall had a sneaky streak, and he could live without the guy strolling back in quietly and unannounced.

After taking his tape-recorder-cum-detector from his pocket, he switched it on. Once its nonblinking assured him that these rooms were as secure as number five had been, he shut off Marshall's TV and walked over to the doorway that led to the other bedroom.

Hayley and Max were sitting together on the side of the bed, facing away from him and clearly oblivious to anything except each other. Hayley had one arm around the boy and was listening to him babble a mile a minute about something.

Sloan didn't even try to make out what he was saying, simply stood eyeing them—Max with his fair hair, Hayley's the color of rich cognac.

The way hers was spilling down her back started him thinking about last night again. About how he'd slipped his hands beneath her hair and cradled her head in them. About how silky-soft her hair had felt against his skin and how smooth her skin had been.

He watched the two of them for another minute, until, for some absurd reason, seeing them sitting close like that made his chest hurt. Finally, he cleared his throat. They both turned toward him at the sound.

His gaze met Hayley's, and when it did his heart slammed against his ribs.

There were no daggers in her eyes this time. Instead, she was gazing at him with the same warmth he'd seen last night. And there was something else. A naked tenderness that made his mouth dry and started hot desire curling deep within him.

Then she smiled, and his heart slammed against his ribs again.

"Sloan," she murmured. "I owe you a very large apology."

CHAPTER ELEVEN

"APOLOGY?" MAX REPEATED, picking up on Hayley's remark.

She looked away from Sloan, who was still standing in the doorway between the two bedrooms, and ruffled her son's hair. "There's just something Sloan and I have to discuss later."

Just something about the way she'd accused him so bitterly, only to discover she'd figured things wrong.

Every time she thought about how nasty she'd been she felt guilty all over again. After he'd done so much to make this situation easier for her and Max...

Stockholming, an imaginary voice whispered. It was almost inaudible, though, not anywhere near as loud as in the beginning.

The longer this went on, the more good she could see in Sloan—and the less she could believe that her feelings for him were nothing more than the manifestation of some syndrome.

When Max began jabbering again, her thoughts remained on Sloan. She still couldn't understand how he'd gotten mixed up with Billy Fitz. Yet despite the fact that he was, he'd done so much for her that she should be grateful until the day she died. She certainly shouldn't have...

Died. She backtracked to the word, unable to stop herself from visualizing it. And when she did, that terrified feeling she'd become so accustomed to recently came rushing at her again. She just couldn't shake the fear that neither she nor Max would get out of this alive.

Oh, she kept telling herself that if Billy was planning on killing them he'd have done it by now. Because once he'd made good his escape, she'd been of no more use to him.

Yet as sound as that logic was, he'd changed his mind about leaving her with the guards. And she had no reason to believe he wouldn't change it about something else.

Closing her eyes, she forced her fear to the back of her mind and ordered it to stay there for a while. Then, when Max paused to take a breath, she looked over at Sloan once more.

"Marshall won't be gone forever," he said quietly.

She nodded. She realized they might not have much time, but Max was already launching into another monologue. He obviously needed a little longer to completely unwind. And if they waited until he did, it would be a lot easier for them to talk.

Finally, a couple of minutes later, he seemed to have finished telling her everything he'd been saving up.

"Wow," she said after he was silent for a few

seconds. "You've had so much excitement recently that you must be really worn out."

"Uh-uh!" he insisted, shaking his head.

"Well, *I* am. So how about if we find some cartoons on TV? Then we'll just curl up and watch them for a while."

"I'll find them." Sloan sat down on the end of the bed and turned on the set, making her wonder whether he figured she'd sneak a peak at the news if she did the looking.

Of course, if she thought she could get away with it she just might. Earlier, he'd mentioned there was speculation she'd helped Billy escape. And she was very curious about exactly what was being reported.

While Sloan began flipping through the channels, she propped the pillows against the headboard. "That air-conditioning's kind of cold," she said as Max snuggled into one of them. "Why don't I tuck this blanket over you."

She gave him a kiss, then sat on the bed with him while he watched a few minutes of a *Road Runner* episode. Just as she'd suspected, it didn't take any longer than that for his eyes to close. Another minute and he was asleep.

"Sloan?" she said quietly.

He glanced at her, then at Max. "Let's go into the other room so our talking doesn't wake him."

He started off before she could tell him that Max slept as hard as he played. That once he'd fallen asleep, the sound of a truck crashing through a wall probably wouldn't wake him.

She slid off the bed and headed across the room,

glancing back at Max as she reached the doorway, then continuing into Keith Marshall's room, where Sloan was standing in front of the window, staring across the courtyard.

She waited for him to turn toward her, trying to keep her gaze from lingering on his broad shoulders but not quite able to manage it. There was something equally mesmerizing about the way his dark hair curled slightly onto his neck. Something that started a tiny fluttering sensation around her heart.

Fluttering. The word began to play in her brain, making her remember the funny, old-fashioned phrase Peggy had used the first time they'd talked about Sloan.

"Sets the ladies' hearts aflutter," she'd said.

At the time, Hayley had firmly denied that he'd set her heart aflutter. But there was no denying the sensation was alive and flourishing right now—busily reminding her, yet again, just how wonderful she'd felt when he'd held her and kissed her.

And it seemed as if all she had to do was look at him, at his chiseled face and deep blue eyes, to make the fluttering grow stronger.

"So," he said, finally turning to face her.

"So," she repeated. Then, since procrastinating wouldn't make this any easier, she forced herself to go on. "First of all, as I said…I owe you an apology. You *did* think Billy was going to leave me behind with the guards. And I apologize for not believing you. And…for the things I said."

"Well…"

She waited, feeling as though the room had no

air. Then Sloan gave her one of his slow, easy smiles and she was able to breathe again.

"I guess most people would have assumed I knew what Billy had in mind," he said. "As for the rest, you hadn't exactly been having a good day. So let's just forget about it."

She wanted to walk straight into his arms. If he'd held them out she would have.

Somewhere deep inside, she recalled promising herself that she'd never, ever allow a repeat of what had happened between them last night. But right this moment, the way he was looking at her made her feel so warm and liquid she didn't care about anything she'd ever promised herself.

"What made you decide I was telling the truth?" he asked.

He hadn't held out his arms, she hadn't walked into them and her momentary insanity had passed.

Thank heavens, she said silently. But if keeping her distance from him was the right thing to do, why was that fluttering sensation around her heart telling her just the opposite?

"Hayley?" he prompted.

"Billy came over to talk to Keith Marshall while you were gone," she explained. "And Marshall wasn't pleased that you were bringing Max here. He said that first they had a woman they weren't expecting, now they were getting a kid, too."

Sloan nodded. "It's hardly surprising he was annoyed. Billy didn't bring him along to play babysitter, and it's not something he'd like."

"That's about what he told Billy. And Billy said they had to play things by ear. But..."

"But?"

"I..." She paused, unable to go on. The fear she'd ordered to the back of her mind had crept right up to the front again.

"If Billy's playing things by ear," she finally managed to say, "how do I know he won't change his mind and decide to kill Max and me?"

"He won't. Don't even let yourself think that's a possibility."

"Sloan, I know you're trying to keep me from worrying, but you can't be sure *what* he'll do. Not really sure. No one can."

She simply gazed at him after she'd finished speaking, and she didn't know which of them moved first, but suddenly he was holding her.

"I'm sure what I'll do," he said against her hair. "And I won't let him hurt you. Not you and not Max."

Her cheek resting against the solid breadth of his chest, she wished she could stay in the circle of his embrace until everything in her world was back to normal. He felt so reassuringly alive, so warm and virile, that she could almost feel his strength flowing into her with each beat of his heart.

It would be incredibly easy to let herself pretend he could protect her from anything. But she knew that wasn't possible. She knew too much about Billy Fitz to believe it was.

"Hayley?" Sloan murmured, moving backward a couple of inches.

He cradled her face in his hands and looked at her. "I'd kill Billy before I let him hurt you."

She could almost see her last lingering concerns about the Stockholm syndrome fading away. This wasn't a case of Sloan only *seeming* sincere. Or of him and Billy playing good guy-bad guy with her. She hadn't fallen prey to any syndrome. She was certain of that now. Sloan was telling her the truth. Everything he'd told her lately had been true.

She didn't know whether it was something in his voice or the words themselves that had convinced her, but she was sure that if Billy went too far Sloan really would try to kill him.

Then where would he be?

In prison, she silently answered her own question.

Either in prison or dead.

Without letting herself think about what she was doing, she put her arms around his neck and drew his lips to hers.

He kissed her deeply, exploring her mouth so possessively that her blood swiftly spread the heat of longing through her entire body.

Her yearning growing with each passing second, she pressed herself against him and slid her hands across the muscles of his back, loving the way his body felt.

"Oh, Hayley," he whispered, trailing kisses down her throat while his hands found her breasts.

The intimacy of his touch engendered a greedy hunger in her, and when his lips met hers again the hot sensations of his kiss almost undid her. She slid her hands lower and pulled his hips even closer, pressing her body to his and moving against him with a need that felt insatiable, the most basic need of a woman for a man.

Not for just any man, though. Only for this man, who was hard with wanting her. This wrong man.

She kissed him with every bit of the passion he'd aroused in her, trying to kiss away the fact that he *was* wrong for her.

She couldn't. But right or wrong, he was the man she was aching for. And she was so hungry for him that she couldn't think about anything except having him inside her.

Anything except that and Max—who was right in the next room. So they had to stop. They couldn't possibly—

"Sloan?" Keith Marshall hollered. "Why the hell is the door locked?"

She leapt away from Sloan, while Marshall began pounding on the door so hard she was sure his fist would come right through it.

Swearing under his breath, Sloan strode quickly across and opened up. As he did, her fingers flew over her hair and straightened her suit.

"Sorry," he told Marshall. "Just habit. I always lock doors when I close them."

"Mommy?" Max called from the other room. "Mommy?"

"I'll be there in a sec, darling."

"We were in the other room," Sloan said as Marshall looked suspiciously from one of them to the other. "Watching cartoons with the kid. It took a minute to get to the door."

SLOAN STOOD STARING OUT the window of Marshall's room, doing his best to look nonchalant even though his gut was in knots.

When Hayley had gone back to the other bedroom he'd stayed in here, hoping that would make Marshall figure he had nothing to be suspicious about.

It hadn't done the trick, though, and for the past few minutes he could practically hear the guy arguing with himself, trying to decide whether he should keep his mouth shut about that locked door or tell Billy he thought something was going on between Sloan and their hostage.

The call had to be a tough one. Even though Marshall was a favourite of Billy's, Billy wouldn't like him bad-mouthing someone else he trusted. He tended to take that sort of thing as a personal insult.

Just as Sloan was telling himself that at least Marshall hadn't looked in the window, didn't know *for sure* what had been happening, the guy said, "You mind staying here a little longer? When I was talking to Billy I forgot about something I meant to ask him."

Damn. Marshall had decided to speak his mind. And it would be enough to start Billy worrying.

"Sure, no problem," Sloan said. "But it's past five, you know. I was thinking one of us should go find a take-out place."

"Yeah, well, I'll mention it to Billy. So…I'll be back in a couple of minutes. And do me a favor?"

"What?"

"Don't lock the door this time."

Sloan forced a grin. Then, the second Marshall was gone, he headed for the other room. Max had fallen asleep again, but Hayley was wide-awake, sitting on the side of the bed and looking half-scared to death.

She gazed up at him and whispered, "He's going to tell Billy he thinks that you and I…isn't he?"

"That's my guess."

"How will Billy react?"

"He'll probably tell Marshall he's imagining things. It'll get him wondering, though."

Hayley nervously licked her lips. While she'd been sitting there she'd come up with an idea, but she was afraid to talk to Sloan about it. Regardless of what had been developing between them, he still worked for Billy. And even if his feelings for her really did run deep enough that he'd do almost anything to keep her from harm, she had a horrible feeling that "almost anything" wouldn't include what she wanted.

But she didn't see how she could possibly get away from here without his help. And if she asked him for it, what would be the absolute worst thing that could happen?

Would he tell Billy?

She watched him for a moment, slowly rubbing his jaw as if lost in thought, and felt certain he wouldn't say a word. Because he knew how Billy would react. And he wouldn't want her facing the repercussions.

So the worst thing would be that she'd ask and he'd say "No way." Which wouldn't leave her any worse off than she already was.

But if that was really true, why was she so afraid to open her mouth?

She thought she knew the answer, and it had her shaking inside.

As much as Sloan had done to make things easier for her, nothing had involved crossing Billy. But this would. If he helped her escape he'd be choosing between them—aligning himself with her rather than Billy Fitz. And if he did that… Her thoughts started racing so fast they were suddenly tumbling over one another.

What if he began by crossing Billy on this and ended up changing his entire life? What if he decided he no longer wanted to be in bed with the bad guys? If he began working for legitimate clients?

She knew she could bring herself to forget all about his past if only he'd… But this simply wasn't the time to speculate about things like that…about whether the two of them would ever…

Because she had a horrible feeling that he was going to tell her "no." A horrible feeling that thinking there was even a chance his feelings for her were stronger than his allegiance to Billy was crazy.

And that, of course, explained why she was afraid to ask him to help her.

Finally, screwing up every ounce of her courage, she said, "Sloan?"

"Uh-huh?"

"What you told me earlier? That you'd kill Billy before you'd let him hurt Max or me?"

"I meant it."

"I know you did."

He smiled at her when she said that, and her pulse rate accelerated. His gaze was so intimate it made her think that maybe he *would* say, "yes."

"But if it came down to your actually having to try," she managed to continue, "well…there are four of them with guns and only one of you. Which means the odds are that you and me and Max would all end up dead."

He gave her another smile, but this one was strained.

"I sense a decided lack of confidence."

"Oh, Sloan," she murmured.

She wanted just to wrap her arms around him and hold on tight. Instead, she reminded herself that Keith Marshall could walk back in on them any second. And this might be the last chance she'd get to talk to Sloan alone.

"I…Sloan, with Marshall over there blowing the whistle on us, I just can't help being afraid that… And I was thinking… If you helped us, Max and I might be able to get away."

His expression said he thought he must have misheard her.

"If we just got to the highway—" she hurried

on before he could say a word ''—somebody would stop for a woman with a child. In no time.''

''Dammit, Hayley, that idea's absolutely insane!''

''No, it's not. If you created some kind of diversion…did something that would give us a few minutes to make a run for it…''

She hadn't thought as far as a specific diversion, so she left it at that and simply watched him, holding her breath and waiting for his response.

When he slowly shook his head, it was all she could do to keep from crying.

''I can't,'' he said quietly.

''But as long as Billy didn't know,'' she persisted—aware it was futile yet unable to stop herself. ''As long as it didn't look as if you'd had anything to do with it…''

Sloan swallowed hard, doing his damnedest not to let his feelings show. He was almost tempted to figure out if there was any possible way. But even if there was it would be too dangerous. For all of them.

''Hayley, you'd end up dead,'' he told her. ''And so would Max.''

''We might end up dead if we stay here! I mean, maybe you were right. Maybe Billy really did intend to let us go before. But now, if Marshall gets him worried enough who knows what he'll do?''

He gazed at her, the urge to sit down beside her and simply hold her so strong he could barely stop himself. But he knew what would happen if he got too close to her.

He'd smell the intoxicating scent of her perfume, feel the warmth of her body heat, and in about three seconds flat his brain would turn to mush and he'd agree to what she wanted. And he couldn't.

He hadn't been exaggerating, not just trying to scare her off her idea. If she and Max made a run for it they probably would end up dead. Neither Billy nor any of his men would think twice about shooting them.

And if by any chance they *did* get away, Billy would never just shrug and forget about them. So they had to stay right here.

"Hayley, there's simply no way," he told her. "You'll have to trust me on this. I know Billy a whole lot better than you do. Regardless of how suspicious Marshall makes him, you're far more likely to be okay if you don't try anything."

Besides, he added silently, he had a job to do. One that wouldn't be completed until he'd helped Billy rendezvous with the Pelican. And he couldn't risk screwing up that get-together because Hayley did something crazy—like calling the cops—if she actually did manage to escape.

"That was a definite no?" she whispered, her voice catching. "You really won't help me?"

"Just trust me, okay? Play it my way and you'll be fine. I swear you will. I…" He stopped himself from saying more. All he could do was what he'd already promised. Keep her and Max safe even if it cost him his life. And he *would* do that because…

As hard as he fought against letting the thought

form, he couldn't. He'd keep them safe because he'd fallen in love with her.

He'd desperately tried not to admit that to himself, yet he knew it was true. As true as the fact that they had no future. Not together.

But he'd known *that* all along. He just had to make himself face it.

"Hayley," he said again. "Promise me you won't try anything. Promise you'll sit tight."

When she bit her lower lip, he knew she was biting back more tears.

"Promise," he repeated.

Finally, she nodded.

"Okay," he said softly. He'd have preferred to hear the words, but a nod was probably the best she could manage.

He stood there for another minute, searching for something to say that would make her feel better, but before he came up with anything the front door of Marshall's room opened.

When the man walked in, he looked through into the other bedroom. "Sloan, Billy wants to see you," he announced.

CHAPTER TWELVE

SITTING ON THE EDGE of the bed, Max curled up asleep behind her, Hayley was trying her best to think through her fear and decide what to do.

Sloan's refusal to help had hurt. Badly. And she felt incredibly stupid for deluding herself that he cared more for her than he did.

For all she really knew, he didn't care one bit. Maybe he was just a good actor. Maybe she'd fallen in love with a man who was as much of a psychopath as Billy.

Fiercely, she told herself she had *not* fallen in love with Sloan Reeves. What she'd done was fallen prey to the Stockholm syndrome. Earlier, when she'd decided she hadn't, she'd been completely wrong.

As for him loving her, there was simply no way. If he did, he'd have agreed to help. Because it was patently obvious that she was right and he was wrong.

Even though trying to escape would be dangerous, doing nothing would be *more* dangerous. So with or without his help, she had to try to get out of here.

There. She'd made her decision and it hadn't been nearly as hard as...

Hayley, promise me you won't try anything. Promise you'll sit tight.

She could hear his words as clearly as if he were in the room with her again. But her nod had hardly constituted a real promise.

Even if it had, Max's life was at stake. And she'd break any promise she'd ever made if she thought it was the right thing for him.

After checking that he was still asleep, she pushed herself up off the bed and headed into the bathroom. Without closing the door, she cautiously turned the lock. If it was a noisy one, she'd better find out before she did anything more.

It wasn't. The click was barely audible.

She waited without breathing for a moment, but the only sounds she heard—aside from the thudding of her heart—came from the television sets. Hers was tuned to a nature show. In the other bedroom, Keith Marshall was watching something with a grate-on-the-nerves laugh track.

Closing the door, she turned toward the frosted bathroom window. Its size was a good omen. But when she tried the lock she almost broke her wrists making it turn. If Marshall had tested it, he'd probably figured there was no way she'd get it unlocked.

The window, itself, was less of a challenge. It pushed up with relative ease, and far enough that she shouldn't have any trouble getting through. That made a second good omen.

She slid the window back down, just in case

Marshall didn't react the way she expected him to, thinking that if only Sloan had agreed to help…

But he hadn't. And she simply couldn't let thoughts of him keep popping into her mind and distracting her. Until she and Max were safe, she had to stay firmly focused on what she was doing.

Back in the bedroom, she leaned over him and shook his shoulder firmly enough to wake him. "Hey, sleepyhead," she murmured. "Rise and shine."

He opened his eyes, then slowly rubbed them.

"Max, are you awake enough to listen?"

He nodded.

"Good, because you have to listen very carefully. I need you to do something without asking any questions, okay?"

"Why?"

Oh, Lord. His expression warned her he was good for a hundred questions in a row. And if he didn't cooperate this wouldn't work and they'd both end up dead! But if they stayed here they'd probably end up just as dead!

She ordered herself to calm down, then said, "No whys, Max. It's really, really important that you just do exactly as I say. No questions. No talking at all. Can you do that?"

He sat up, nodding more slowly this time. She could tell he'd picked up on her fear, but there wasn't much she could do about hiding it when she was so frightened she could hear her heart pounding in her ears.

"Good boy." She leaned closer and did up an

undone button on the Yankees shirt Sloan had bought him, trying to act as normal as possible.

"There," she said, giving the button a little pat. "Now, all I need you to do is go into the bathroom and close the door. But don't lock it. Just wait for me. I'll be along in a minute. I'll probably be alone, but if anyone's with me, I—"

"You mean Sloan?"

"I mean anyone at all. If I'm not alone I want you to pretend you're sick. Pretend you feel like throwing up."

"But—"

"Hey. You're not supposed to talk, remember? So just scoot," she added, pressing her fingers against his lips.

He hesitated for an instant, then climbed off the bed and started for the bathroom. After a couple of steps, he wheeled around and came back for his Yankees cap. Clutching it to his chest, he scurried back toward the bathroom without even glancing at her again.

Praying she was up to this, she walked over to the doorway and looked into the next room at Keith Marshall.

For a moment she couldn't make herself speak, but she finally managed to say, "Keith? Max is sick."

"Terrific," he muttered, his glance not wavering from the TV.

"Yes, well, I'm telling you because he says he's going to throw up. So I figured I'd better let you know we'll be in the bathroom until he's finished."

"Don't lock the door."

"No. I won't." She turned away and practically raced across the room.

When she opened the bathroom door, Max looked ready to start crying, so she whispered, "It's okay, darling. We're just going to have an adventure."

"What kind of 'venture?" he asked suspiciously.

"Well," she said, locking the door, "I'm going to climb out the window. Then you'll stand on the toilet seat and I'll help you out, okay?"

"But why? Why can't we go out the real way?"

"Because...because we can't."

"'Cuz we're runnin' away? And we don't want that man to know?"

"Yes. That's exactly it. The adventure is running away without letting anyone know. So we've got to be as quiet as mice."

"Mommy, I'm scared."

She gazed at him, her heart filled with an almost immobilizing combination of love and fear. What if she was doing the wrong thing? What if, in trying to keep him from harm, she ended up making things even worse than they already were?

Telling herself this was no time for doubts, she said, "It's all right to be scared, Max. I know everything's been really strange lately, but I promise we'll be back to normal very soon. Okay?"

His lips were quivering and his eyes were dark with tears. Even so, he gave her such a brave nod it made her chest ache.

"Okay, here goes, darling."

After hiking her skirt up around her hips and lifting her leg over the window ledge, she scrunched her head down and started to maneuver the rest of herself through the opening, trying not to think that Max's "scared" didn't even come close to describing *her* emotional state.

She felt as if an enormous black dragon were looming over her, ready to devour her whole at any second. And, maybe worst of all, she'd grown so used to the feeling that she was starting to think it was normal.

Getting through the window was a tighter squeeze than she'd anticipated, but she made it. When she reached back in for Max, he scrambled up onto the toilet seat and wrapped his arms around her neck.

"Hold on," she whispered. Then, holding on hard herself, she pulled him to freedom.

"That was perfect," she said as his feet hit the ground. "Now we've got to run. Come on."

Grabbing his hand, she started for the stand of trees out back of the motel—cursing her high heels as they dug into the earth with each step. But this was the only way to go. The property between the motel and the highway was wide-open space. Anyone looking out would see them there. So they'd have to cover some ground first, then head for the highway and flag down a ride.

"SO THAT'S WHAT MARSHALL told me," Billy concluded. "Is it true?"

Sloan slowly shook his head. Billy had pussy-footed around for a bit, but he'd finally launched into a word-by-word replay of what Marshall had said. And he'd said a lot.

He'd told Billy he was certain they had something serious to worry about, because he'd practically caught Sloan and Hayley in bed together. He'd even suggested that Sloan might try to help her escape.

But at least Billy had asked for Sloan's side of the story.

"Marshall's got an awfully active imagination," he said, still figuring out the best way to play this.

"Oh?"

Deciding, he gave Billy a boys-will-be-boys grin, accompanied by an "aw shucks" shrug.

"Okay, maybe Marshall caught me leering at her or something, I don't know. But I guess he could have, because you were right. I *do* kind of have the hots for her. She's got a great body. But there's sure nothing more to it than that. Ball-breakers scare the hell out of me."

He could feel himself relaxing a little when Billy grinned back. He'd picked the right approach. Billy had no trouble relating to a guy wanting to have sex with a woman he didn't even like.

"Marshall just read a lot more into finding that door locked than he should have," he added. "I mean, the kid was in there with us, for Pete's sake."

Billy eyed him for a few seconds, then nodded. "Yeah, I knew Marshall must be off base. So why don't we see what the network news is saying about me.'' He picked up the remote and flipped from CNN to another channel.

''Good idea. Then maybe I should go get us all some pizza or something.''

''Yeah. Or maybe Popeye's Chicken and Biscuits,'' Billy said, his eyes not leaving the screen. ''What they called chicken at Poquette tasted like dried shoe leather. And I figured they got their biscuit recipe confused with one for cement blocks.''

Sloan laughed, pretty sure he was completely off the hook. The only problem was, you could never be entirely certain what cogs were turning in Billy's mind.

''Here it is.'' He leaned forward as a photograph of him appeared on the screen.

The announcer had barely started the intro to the story when they heard someone trying the locked door.

Billy was already drawing his gun as Marshall hollered, ''Billy! Open up!''

Sloan's blood froze. Marshall was supposed to be guarding Hayley. So why was he out there? Unless she hadn't listened. Unless she'd somehow gotten Max out of that room and taken off.

''Make sure he's alone,'' Billy was saying. He quickly moved to the bathroom doorway, his gun in his hand.

Right. Not alone. Maybe that was it. Maybe the cops had tracked them down and forced Marshall to call Billy out. Dammit! He didn't know which scenario would be worse.

He strode across to the door, his heart hammering, and checked the peephole. When he saw no one but Marshall, he edged over to the window and peered cautiously into the courtyard.

Still only Marshall.

"I don't see anyone with him," he said, glancing at Billy.

"Okay. Open up."

After stepping back to the door, he unlocked and opened it.

Marshall practically bowled him over on his way in.

"She's gone," he announced.

"What?" Billy's face grew pale.

Sloan told himself he had to play this right—had to seem concerned about the potential consequences of Hayley's getting away, not about her and Max's safety.

"She told me the kid was sick and took him into the bathroom," Marshall was explaining. "It was only a minute or so before I went to check, but they'd gone out the window and I couldn't see them. They're probably just hiding right around the building, but—"

Billy swore, cutting off the rest of the explanation. "How could you be so damned stupid?" he demanded, pointing his finger at Marshall. "Instead of taking you with me, I oughta—"

"Go easy, Billy," Sloan interrupted. "I'm the one who's gotten to know her best. It should have occurred to me she might try something like this. If I'd been thinking, I'd have warned Marshall."

Both men looked at him, Marshall's expression showing surprise that Sloan had volunteered for some of the blame. But it might help if Marshall felt indebted to him.

If they caught Hayley and there was any discussion of what her fate should be, he'd want the guy voting his way. Taking a little blame off Marshall's shoulders now might pay dividends later.

"We're wasting time," Billy finally snapped. "Go find her," he added to Marshall.

Without another word, Marshall took off.

"And he was worried that she might escape because I'd *help* her," Sloan reminded Billy as Marshall closed the door.

"Right," Billy muttered. "But look, you go tell McIver and Dunne what's happened. I want the three of you looking, too."

"Fine."

"Get her," he added as Sloan turned away.

"I will," Sloan said over his shoulder. He *had* to get her. Because if one of the others did, she might not come back alive.

"Mommy, my side hurts," Max cried, tugging on Hayley's hand. "I can't run anymore."

"Can you just keep going until we reach that bush up ahead? Then we'll stop and rest."

Her side was hurting, as well. And she was so winded she was practically gasping. They hadn't gotten far from the motel before the heel of first one shoe and then the other had broken off, so running had been tough.

But they'd done what they had to. She'd guess that in the past ten minutes they'd covered over a mile. And, despite the fact that the land was pretty much open country, they weren't full of bullet holes. She only wished there were some guarantee she could keep them that way.

By now, though, Keith Marshall must have discovered they were gone. And as soon as he had, Billy would have mounted a search. Sloan had mentioned that there were a couple of Billy's other men at the motel, which meant there'd be at least three of them searching for her.

Plus Sloan, no doubt. And whether he caught up with her or one of the others did, the result would be the same. She and Max would either be dead or back at the motel, and… But that wasn't something she should let herself think about.

"Here," she said as they reached the bush. "We'll sit down for a few minutes." She sank to the ground beside Max, no longer even trying to prevent her suit from getting filthy. It already was.

"I wish I had a drink," Max said.

"I know. I wish I had one, too."

"My throat's too dry to talk."

"Mine, too." She wrapped her arm around his shoulder and gave him a squeeze. "So we'll just be quiet and rest for a bit, okay?"

"Okay." Max rested for about ten seconds before he picked up a stick and started poking at some weeds.

Hayley watched him for a minute, then looked across the stretch of open land toward the highway.

It was only about the width of a football field away, so they could reach it in no time at all. The question was, would heading for it really be the smartest move?

There wasn't a solid stream of traffic, but the road was far from deserted. And they only needed one person to offer them a ride.

On the other hand, when she'd thought that almost anyone would stop for a woman with a child, she hadn't envisioned herself looking the way she did at the moment—seriously disheveled, to put it mildly.

Aside from the condition her clothes were in, she was drenched in perspiration and her hair had to be a total mess. And Max was in no better shape. After stumbling a couple of times, he looked as though he'd been rolling in dirt. All of which meant that it might be a while before someone stopped. And what if, before anybody did, one of Billy's people came along?

Despite the heat, that thought made her feel as if an ice cube were slithering down her spine. Yet she could hardly ignore a possibility that was only too likely to become reality.

Glancing back in the direction they'd come, she slowly scanned the terrain.

She couldn't see anyone, but she was certain they'd be hunting for her on foot. At least one of them, though, would be cruising the highway. So what should she do?

The next town, Gonzales, was ten miles from the

motel. She'd spotted a sign giving her that information just before they'd reached Billy's hideout. And nine more miles was an awfully long hike. Especially for a six-year-old and a woman with wrecked shoes. Especially when a crew of determined men were pursuing them.

Viewing the situation from that perspective, they really had no choice. They'd have to take their chances with the highway.

Praying she'd come to the right decision, she said to Max, "Are you up to moving on? Just as far as that road?"

"I guess."

"Good, then we'll go see if somebody will stop and give us a ride."

He gazed at her uncertainly. "You mean a stranger?"

She nodded. "Sometimes it's all right to take help from a stranger. You just have to be a lot older than six before you can decide when it is."

THERE THEY WERE! Two figures up ahead on the shoulder of the road.

Sloan had been certain Hayley would make for the highway at some point. That, of course, was why he'd told the others he'd search along it.

He eased off the gas, warning himself not to feel *too* relieved. He might have been the one to find them, but that didn't change the fact Billy was fit to be tied. Which would hardly be a minor problem to deal with.

Hayley waved as he drew nearer, trying to flag him down, obviously not yet aware he was the driver. But from the distance, she wouldn't be. Not when he'd taken one of the cars that had been parked at the motel, rather than his Jeep.

A second later, she froze. Beside her, Max began to grin and wave.

Wishing that Hayley were even a quarter as pleased to see him as her son apparently was, Sloan pulled to a stop a few yards from them. Sticking the keys into his pocket, he got out of the car and started toward them—wondering how she could still look beautiful when she was in dire need of both a shower and fresh clothes.

The thought reminded him that he'd picked up a few things for her when he'd gotten the Yankees stuff for Max. At least she'd have something to change into.

"Let's go," he quietly said, reaching them.

"It's Sloan, Mommy," Max pointed out when she didn't move. "He's gonna give us a ride. We won't have to go with a stranger."

"Sloan, don't do this," she murmured, her eyes shimmering with tears.

He swallowed hard, tempted simply to pile the two of them into the car and drive until half a dozen states lay between them and Louisiana.

But taking off would only be a short-term solution to a long-term problem. And if they chose it, sooner or later they'd all end up dead.

"Just leave us here," she pleaded. "Tell Billy you didn't see us."

"Mommy?" Max said, anxiously gazing up at her. "What's wrong?"

"Max, would you mind waiting in the car?" Sloan asked. "Give me a minute to talk to your mom alone?"

The boy looked at Hayley again.

She shot Sloan one of her "pure hatred" glares, then nodded to Max.

"Listen to me," he said as the boy headed away. "What do you think would happen if I *did* leave you here? If I said I hadn't seen you? Do you figure Billy would just forget about you? Because there's not a chance in hell he would."

He paused and stood gazing at her, willing her to believe the truth of what he was saying. As much as she didn't want to go back to the motel, the only way he could keep her alive was to keep her with him. If she was off running and trying to hide on her own, she wouldn't have a prayer.

"If we don't find you fast," he continued, "Billy will call on everyone he knows to start looking for you—including his friends in the NOPD. And that means if you went to the cops he'd hear about it. You'd be signing your death warrant for sure."

"But I wouldn't go to them! Billy made it only too clear what would happen if I crossed him."

"Then why on earth did you run off? You don't count that as crossing him?"

"I…if he'd left me at the escape scene the way

he said he would… Surely it's obvious even to him why I was scared he'd change his mind about something else. But if he's afraid I'll go to the police, he shouldn't be. Because I won't. There's just no way. I mean, I realize I'll have to talk to them eventually. Lord, I realize I might end up in jail eventually. But Billy knew they'd probably figure out I'd helped him. He told me how to play things if that happened. You know he did.''

"Yes, but—''

"And you said he's leaving the country. I can avoid talking to the police until after he's gone. Sloan, if you let us go, Max and I will lay low for a while. And when we surface I'll play by Billy's rules. I won't implicate any of his people. I know he wouldn't stand for it. And there's no way I'd jeopardize Max's life.''

"Dammit, Hayley, maybe you mean all that, but if I don't take you back he won't know *what* you intend to do. So he'll send people looking for you with orders to kill you.''

"But you could *tell* him. You could tell him we had this talk and—''

"And what? Tell him I found you and then just took it upon myself to let you go? After he told me to bring you back? Hell, that would make me number one on his hit list. You and Max would be demoted to second and third.''

"Then say you didn't see any trace of us! If you leave us here we'll get a ride with a real person. And—''

"Hayley, you're not listening. If you actually did make it away from here, Billy would have a whole army of people searching for you. It's more likely, though, that you wouldn't make it away—that before any *real* person stopped, Marshall or one of the others would spot you. And you're a lot better off with me than you'd be with one of them."

"Oh, right!"

The look of utter loathing she gave him pierced his heart. If only he could just leave her here and let her get her ride. If only things were half as simple as she assumed.

"Right," she said again. "We're a whole lot better off with you. Even though you're going to take us back to that motel, just the way the others would. And then what? Then Billy will kill us," she continued before he could utter a word. "I was already convinced he would. If I hadn't been, we wouldn't have tried to escape. And now that we have…"

"He's *not* going to kill you."

Hayley merely shook her head, looking so wretched it was all Sloan could do to keep from wrapping his arms around her. But she was back to hating him again. If he made a move to console her, she'd spit in his eye.

So, instead, he merely repeated what he'd just told her. "He's not going to kill you." He took his cellular from his pocket. "Because I'm going to make a deal with him before we go back."

And if he couldn't manage to do that, he damn

well *would* simply get in the car and drive away with them.

He'd have no other choice. They'd take off and he'd worry about the consequences later. Because despite all his efforts not to, he'd fallen in love with Hayley.

CHAPTER THIRTEEN

HIS OWN CELL PHONE in his hand, Sloan hesitated before punching in the number for Billy's.

He'd managed to figure out a pretty good story to feed the man if Billy proved so angry he wanted Hayley dead. But it wouldn't hurt to spend another minute psyching himself up by thinking about the advantage he had.

Billy might have spent his entire adult life dancing with the devil, and under most circumstances you couldn't trust the man very far, yet when he gave his word he *did* keep it. Sloan had never known him to go back on it.

There's a first time for everything. The thought flitted through his mind before he could stop it.

But the risk of Billy breaking his word was a lot lower than the one Hayley and he would face if they ran.

And even if they managed to avoid being found, taking off would mean the end to Sloan's life as he knew it. Things would be far, far better if he could convince Billy to promise...

If. He slowly shook his head. It was an awfully big if. But this was something he simply *had* to do. Because...

His gaze drifted toward the car, where his "because" was waiting with her son. Max was in the back, Hayley in the front—more or less.

She'd kicked her shoes off onto the shoulder of the highway and was sitting sideways in the passenger seat, watching him, her bare feet on the ground, her bottom lip caught nervously between her teeth.

He'd asked her to wait there so she wouldn't hover over him, making him even more anxious than he already was. But apparently she intended to try her hand at lipreading.

Turning his back to her, he began imagining how his conversation with Billy would go. Billy wouldn't be expecting him to call, so when his phone rang he'd hope it was the Pelican making contact.

He'd be disappointed that it wasn't. But he'd be relieved to hear Sloan had caught up with Hayley. And then...

And then Sloan simply didn't know. Exactly how he played things from there would depend on Billy.

Finally, telling himself to just get on with it, he punched in the number.

"Yes," Billy answered on the first ring.

"It's Sloan. I found them."

"Good, I knew one of you would. So you'll be back here in what? A few minutes?"

"Unless you want me to get some takeout first."

"No. I'll send one of the boys for something later. Right now, I just want that woman."

"Okay. But what do you figure on doing with her?"

A moment's silence followed, before Billy said, "Why are you asking?"

"I want to be sure you don't have any thoughts about killing her. Or the kid."

"Oh? You don't think that would be the smartest idea? Considering what she just did?"

"No, I don't. Because it could cause me a real serious problem."

The silence was longer this time, so long that Sloan caught himself counting off a second with each pounding beat of his heart.

"You want to explain that?" Billy said at last.

"Someone I know saw me with the boy," he lied. "After I'd picked him up from Sammy and O'Rourke. He needed a bathroom, so I stopped at a burger place. And damned if we didn't run into a friend of a friend.

"I told the guy Max was my nephew," he continued when Billy said nothing. "And he'll probably never give a second thought to having seen us—unless the kid ends up dead and his picture's splashed all over the place."

"It's already been on TV."

"Well, if this guy saw it he didn't recognize him. But if Max turns into a murder victim, and someone can put me together with him only hours before he was killed... "

"Dammit, Sloan, she ran! If she ran, she'll talk!"

"No. She won't. She'll do exactly what you told her to. If I had the slightest concern that she wouldn't... Hell, where would I be if she went to the cops? I'd be in so deep I'd spend the rest of my life behind bars. There's just no way she'll open her mouth, though. She's perfectly clear on what will happen to her and the boy if she does.''

''But she took off, dammit! I can't—''

''Billy, she didn't run with any ideas about causing us grief. She was just afraid you might change your mind and decide to kill them. But if I bring them back and everything's fine, she'll be convinced that she really doesn't have anything to fear. Not as long as she keeps quiet.''

''How can you be so damn sure?''

''I just am.''

''You just *are*,'' Billy muttered. ''Dammit, Sloan, shutting her up permanently makes a lot more sense. Then none of us would have to worry about her ever talking.''

''No, but I'd have something worse to worry about. You kill her and it might come back to bite me in the butt. If it wasn't for that, I wouldn't give a damn what you did. But I don't want the payback for helping get you out of Poquette to be someone linking me directly to a murder. Not the kid's and not hers. And, look, if it would make you feel better, I'll take over watching her until you're out of the country.''

''Well, I sure as hell wouldn't trust Marshall with the job again. I'm starting to wonder if I'm making a mistake by taking him along.''

Sloan began to breathe a little more easily. It sounded as if Billy was starting to buy in. ''I'm not

Marshall," he pressed on. "I'll watch *her,* not the damn television. And if she tries anything else I'll kill her myself. But she won't."

"I don't know. I just don't like—"

"I know you don't, but listen to me, okay? You'll be in South America. I won't. And I sure as hell don't want to be on the hook for something as serious as murder. Not when it's avoidable. Besides, you had a deal with her. She helped you escape and you wouldn't harm them."

"We had a deal *before* she ran."

"So? You kept her with you after the escape. That wasn't part of any deal she agreed to. The way I see it, those two things cancel each other out. And hell, Billy, you've always been a man of your word. Isn't that how you want people to think of you when you're off lying on your beach? You don't want to retire on a sour note. We both know that. So why not just say you'll be cool when I bring them back."

He thought about bluntly pointing out that Billy owed both him and Hayley big-time, but resisted the temptation. Billy knew they were the ones he had to thank for being in that motel right now instead of in a prison cell. Besides, there was a limit to how far you could push the man before he got donkey-stubborn.

In view of that, instead of saying another word, Sloan simply waited.

THE INSTANT SLOAN TOOK the phone from his ear, Hayley was out of the car and heading toward him—her heart beating a terrified tattoo.

Billy's not going to kill you, he'd said. *Because I'm going to make a deal with him before we go back.*

But she still didn't want to go back to that motel, whether Sloan had made his "deal" or not.

Reaching him, she glanced back at the car, checking that Max had stayed put as ordered. Then she said, "Well?"

"Everything's fine. Billy just wants to keep you with him a little longer. Until his plans for getting out of the country are finalized. Just so he's entirely certain you can't say anything to—"

"Sloan, I won't! I've told you that a hundred times. And how can you be sure everything's really fine? How do you know that if Max and I go back Billy won't—"

"Hayley, I realize how frightened you are, but—"

"Frightened? Try petrified. Why can't you see that if you'd just let us go—"

"No. Look, Billy gave me his word and—"

"And you believed him."

"Yes, I did. And even if I had any doubts about him keeping it—which I don't," he added quickly, "the bottom line hasn't changed. If I let you go, his people will find you and kill you. As bizarre as it might sound, you'll be safer if I take you back."

"But—"

"Hayley," he said quietly, "please just trust me. You and Max are going to be all right."

She stood gazing at him, her heart thudding, telling herself this wasn't the first time he'd asked her to trust him. And thus far she and Max were all right.

But how could she trust him now, when he was delivering them back to Billy Fitz? How could she believe he was doing what was best for them when he might simply be feeding her a line? When his only real concern might be doing what was best for Billy?

For all she knew, Billy hadn't even promised not to kill them. Maybe Sloan had just said that so she'd go along with him, like a meek little lamb to the slaughterhouse.

The analogy made her shiver.

"Okay?" Sloan said quietly.

She gave him a miserable shrug in reply. Of course she wasn't okay. But they were going back. End of story. Or, rather, end of chapter. The end of the story would come once they reached the motel—and she found out what Billy was really going to do. If she let herself think about that, though, she wouldn't have a prayer of keeping up a brave face for her son.

Wordlessly turning away from Sloan, she started for the car.

"Don't forget your shoes," he said.

She looked down at them sitting on the shoulder, then shook her head. She was better off in bare feet.

When she climbed into the car, Max said, "Are we going now?"

"Yes."

"*Where* are we going? Home?" he demanded as Sloan slid into the driver's seat.

Glancing across the car, she caught his gaze and held it a second. Once she let it go, he turned toward Max, his expression uneasy. "We're going back to the motel."

Max eyed him for a few moments, then looked at Hayley. "But how come? You said we were running away."

How come? Good question. Because Sloan was on Billy's side, not hers? Because when it came to choosing between her and Billy—

"How come, Mommy?"

"Because...Sloan convinced me we should stay there for a while longer."

"How *much* longer?"

"Just a little while," Sloan told him.

"With that man who was there? That Keith? He scares me."

"Then how about if I stay in the next room to you, instead of him?" Sloan asked.

"Well...yeah, I guess that'd be okay."

Hayley swallowed hard, wondering whether anyone would actually end up staying in the next room to them. Or if, mere minutes from now, they'd both be dead.

THERE WAS NO SIGN of anyone in the motel office when Sloan drove by, which had to mean that Marshall, McIver and Dunne were still out searching for Hayley and Max.

That was good, he told himself. He was ninety-nine-percent convinced Billy would keep his promise, but even if he didn't, he wouldn't try anything without his backup men around.

And with a little luck, his reaction when he saw Hayley would reveal whether they had anything to worry about on the Billy-breaking-his-word front.

Trying not to think about what a good actor the man was, Sloan looked at Hayley. The way she was staring straight ahead, her face pale and her lips pressed together, made him want to reach over and give her hand a squeeze. He didn't, though.

If she had a choice between him and a two-thousand-pound gorilla touching her, she'd probably prefer the gorilla. Besides, Max was hanging over the back of her seat, and Sloan didn't want to encourage more of his questions.

"We'll just check in with Billy," he said, pulling up in front of unit twenty.

Hayley glanced at him then, but didn't say a word. She didn't have to. Her expression told him exactly how frightened she still was.

He cut the ignition, then reached under the seat to where he'd stashed his Glock.

"That's a gun!" Max exclaimed, practically in his ear. "How come you had a gun under there?"

He looked at Hayley again as he stuck it in his belt, but she clearly wasn't going to help him out. She'd gone back to staring straight ahead.

"Sloan? How come you had a gun under there?"

"Oh…it's just in case we come across another snake. Let's go," he added, getting out of the car before Max came up with something else to ask about.

Halfway to the door, he stopped and waited while Hayley reluctantly climbed from the car.

"Come on," he said as she took her son's hand. "It really *is* going to be okay."

"What is?" Max demanded.

"Oh…you know, everything." He turned, walked the final few steps to Billy's door and knocked.

"It's Sloan," he called when there was no response.

Another good minute passed before Billy opened up, his cell phone in his hand and a major grin on his face.

"I just got the call," he said, his gaze barely flickering past Sloan to the others. "Right after you and I were done. I'd just clicked off and he phoned."

For half a second Sloan didn't realize who Billy was talking about. Then the light went on. He'd heard from the Pelican.

"Come in," he said, backing into the room. "I'll tell you the details."

He glanced at Hayley and Max, then said, "There's no one here to keep an eye on them. But my bathroom doesn't have a window, so they can wait in there."

"I won't try anything again," Hayley said earnestly. "I hope Sloan explained that—"

Billy impatiently waved off the rest of her words. "Just take the kid in there."

She'd barely closed the door behind them before he said, "We're on for tomorrow afternoon. Two o'clock. Flying out of a private airfield not far across the Mississippi state line. I've got the instructions," he added, waving the piece of paper in his hand.

"We turn off Highway 61 just beyond some town called Woodville and we're practically there. He said it's the only airfield around. We can't miss it."

"Terrific," Sloan said, thinking the call had been timely. Billy was so excited the arrangements were set he couldn't care less about Hayley and Max.

And he'd be gone tomorrow. So just as long as his men didn't convince him not to leave any loose ends, things would probably be okay.

"We'll be going in a Lear," Billy was saying. "He told me, 'You have the rest of my money, and I'll have a Lear jet.'"

"Terrific," Sloan said again.

"His money's right there." Billy pointed at one of the suitcases parked against the wall. "And you'll come along to see us off, won't you?"

"I wouldn't miss it for the world. But what about them?" he asked, nodding toward the bathroom door.

Billy shrugged. "They'll come with us."

A chill ran down Sloan's spine. "You don't think they'd be in the way?" he said as casually as he could. "Maybe you should just leave them here and—"

"Not a chance. *You* might be sure she'll never

open her mouth, but I'm not. We drive out of here, she gets on the phone and we're dead.''

''So tie her up before we leave. But—''

''And what if she somehow gets free? Or someone happens to pull in here and finds her?''

''Billy—''

''Uh-uh. If you want to spend the rest of your life knowing there's someone around who could put you away, that's up to you. But I'm not taking any chances until that Lear's flying high. You can set her free after I'm gone if that's what you really want. But sleep on it tonight, huh? 'Cuz I figure you'd be making a big mistake.''

Sloan silently counted to ten, telling himself not to let Billy realize how anxious he was. ''You're right,'' he said at last. ''I'll give it some more thought. But you know what just occurred to me?''

''What?''

''The Pelican would have a fit if you showed up with Hayley. I mean, he's not going to worry if I'm there. He'll expect you to have a driver, and considering I'm the one who set things up with him… But we know he's secretive about his identity. So if someone like Hayley saw him—could describe him—he'd never let her just…''

The evil smile that crept onto Billy's face stopped Sloan midsentence.

That bastard! He'd given his word that *he* wouldn't kill Hayley and Max, but he was setting things up so the Pelican *would*.

AFTER THE OTHERS had straggled back from searching for the runaways, McIver had gone off to get some food and beer. Now Billy's motel room was strewn with empty cans and pizza boxes, and the smell was really getting to Sloan.

Or maybe it wasn't the smell at all. Maybe he was feeling sick to his stomach because he was so worried.

He glanced at the bathroom door, wishing once again that he could get Hayley and Max across the courtyard to the other rooms. Billy had given them a pizza, so they wouldn't be starving, but they had to be damned tired of being cooped up.

"Sloan?" Billy said. "You're sure you don't want to fly south with us tomorrow? Spend the rest of your days on a beach?"

He manufactured a smile. "As tempting as that sounds, I'll pass. I'm not really the beach type."

"Well, I guess maybe that's all for the good. Brendan would have a fit if I took you with me. He'll need your help after I'm gone."

Sloan let that pass. There wasn't much chance he'd end up helping Brendan, though. Things just weren't likely to play out that way.

And assuming they didn't, what would he do?

He'd been asking himself that question for a while now. And he'd been giving the possible answers a lot of consideration, especially since he'd realized how hard he was falling for Hayley.

He let his thoughts drift down that road for a minute. Then, telling himself they had to get through tomorrow before he spent any more time thinking about the future, he tuned back into

Billy—who was rambling on some more about how great life would be in South America.

When Billy paused for a slug of beer, Marshall said, "What if someday they change that extradition-treaty thing? What if someday we're all lying in the sun and a bunch of feds come strolling along?"

"What if you stop trying to get us worried about something that'll never happen?" McIver said.

"It *could* happen. And I just don't like leaving her alive when she knows so much," he added, nodding toward the bathroom.

"I told you, I gave her my word," Billy snapped. "So I don't want to hear any more about it."

McIver grinned. "Marshall's just pissed off because they got away on him."

"Yeah," Dunne added with a grin of his own. "Maybe we shouldn't take him with us, Billy. He's not as sharp as he used to be."

Marshall grabbed one of the pizza cartons and heaved it across the bed at Dunne, while Sloan swore under his breath. He needed some peace and quiet to figure out what the hell he was going to do about tomorrow. He sure couldn't think while these guys were acting like a bunch of morons.

He listened to McIver and Dunne take a few more gibes at Marshall, then he stretched and pushed himself out of the chair. "I'm beat," he said in response to Billy's questioning glance. "Why don't I take our prisoners and go."

"I nailed all the windows shut over there," Marshall told him. "While McIver was out getting the pizza."

"Kinda like nailing the barn door shut after the horses have bolted," Dunne pointed out.

Marshall scowled at him.

Sloan didn't say a word. He could live without more discussion about whether Hayley might try to make another run for it.

"Yeah, maybe we should all call it a night," Billy said. "We've got a big day ahead of us tomorrow."

If he only knew *how* big, Sloan thought.

DUSK WAS GATHERING by the time Sloan left Billy's room and headed across the courtyard, Hayley and Max in tow.

They'd obviously spent some of their time in that bathroom getting cleaned up. They no longer looked like escapees from a prison work crew. They sure didn't look happy, though, and Max was clearly tired.

Sloan hoped that meant the little boy would fall asleep as soon as Hayley put him to bed, because they had to talk. But before they did, he had to decide exactly how much he was going to tell her.

If he followed the rules, it would be absolutely nothing. But if he followed the rules, she'd likely end up dead. Both her and Max. And if that happened, he'd never be able to live with himself.

He stopped at the car he'd driven earlier and

opened the back door, saying, "Tom and Dick gave me the clothes and things they got for Max."

Once he'd set the two plastic bags on the ground, he reached back in for the shopping bag. "And when I was buying the Yankees stuff," he added, glancing at Hayley, "I picked up a few things for you, too."

She gazed at him for a moment after he'd closed the car door, obviously knowing she should thank him but not wanting to. It made him think that, if he were in her position, he'd have a hard time feeling grateful, too. Even though her worst fears hadn't materialized, she was still frightened about being back in the motel. And he was still the one who'd brought her back.

"Unfortunately," he said, glancing at her bare feet, "I didn't know you were going to leave your shoes on the side of the road."

"I couldn't walk in them the way they were. But…thanks for thinking to get me what you did."

He simply nodded, and neither of them spoke again until they'd walked the rest of the way to number eleven.

As he opened the door and the air-conditioned air greeted them, she ruffled Max's hair and said, "I don't know which of us needs a bath more."

"I'm too tired for a bath," Max told her. "'Sides, I washed my face real good."

"I know, but the rest of you—"

"M-o-m-m-y. I'm r-e-a-l-l-y tired."

She ushered him inside, saying, "I'll tell you

what. How about if we do a little more work with a facecloth but save the bath for morning. Deal?''

He nodded. ''Deal.''

''Okay, you scoot into the other room and get out of those clothes. I'll be there in a second.''

As he headed away, she looked at Sloan. ''I...I've been trying to decide whether to tell you this or not, but—''

Silencing her with a gesture, he took his ''tape recorder'' out of his pocket and turned the detecting mode on. The warning light didn't begin flashing, but it made sense to just leave the thing on. He wouldn't put it past any of Billy's guys to wander over with a high-power mike.

When he set down the recorder, Hayley was eyeing him strangely.

''You think they'd actually care what I say?''

He merely shrugged. ''What were you starting to tell me?''

''I...oh, that it wasn't hard to hear through that bathroom door. I heard almost everything all of you were talking about.''

''I see,'' he said, not really surprised she'd been eavesdroping. He'd assumed she'd try, and the others probably had, as well. But given that they'd soon be out of the country, they wouldn't have cared.

''You figure this Pelican person might kill Max and me, don't you. I mean, if Keith Marshall doesn't convince Billy he should do it before we even get to the airfield.''

"Well…first off, you don't have to worry about Billy. Marshall won't make him change his mind. As for the Pelican…" Sloan paused, then squared his shoulders and lied through his teeth. "You've got nothing to worry about from him, either."

"Oh? That isn't what I gathered when you were talking to Billy."

He shrugged again. "I don't always tell Billy the whole truth and nothing but. I had my reasons for saying what I did. Let's just leave it at that. Nothing's going to happen to you and Max, though. We'll deliver Billy and his boys to that airfield, they'll take off and then I'll drive you back to New Orleans."

"You're sure? What about the part where Billy said you'd be crazy to just let me go? And you told him you'd give it some more thought."

"That's what he wanted to hear."

"Ah."

For a long moment, her dark eyes held his gaze. It made him hot inside; it also made him glad he'd lied. He'd eventually have to tell her the truth. At least some part of it. But for the next little while, maybe she could just relax a bit.

She finally took the bags from him and headed for the other bedroom. Once she'd vanished through the doorway, he lay down on the bed, his hands behind his head, and began to give the situation some serious thought.

Faintly, from the other side of the wall, he could hear the sounds of Hayley helping Max get ready for bed. Water running in the sink, the whisper of their voices.

After a few minutes, Max called, "Sloan?"

He pushed himself up and walked across to the doorway. Max was in bed; Hayley was sitting beside him on the edge.

"Max wants you to help tuck him in," she said.

Her words elicited a strange feeling in his chest.

"And read me my story," Max said.

"There were a few books in the bags," Hayley explained, gesturing to where they sat on the bedside table. "And if you wouldn't mind... I'm really dying for a shower."

"Sure. I wouldn't mind."

"Good. Thanks." Giving him a brief smile, she rose and headed into the bathroom.

"This one," Max said, reaching for the top book, then patting the bed where Hayley had been sitting.

As Sloan eased himself down and took the book, he could hear Hayley turning on the shower. Suddenly, he was imagining her naked.

"So what are we reading?" he said, forcing himself to focus on the book. "*The Hunt for Rabbit's Galoshes.* Well, that sounds exciting."

"It is. And I can read some of the words myself. But I'll let you do them all."

Sloan couldn't help smiling. It sounded as if getting to read all the words, without Max's help, was a special treat.

When he opened the book and began the story,

Max snuggled down under the covers. After only three and a half pages, the little boy was asleep.

Sloan simply sat watching him then, that strange feeling still in his chest. In the bathroom, the sound of running water eventually ceased.

He heard Hayley pulling back the shower curtain and couldn't stop himself from imagining her naked again. It was enough to make him hard with arousal, and if she came out of the bathroom with only a towel wrapped around her...

He rested the book strategically on his lap and waited, wondering how large the motel towels were.

When the bathroom door opened, she emerged wearing the yellow sleeveless shirt and the shorts he'd bought for her.

Trying to ignore his disappointment, he told himself it was just as well she'd gotten dressed.

"I feel so much better," she said, combing her wet hair with her fingers. "I didn't think it would take him long to fall asleep," she added, smiling down at Max.

"The bad part," Sloan told her, "is that we barely got into the story. I'll never know whether rabbit finds his galoshes or not."

That made her laugh. She had a wonderful laugh—warm and silvery—and he realized this was the very first time he'd heard it.

He didn't want to think about what that said, about how dreadfully unhappy she'd been since he'd met her. He also didn't want to think about what they had to discuss. But he'd decided he had to fill her in about everything. Otherwise, come tomorrow, she and Max would be sitting ducks.

CHAPTER FOURTEEN

HAYLEY TUCKED THE BLANKET around Max, glanced over to make sure the courtyard door was securely locked, then turned off the overhead light and trailed anxiously into the adjoining room after Sloan. When he'd said there was something they had to talk about, her intuition had warned her it wasn't something she was going to like.

"Close that door, would you?" he said.

"Our talking won't wake Max. Nothing ever wakes him during the night."

Sloan shook his head. "If this was the one time it did, he might repeat the wrong thing."

Her anxiety increasing, she stepped back and shut the door between the two rooms.

"You might as well sit down," Sloan said. "This could take a while."

There was only one chair, and since his jacket was lying across it she perched on the edge of the bed, then watched him pace over to the window and look out into the night.

To make sure no one had an ear to the door? she wondered.

He checked that the bolt was slid into place, then

said, "I'm going to turn off the light. So if anyone wanders over, we'll see him coming."

When he flicked the switch, pale moon shadows drifted into the sudden darkness of the room. He became a black silhouette in their gossamer light.

"I don't quite know how to start," he said, gazing in her direction. "Except to say I've decided to tell you a lot of things I shouldn't."

Her eyes gradually adjusting to the dimness, she waited for him to continue. When he didn't, she said, "I'm good at keeping secrets."

"I've gathered that. But I want your word, on Max's life, that you'll never repeat any of it."

"All right, you've got it."

He was silent for another long moment. "Okay, here goes," he said at last. "When there's a drug bust or a takedown—"

"Drug bust? Takedown? Sloan, what are you—"

"Just listen, okay? Let me get this all out before you ask any questions."

"Okay," she said uneasily.

"When there's any sort of major police action, it all happens in seconds. Everyone's adrenaline is pumping like crazy and things get unbelievably confusing. That's why the bureau's jackets have FBI stenciled on them in enormous letters. So the agents can tell who's who. Then, hopefully, they don't shoot one another."

Hayley nodded. By now she had a pretty good idea where he was heading, and her intuition had been right. This wasn't something she was going to like.

''Anybody who makes a wrong move can easily end up dead,'' he continued. ''And I don't want you making any wrong moves tomorrow. Because there's going to be a takedown at that airfield.''

''What?'' she whispered. But how did he—

''Hayley, not even my parents know this, and if the wrong people ever find out I'll be dead. I'm a federal agent.''

''What?'' she whispered again.

''Deep undercover, obviously. They recruited me while I was still in law school, specifically to take over from an agent who'd infiltrated the Irish Mafia years before. He'd been keeping the Bureau informed about the family's activities for a long time, but he was ready to retire. Before he did, though, he convinced Billy that he needed a sharp young lawyer looking out for his interests. And—''

''Wait.'' Hayley's mind was whirling too fast to register half of what Sloan was saying. But he was telling her he was one of the good guys? When all along she'd believed... And that wasn't true?

As she gazed across the moonlit room at him, her thoughts raced even faster. If he wasn't actually on Billy's team, then all the feelings she'd been doing her best to deny...even though they'd kept on getting stronger and stronger...

She closed her eyes, certain a floodgate had just opened inside her and all those feelings she'd been trying to repress were rushing through it.

But even as every single one of them was making its way to freedom, an imaginary voice whispered,

Hey, wait a minute. What if he isn't telling you the truth?

"Are you wondering if you should believe me?" he asked.

She looked over at him, her face growing warm. "Is what I'm thinking that obvious? Even in a dark room?"

"No. But either I'm lying now or I've completely misled you all along. And you're too smart not to wonder which it is."

She said nothing, merely waited.

"I don't have any bureau I.D. to show you," he continued. "When you're undercover, you sure don't carry anything that says you're a fed. But if I tell you the rest of the story, that should help."

"All right," she agreed, wishing he hadn't turned off the light. If his expression revealed any clues to truths and lies, she'd never catch them with only moonbeams to see by.

"Billy's escape was a setup," he said.

She almost interrupted right there. Her son had been kidnapped as part of a setup? Biting her lip, she ordered herself to simply listen.

"Billy had heard about this Pelican," Sloan continued. "I assume you gathered what his specialty is? Smuggling criminals out of the country and establishing them in new lives?"

"Yes. I gathered."

"Well, he does such a good business that he's on the bureau's Most Wanted list—although we only know his code name, not his real identity. At any rate, when Billy decided he was going to try to escape, he asked me to contact the guy. My superiors gave me the green light to play along and see where it got us. They figured that at the very least we'd put some of Billy's boys away for their part in a prison break. But what they were really hoping we could do was nail the Pelican.''

"So you contacted him," she prompted when Sloan paused.

"Uh-huh."

"How?"

"Well, the hows in this don't really matter. What's important is that when he and Billy hook up tomorrow, a squad of special agents will be lying in wait. They'll drop their net on everyone at once."

Or else they'll blow it, Hayley thought, her heart starting to hammer.

TV images from a few years back flashed through her mind. Images of that standoff in Waco, Texas. The feds trying to force a whole bunch of cult members out of a building.

All kinds of people had ended up dead, and that certainly wasn't the only operation the bureau had ever screwed up. What if they did that tomorrow, when...

"Oh, Lord," she whispered. "We can't take Max into something like that."

"We have no choice," Sloan said quietly. "If we said you'd just as soon not go along for the ride, Billy would say, 'Too bad.' And we can hardly tell him why we don't want you at that field—because

I'm a fed and he'll be walking into a trap. Not unless we want him to kill all three of us on the spot.''

"But a six-year-old child? Sloan—''

"Billy doesn't care, Hayley. Period. You and Max will have to be there and we'll have to cope.''

She slowly shook her head. Just thinking about exactly what they might have to cope with was making her cold all over.

"It'll be okay. While McIver was out getting the pizza, I went for a walk and called my superior. I had to give him the details about the rendezvous, but I also told him that you and Max would be along. So the team will know.''

"What you're saying is they'll *try* not to shoot us.''

"Hayley—''

"But you can't even say *that much* for Billy's team.''

"It'll be okay,'' he said again. "Let me finish explaining how this situation developed, though. Then we'll talk about tomorrow.''

"All right,'' she made herself say. Then, as he began speaking once more, she did her best to force those Waco images from her mind.

"When I made contact with the Pelican,'' he continued, "he said he'd be happy to take care of things if Billy managed to get himself out of prison. But there really wasn't much of an *if*, given that the bureau wanted him out. That's why I was so sure Warden Armstrong would approve the trip to the med center, and that he'd let you go along. Because as soon as he hesitated, a couple of feds paid him a visit.

"And those guards in the van with you were actually special agents. We didn't want to risk using real guards who might have tried to prevent the escape. Billy was our decoy. We did everything we could to help him."

"Including letting his people kidnap Max," she couldn't keep herself from saying.

Sloan turned toward the window and gazed out for a moment. Then he pulled the curtain closed and walked slowly over to the edge of the bed. When he sat down a foot or so from her, her heart skipped a beat. If only he could explain the kidnapping away. If only—

"Hayley, I've told you before, I'm in no position to *let* Billy or his people do anything. I've also explained that taking Max wasn't something I wanted, and that's the God's honest truth. But when Billy and I decided we'd use you to help him, he—"

"Use me."

He was silent for a couple of beats, then said, "That was a poor choice of words."

But an accurate one. Using her was precisely what he'd done. And she found that very difficult to reconcile with her feelings for him.

"At any rate," he continued, "kidnapping Max was Billy's plan B right from the start. As soon as he learned you'd recommended against the transfer, he told Brendan to put Max under surveillance and figure out the easiest way to snatch him."

"I see," she murmured.

Now that the floodgate had opened, it would be impossible to pretend the feelings it had released didn't exist. But she couldn't simply forget about what Sloan had done, so she needed to understand how he could have done it.

"Do you often use innocent people?" she asked, keeping her voice as free of emotion as she could. "Women and children?"

He shook his head. "Not often. But sometimes I have no choice."

"Oh?"

"Hayley, the bureau fights organized crime. Our methods can't always be squeaky clean. If they were, we wouldn't have a prayer of coming out ahead of people like Billy. Or this Pelican."

"I guess I know that. I mean, I *do* know it. Intellectually, that is. But when it comes to Max..."

"I didn't want to use you," he said quietly. "Neither you nor him. But things didn't fall as nicely into place as I'd hoped.

"When Billy first decided that grabbing Max was the best way to make you cooperate, I convinced him we should go a different route—get you to recommend that damned transfer. You were never even supposed to realize you'd played any part in the escape. That recommendation would have been your only involvement. You threw a wrench in things, though. And when you did, Billy put the wheels in motion for the kidnapping."

"But you could have prevented it! You knew

beforehand. The bureau could have kept it from happening.''

''No. It's just not that simple. If the bureau could prevent every crime it knew about beforehand, the crime rate would plunge. But that's not how things work. In most cases there can't be an arrest until after a crime is committed.

''And once Billy decided he wanted Max snatched, it was going to happen. With or without my involvement. If not on the first try then on the second. Or the third. Hayley, I understand how Billy's mind works, and the best thing I could do was what I did. Suggest who should grab Max and where he should be held. And volunteer to act as the go-between.''

She nodded slowly. She still hated what had happened to her son, yet Sloan's explanation made sense. And it made her wonder whether she'd have done any differently if she'd been in his position, with his job to do.

''I did the best I could under the circumstances,'' he said as if reading her mind. ''And…the bottom line is that both you and Max are still alive.''

Thanks only to him. Because he'd convinced Billy not to kill them.

''But will we still be alive after tomorrow?'' she couldn't stop herself from saying. ''After the take-down? I mean, if there's a field full of men with guns…''

''The feds will know which one I am. They'll have been told I'll be wearing white pants and a green shirt. So the safest thing for you and Max to do is stick close by me.

"That's why I had to tell you all this. Because I knew that if you still thought I was on Billy's side and those feds suddenly appeared, you might figure you should make a run for it or something. And I couldn't risk you getting shot in the confusion. Couldn't risk it because…"

She gazed at him, certain he'd been going to say "because I love you." It made her feel as though a whirlwind had suddenly picked her up and she was sailing through the air with no idea where she'd come down.

"Anyway, that's why I had to tell you the truth," he said. "So you'll know how to react tomorrow."

The truth. They were back to where his explanation had started—to whether she should believe this new version of reality.

Was there even a remote chance it *wasn't* the truth?

She didn't think so. Surely nobody could invent such an involved story. And what would be the point?

Besides, unless Sloan actually was a fed, he wouldn't know about the takedown. And if he was truly on Billy's side, he wouldn't be leading him into a trap.

"Won't being there tomorrow blow your cover?" she asked as the question occurred to her.

"Probably. Barring something unexpected. Ostensibly, I'll be helping Billy escape, so no one would ever believe the feds just let me walk. Which means that if I don't end up behind bars, everyone will realize which side I'm *really* on."

"Then why be there?"

"Billy asked me to. If I finagled my way out of it, afterward he'd figure I had something to do with what happened."

"Assuming he comes out of it alive."

"If he doesn't, his son will suspect something wasn't kosher. Billy's told him I'll be going along, so if I don't..."

"And after your cover's blown? What then?"

"I'll get a new assignment—have a completely different identity and work in another part of the country. It's probably time for a change anyway. But even if it wasn't, the situation's different now.

"Maybe, if things were the way they were supposed to be initially, I'd figure out a solid reason for not going along tomorrow. But with you and Max involved, I have no choice. You'll be a lot safer with me around."

No doubt they would be. But she very much wished she'd known how things really stood long ago. If she had... Before she could finish that thought, Sloan said, "What happened to the vest I gave you?"

"I hid it. In the room I was in at first. Under the sink."

"Good. I'll get it later. At least you'll have that."

"But..." She couldn't go on. Max and Sloan wouldn't have vests. And if a bunch of men were shooting at one another...

"Hayley?" Sloan rested his hand on hers. "I'll

be okay. I know how awful this has been for you, but it's almost over. And everything will turn out all right."

"You don't *know* that," she murmured. "Oh, Sloan...I'm just so scared."

He moved closer and wrapped his arm around her shoulders, drawing her to him.

Trying not to let her tears escape, she pressed her cheek against the hard warmth of his chest and breathed in his scent. It made her think of fall leaves. A crisp, sunny day back in Pennsylvania. The enormous maple trees at her parents' place, where she'd always been safe.

But that world was light-years away. Here, she was anything but safe. And the situation was impossible. How could Sloan have turned out to be one of the good guys only now, when they both might be killed tomorrow?

And Max. She pictured him fast asleep in the next room and her tears spilled over.

She couldn't let her son die. Yet she might not be able to prevent it.

"Hayley?" Sloan brushed away her tears. "Hayley... Please don't cry. We've made it this far and we'll make it the rest of the way."

She wanted to believe him so badly it hurt.

"You think I'd go and fall in love with you, then let anyone kill you?" he whispered.

Fall in love with you. The phrase wrapped itself around her heart.

"Is that what you've gone and done?" she asked, inching away so she could look at his face.

"Absolutely."

He captured her hand in his and the tightness in her throat eased a little. If he loved her... If they actually did make it through tomorrow...

She sat staring into the darkness of the room, struggling to sort through her emotions. She didn't doubt that what she was feeling for Sloan was love—even though it was awfully hard to believe she could fall in love with a man who'd had anything to do with kidnapping her son.

But when he'd said that—with or without his involvement—Billy's people would have grabbed Max, it had rung true. And assuming it was, she should count her lucky stars he *had* been involved.

She considered that, realizing she hadn't completely absorbed all the facts about the "new, improved" Sloan Reeves. That was hardly surprising, though, since it meant turning her way of perceiving him around a full hundred and eighty degrees.

Finally, she looked at him again.

"You okay?" he asked softly.

"I'm getting there. And you know what?"

"What?"

"By this time tomorrow night, I'll be perfectly okay."

"Good," he said. Then he drew her to him and kissed her.

The warmth of his lips did wicked things to her insides and made her nerve endings sing. But when he deepened the kiss, easing her down on the bed and pressing her against the mattress with his body, she tensed for a second—thinking about Max in the next room. And Billy just across the courtyard. And the others all somewhere nearby.

The door to outside was bolted, though, and Max would sleep through until morning. And now that she knew the truth about Sloan, knew he *wasn't* the wrong man... Surely nothing that felt this good could be bad.

"You smell like soap," he whispered, breaking their kiss and brushing her still-damp hair back from her face.

"Couldn't have anything to do with my shower, could it?"

He smiled—such a sexy smile it sent a shiver of anticipation dancing down her spine. Then his fingers found the buttons on her blouse and yearning welled up inside her.

Slowly, he undid the buttons, watching her in the darkness, his gaze so mesmerizing she could scarcely breathe. When he unhooked her bra and lowered his mouth to her breasts, need flooded her.

She slid her hands up under his shirt and across his back, feeling herself growing liquid with longing.

"Just a sec," he murmured, getting up and quickly removing his clothes.

The sight of him naked inflamed her desire. She wanted the heat of his body against hers and the hardness of him inside her.

"You're wearing too much," he whispered, reaching to help her remedy that.

Then he was lying next to her, and being with him like this was fantasy made real. He rested his fingers on her cheek and slowly traced the line of her nose. It made her smile, and he smiled in return. Lord, but she adored his smile.

Possessively, he moved his fingers lower, over her breasts...down across her stomach...over her hip...making her feel as if a lazy current of warmth was oozing through her body.

His hand came to rest on her inner thigh, and he gently slid his fingers upward, filling her with pleasure. Skin against skin, flesh against flesh, his mouth on hers. She could taste desire in his kiss, mingling with her own.

He caressed her until her heart was beating so hard she could feel its thudding through her entire body, until the fire of her need made her as hot as sand on a sun-drenched beach.

His breathing grew faster and faster, hot against her skin while the air in the room grew impossibly heavy—until it was hard to breathe at all.

"Sloan," she finally murmured. "Sloan..."

He shifted position and sank into her, his urgency matching hers. She wrapped her arms tightly around him and arched against him, feeling as though she were part of him, wanting the all-consuming sensations to end, yet wanting them to go on forever.

Then he cried her name, and in the same timeless moment she came—with a shattering sensation of falling through the darkness of eternity with the man she loved.

Falling and falling, a series of afterwaves seizing her body. They sent fresh shudders of such pure ecstasy through her she thought she might die. Then she gradually began to lose speed and drifted, ever so slowly, back to reality.

Sloan was resting heavily on her, his heartbeat pounding against her skin. She gave his shoulder a lingering kiss, feeling so happy that when her fears began tiptoeing around the room once more they seemed mere shadows of what they'd been earlier.

He started to move away from her, but she clung to him, loving the hard heat of his body. And when he finally did shift onto his side, she snuggled her back so closely against his chest that not the tiniest draft of air could find its way between their sweat-slicked bodies.

She felt warm and wonderful and loved. Utter bliss would be never having to move from the tangled sheets of this bed.

''Feel okay?'' he said at last.

She smiled. ''Yes, but the timing's all wrong. I wasn't supposed to be feeling so *perfectly* okay until tomorrow night.''

THE BEDSIDE CLOCK read a little past 6:00 a.m. and the first fingers of dawn had already stolen in through a crack between the curtains. That meant Hayley had lingered in Sloan's bed as long as she dared—regardless of how sublime being with him made her feel.

Max would undoubtedly sleep for at least another hour, probably longer, but she didn't want to take the slightest risk that he'd get up and find her in here.

Telling herself she could stay where she was for one more minute, she concentrated on resisting the urge to reach out and trace Sloan's chiseled jaw. He looked so deliciously sexy, with his hair tousled and a dark growth of beard, that her fingertips positively itched to touch him.

That would wake him, though, which would be bad. Given the day that lay before them, the more sleep he got the better.

The day that lay before them. She'd been making a concerted effort not to think about what might happen at that airfield this afternoon. But during the night, those fears tiptoeing around the room had busily multiplied. And for the past little while she hadn't been able to keep from worrying for more than three minutes straight.

All we have to do, she silently told herself, *is make it through this single day.*

And it wouldn't even be the entire day. The rendezvous was at two. Shortly after that, everything would be over. One way or another.

When those words echoed in her mind, making her shiver inside, she told herself to stop thinking and get moving. But the moment she began to ease out of bed, Sloan pulled her back to him and nuzzled her throat, his beard enticingly rough against her skin.

"I thought you were asleep," she whispered, trying to ignore the hot wave of desire rushing through her. This was neither the time nor the place—although she fervently wished it were.

"Uh-uh," he said sleepily. "I was lying here

thinking I forgot to get that vest last night. I'd better do it now, before anyone else is up.''

He started to push himself out of bed, then stopped and gave her a smile so warm she felt its heat all the way to her toes.

''Or maybe that can wait a few more minutes,'' he said.

Snuggling back down beside her, he kissed her. Thoroughly enough that the thought of staying right there for a little longer began to seem like a truly excellent idea. But she knew, deep down, it wasn't.

''I'm afraid we'd better put this thought on hold,'' she made herself say. ''In case Max wakes up early.''

''Yeah,'' he said reluctantly. ''I guess you're right. Just don't forget where we left off. We'll pick up there later.''

As he climbed out of bed and started collecting his clothes from the floor, she couldn't keep from wondering if there'd actually be a later for them.

Instead of voicing her fear, though, she simply said she was going to hit the shower.

Sloan nodded, then surreptitiously watched her get out of bed. Not only was she absolutely gorgeous, she was the most wonderful woman he'd ever known—and he was having a lot of trouble believing she really felt the same way about him as he did about her.

But last night she'd told him she loved him, whispering the words over and over against his skin, her lips soft and her breath warm. She'd repeated them so many times that he'd stopped counting. And started believing.

She loved him, and there wasn't a shred of doubt that he loved her. Which, of course, led to the question of what the hell they were going to do about it. Assuming they were still alive at the end of the day.

CHAPTER FIFTEEN

SLOAN WAITED UNTIL HAYLEY disappeared into the other room before opening the door to the cool morning air. As he started along the row of units, his thoughts returned to the question of where the two of them went from here.

For most people the answer would be easy. But not for them. Not for him, at least.

The last thing he'd meant to do was fall in love with Dr. Hayley Morgan. Hell, he'd never intended to fall in love with anyone—an intention that had made a whole lot of sense.

He lived with the constant risk of his cover being blown. And when that happened to special agents, they generally ended up dead.

This time, with advance knowledge, he was in a far better position than he might be. But after the takedown, the first thing he'd have to do was get far away from New Orleans. Fast.

It would never be safe to return, and if he asked Hayley to pull up stakes… Well, he just had no idea how she'd feel about a future with him.

She hadn't had time to give much thought to the big picture. But once she had, she'd ask herself some tough questions. Like, did she want to get hooked up with a man who never knew when he might find himself staring at the wrong end of a gun?

That hardly made him prime husband material. Or father material. Or stepfather material.

He thought about Max for a moment, certain it would be very easy to turn things like reading his bedtime story into a regular routine. But, to all intents and purposes, the boy had already lost one father. Losing another…

You're getting way ahead of yourself, he told himself. And hell, the best thing for all three of them might be for him to simply disappear after today.

Never seeing Hayley again would be utter torture. But maybe it was the only real option.

Reaching number five, he glanced around the courtyard, saw no one and tried the door. It was locked, so he dug his handy "pass key" from his pocket and picked the lock in one second flat.

Getting into places he wasn't supposed to was something he'd developed a real skill at. As he'd told Hayley last night, he couldn't always stick to squeaky-clean methods.

Once inside, he headed for the bathroom, opened the cabinet beneath the sink and reached into the back corner where she'd hidden the vest. His pulse skipped a beat when he didn't find it.

He crouched down and peered inside. It wasn't there. So where was it? A single likely possibility came to mind. One of Billy's boys had discovered it.

Swearing under his breath, he pushed himself to his feet and rapidly searched the entire unit. Nothing. *Nada*. Dammit! He'd been counting on her having it to wear this afternoon and now she wouldn't.

That wasn't good. But was there anything else bad about this turn of events?

Whoever found the vest, most likely Marshall, would have shown it to Billy. Was that a problem?

After thinking for a minute, he decided it wasn't. Hayley had known the trip into New Orleans was actually an escape run, so surely no one would consider it strange that she'd worn a bulletproof vest. And working in prisons meant she'd have had easy access to one.

He began breathing more easily, although he still wished she was going to have the vest for today. But he didn't see how he could possibly get his hands on it. He could hardly go to Billy and say, "How about giving me that vest so Hayley can wear it to the airfield. Because odds are we're all going to get shot at."

Imagining Billy's reaction to that wasn't tough. He'd turn purple. And then he'd kill them.

After a final glance around the room, hoping against hope that the vest might have magically materialized, Sloan walked out into the courtyard. He'd taken about four steps when he spotted Marshall, leaning against the hood of a car and watching him.

Uneasiness curling down his spine, he stopped

walking. Something told him the guy didn't just happen to be there. He'd been lying in wait.

"Hey, Marshall," he said. "You're up early."

"No earlier than you. What were you doing in there?"

"Oh, nothing, really," he said, thinking as fast as he could. He needed some sort of reason and—

He breathed a sigh of relief as one came to him. "Hayley lost her makeup bag and thought that's where it might be. So I figured it wouldn't hurt to have a look for her."

"Yeah?"

Marshall's dubious tone made him uneasy again.

"And did you find it?"

Shaking his head, he started walking once more.

"It's funny she thought it might be there. I mean, funny she thought she'd had it here at all."

"Oh?" He stopped a second time.

"Yeah. 'Cuz when she and Billy got here she didn't have a purse with her."

"She must have. You probably just didn't notice it."

"Uh-uh. She wasn't carrying a thing. She must have left it at the escape scene."

Sloan shrugged, feeling like kicking himself but trying to look nonchalant. "Then I guess the makeup bag was in her pocket or something."

"Yeah? That'd be kinda unusual, wouldn't it?"

"Hey, you know women. They're always doing the unusual." He could feel sweat trickling down his back.

"Yeah...but you know what I figured when I saw you going in there?"

"No. What?"

"That you were after the bulletproof vest she hid in the bathroom."

"What?" He gave Marshall his best taken-aback look. "What bulletproof vest?"

"You didn't know about it?"

"No."

"Oh. Well, neither did Billy or me. Not until I found it hidden away. It didn't show none under her clothes."

Sloan shrugged again, sweat pouring down his back now. "Well, that makes three of us who didn't know she was wearing one," he said. "But I guess it's hardly surprising she was. She must have been scared to death that the escape would go south."

"I guess."

He waited a couple of beats. Then, when Marshall seemed content to let the subject drop, he said, "So what are we doing about food today? Breakfast and lunch?"

"Well, I don't know about lunch, but I told Billy I'd get some takeout for breakfast. There's a coffee-and-doughnut place down the highway. That okay with you?"

"Sure. And maybe milk for the kid."

Marshall nodded. "Yeah. Didn't think of milk. Good thing I saw you, 'cuz I was just about to go."

When the man turned away, though, he didn't get into a car. He headed straight for Billy's door.

HAYLEY HAD BEEN on tenterhooks from the moment Sloan arrived back and told her about his encounter with Keith Marshall.

If he hadn't believed Sloan's story about the makeup bag, and it sure didn't sound as though he had, he and Billy would be certain Sloan had gone into that room to get the vest. And his denying he'd even known about it would raise all kinds of questions.

The only good news was that there actually were pockets in her suit. And that they were fairly large. She could conceivably have stuck a makeup bag in one of them, so at least they had a story they could stick to.

But most men knew enough about women to realize they didn't normally carry their makeup in their pockets. And if that didn't occur to Billy, Marshall would point it out.

She glanced at Max, who was still fast asleep, then turned back toward the window and looked anxiously across the courtyard once more.

Sixty seconds after Marshall had come out of Billy's unit and driven off—they'd assumed to get breakfast—Billy had phoned, saying he wanted to see Sloan.

He was still over there. And she was worried sick. She hadn't heard any shots, but for all she knew he was lying dead by this point.

Just as she was seriously wondering whether Billy had a silencer on his gun, his door opened and Sloan stepped outside.

Relief flooding her, she watched him walk across

the courtyard. His expression wasn't revealing a thing.

Before he reached the door, she stepped over and quietly opened it, putting her finger to her lips and nodding toward Max.

"What happened?" she whispered. "What did he say?"

"Not a single word about the vest."

"What?"

"He told me he had another call from the Pelican, confirming things for this afternoon. And he said we're leaving at quarter past twelve, that it's apparently a ninety-minute drive from here to the airfield. Then he just talked about a few other details."

"Like what?"

Sloan shrugged. "Like the fact he wants to go in three cars."

"Why? Two would be enough."

"Hayley, it's not important why. Billy organizes things his way, that's all."

"So then the cars just get left at the field?"

"No. One of them will be my Jeep, and we'll drive back to New Orleans in it. Billy's son will have the others taken care of."

After glancing over to make sure Max was still sleeping, she looked back at Sloan. "But he said *nothing* about the vest? Or the makeup bag?"

"No. He acted as if he didn't even know I'd been in number five. As if Marshall hadn't said a thing."

"He must have."

''Well, that's what I was figuring, too. But maybe he didn't.''

She shook her head. ''That just doesn't add up. I get the impression he doesn't like you much, and he's so angry at me for running that he wants me dead. Plus, when he caught us with that door locked, he was only too happy to go squealing to Billy. So why wouldn't he jump at another chance to cause us grief? Why—''

''Mommy?'' Max said sleepily.

They both glanced over as he sat up in bed and rubbed his eyes.

Sloan said good-morning to him, then added to Hayley, ''There's something I've got to do, but I'll just be in the other room. Maybe we can finish our conversation later?''

She nodded. ''As soon as I get Max organized.''

Sloan headed through the doorway, aware the interruption couldn't have come at a better time. Now he'd have a few minutes to decide whether he should give her a plausible explanation for why Marshall might have kept quiet or tell her the truth—that he was absolutely convinced the guy had spilled everything to Billy.

He walked over to the window and stood gazing out, going over his reasoning once more.

Billy had still been angry at Marshall for letting Hayley get away. Marshall would have seen informing as a way of getting back into the boss's good graces.

Besides which, Hayley was right. Marshall didn't like him. He'd enjoy turning Billy against him, even at this late stage of the game. So Marshall had likely woven his suspicions into a theory.

Sloan had no way of being certain what Marshall had come up with, but formulating a good guess hadn't been tough.

Sloan had gone to retrieve the vest—that was the first thing Marshall would have told Billy, the single fact he'd had to build on. From there, he probably said that Sloan must have wanted the vest because he was afraid Billy intended to kill Hayley. So Sloan was going to help her make a run for it. And, obviously, having the vest would make a safe escape more likely.

Yes, that was exactly the sort of story Marshall would have come up with. And if he'd convinced Billy that his legal adviser intended to cross him because he cared so much about Hayley... Billy with his cross-me-and-you're-dead philosophy...

Sloan unhappily shook his head. Not only was he certain he had things figured right, but he'd bet that Billy had bought Marshall's theory. Because the last time Marshall had gone running to Billy, Billy had asked for Sloan's side of the story. This time he hadn't. This time he'd said nothing at all. Instead, he was merely giving the situation some thought before he decided how to handle it.

But Billy's thinking would be colored by his paranoia. Sloan had seen that happen before, and once suspicion began eating away at him it grew and grew.

"Sloan?" Hayley said from the doorway.

He looked over at her.

"Max is brushing his teeth, then he'll get dressed. That gives us a few minutes."

"Right. Good." But what did he say? Should he tell her that getting shot during the takedown wasn't all they had to worry about anymore? That they were also at risk of being killed by "friendly fire," so to speak?

Certain he had nothing to gain by upsetting her even more than she already was, he said, "What I was going to tell you, before Max woke up, is that I did something for Marshall yesterday, and I think he must have figured he'd return the favor by not saying anything to Billy."

"What did you do?"

"Well, after you ran, when Billy was fit to be tied and hollering at Marshall, I said it wasn't entirely Marshall's fault. That I should have known you'd try something and warned him. It deflected some of Billy's steam onto me."

"And…you really figure…?"

"Yeah, the more I think about it, the more it adds up. Marshall may be a creep, but he's also the kind of guy who hates owing anyone. Besides, if he *did* tell Billy, why on earth wouldn't Billy have asked me what was going on?"

"I don't know."

He shrugged, as if to say, *Well, there you are, then. Marshall can't have told Billy. End of story.*

SLOAN GLANCED at his watch, thinking that even if Billy had decided he wanted them dead he wasn't going to do anything about it until they reached the airfield. If he'd been planning a surprise for here, he wouldn't have left it until the last minute.

"It's almost time?" Hayley asked.

"Just about," he said, looking over to where she and Max were sitting on the bed.

Ostensibly, she was watching cartoons with him. In reality, he'd bet she was so worried that she had no idea what was on the screen.

"Somehow I don't feel appropriately dressed," she murmured. "Nobody's ever told me what to wear to this sort of event."

He knew she was trying to be humorous, but she just wasn't up to it.

"What sort of event?" Max asked.

"Seeing people onto an airplane," Sloan told him.

"Oh. She didn't call it an *event* before. When she said we were gonna go to an airfield, I mean."

Sloan forced a smile, then looked at Hayley again. "I think shorts and a T-shirt are exactly right." He stopped there, not saying that was because she'd be able to run faster in them than in her suit. But those bare feet...

Well, there was just nothing they could do about the fact that she'd wrecked her shoes. Nothing short of asking Billy to stop at a shopping mall, and he'd hardly go for that.

"Sloan?" Max said.

"Uh-huh?"

"How come you've got your gun on in here? No snakes can get in, can they?"

"No, I just don't want to forget it when we leave."

"'Cuz there's snakes at airfields?"

"Sometimes there are." He readjusted the Glock in his belt, wishing he had more than one gun. But he didn't, so he'd have to make do and hope for the best.

After checking his watch again, he turned to the window just in time to see Marshall, McIver and Dunne walking across the courtyard, each toting a suitcase and each with a gun tucked in his belt.

Hell, Max would figure the entire world worried about snakes.

They loaded the luggage into the trunk of one of the cars, then went into Billy's unit. A minute later they reappeared with three more suitcases.

Absently, Sloan thought that Hayley had been right. Since Billy had apparently cut back to three cases, they could easily have done with two cars. But Billy likely figured a convoy would be safer.

In addition to those handguns, there were probably pump-action shotguns, or even machine guns, in the cars. And Sloan had no doubt that Billy would ride in the middle vehicle, so that if a problem came at them from either direction... A problem like a state trooper or two.

The prospect of a run-in like that made Sloan's blood run cold. He really wished this were over.

"Mommy, I gotta use the bathroom before we go."

Sloan glanced across the room again, as Hayley said, "Well, it's good that you thought of it now."

She waited until Max had closed the bathroom door, then quietly said, "Billy didn't tell you if we'd be riding together?"

Sloan simply shook his head. She'd already asked him that about six times.

"What if we're not?" she said, pushing herself up off the bed. "What if Max and I are nowhere near you when the shooting starts?"

He moved closer and wrapped his arms around her—painfully aware this could be the last time he ever held her.

That possibility was enough to start his chest aching. He couldn't have fallen in love with her only to lose her. But if he disappeared from her life, he'd lose her then. It would be in a different way, but he'd still lose her.

Not wanting to think about that, he kissed her hair.

"First off," he whispered against its softness, "there won't necessarily be any shooting. If Billy and the Pelican surrender peacefully—"

"Oh, Sloan, can you honestly imagine Billy surrendering peacefully? Knowing he'd be back in Poquette within hours?"

Of course he couldn't. "Well...the feds won't show themselves until everybody's out of the cars. So the moment you and Max get out, head straight for me. But we'll probably be in the same one. Then you'll have nothing to worry about."

"Nothing to worry about?" she repeated, looking up at him. "I doubt that's *quite* the way things will be."

He had no reply, and since the fear that he'd never hold her again had segued into the fear that he'd never get to kiss her again, he lowered his mouth to hers.

She tasted of toothpaste and coffee, and he couldn't for the life of him understand how that tasted so amazingly good.

Then the toilet started to flush and she quickly moved out of his embrace.

"*Now* is it time to go?" Max asked, coming out of the bathroom.

Sloan checked his watch once more and nodded.

Her heart pounding, Hayley watched him pick up the bags full of Max's things. Then, wishing there were some way to prevent the inevitable, she made herself put on her disguise—a large scarf and sunglasses. Apparently photos of her had turned up on TV, along with ones of Billy and Max.

"Don't forget your Yankees cap," she told Max. Billy wanted him wearing it so he'd look less like his picture.

"I won't." He grabbed it off the bedside table. "I'm gonna wear it all the time, 'cuz it's lucky."

"It is, huh?" Sloan said.

"Uh-huh. Right, Mom?"

She managed a smile. She had no idea when he'd decided it was lucky, but she hoped with all her heart it really was.

"Ready?" Sloan asked.

Not entirely trusting her voice, she merely nodded and reached for Max's hand.

When Sloan opened the door, Marshall, McIver

and Dunne were standing by the cars and Billy was just coming out of number twenty, wearing dark glasses and a straw hat pulled low on his forehead.

As they crossed the courtyard, he said, "Sloan, I'll ride in the Jeep with you. We'll be in the middle. Hayley, you go in the front car with Marshall. McIver, you and Dunne take the kid and bring up the rear."

Her heart stopped.

"Mommy, I want to go with you!" Max said in a loud whisper.

"Let the boy go with his mother," Sloan said.

"No way," Billy snapped. "She won't try anything funny if she doesn't have him."

"I won't try anything if I do have him," she said, doing her best to control her fear.

"Momme-e-e," Max wailed, tears beginning to stream down his cheeks.

She knelt and held him against her, her throat so tight she didn't think she could say another word.

"Billy," Sloan said. "You don't want us driving along with him bawling his eyes out. Think about it. Two guys have a little kid who's crying? Hell, somebody might grab a cell phone and call the cops."

Billy shot Max a black look. "What about riding with Sloan then? You want to come with him and me?"

Max fiercely shook his head. "I wanna go with my mom," he got out between sobs.

"Well, you can't! So—"

"Max, go with Sloan," Hayley managed to say,

not sounding quite as frantic as she felt. She could see Billy growing angrier by the second, and the last thing they wanted was him losing it.

"I'll meet up with you at the airfield," she added, giving him a hard hug.

"But I don't..." Another sob choked off his words.

"Max, please. You like Sloan. You'll be fine with him."

Before he could say another word, Sloan scooped him up and tugged the Yankees cap down onto his forehead. "Hey, you're wearing your lucky cap, remember? So nothing bad can happen. And your mom will be in the car right ahead of us. We won't lose sight of her for even a minute."

"Let's get this show on the road," Billy muttered. "Give me the keys and I'll drive," he added, climbing into the driver's seat. "You're in charge of the kid."

"Now, there's a good deal, huh, Max? How about if we both sit in the back and pretend a chauffeur's driving us?"

Max was still crying, but he'd wrapped his arms tightly around Sloan's neck, clearly resigned to riding with him.

"Let's go," Marshall said to Hayley.

She stood gazing at the Jeep, wanting to get into it so desperately that she couldn't make herself step away from it.

"We'll be right behind you," Sloan said.

He was gazing evenly at her, silently telling her

not to be frightened, but she was so far beyond merely frightened she could barely think straight.

"Hey, you deaf?" Marshall asked her. "I said, let's go."

Her eyes burning with tears, she forced herself to turn and follow him.

CHAPTER SIXTEEN

TO SLOAN'S VAST RELIEF, their little convoy made its way north on Highway 61 and across the state border into Mississippi without incident.

Once Max realized he actually could see his mother up ahead, he calmed down and stopped crying. Billy, however, was wound so tightly that Sloan was afraid he'd snap before they reached their destination.

Every couple of miles, he hallucinated either a roadblock up ahead or a cruiser closing in from behind.

Finally, they hit Woodville, and he said excitedly, "We're almost there. We turn off two miles past the other edge of town. There's no sign, but the road is the first one after a billboard advertising harness racing."

Sure enough, just beyond the far edge of town, Sloan spotted the billboard. Seeing it was enough to start his adrenaline pumping.

They turned down the next side road, and about three miles along it, they arrived at the airfield. It consisted of a limply hanging wind sock and a long, hard-packed dirt strip. That was it. Not even a storage shed, let alone a hangar.

"We're supposed to park at the west end of the runway," Billy said, turning off the road.

When he pulled up beside Marshall, Hayley waved over at them. Her smile looked incredibly forced, but Max didn't seem to notice. He just waved back as McIver and Dunne parked on the other side of the Jeep.

"Where's the Lear?" Billy asked anxiously.

"We're a little early," Sloan said. "It'll be here."

"Can I go sit with my mom?" Max asked.

"No," Billy snapped.

"She'll only be in the other car for a few more minutes," Sloan told him. "Only until Billy and his friends are ready to go," he added, uneasily surveying the scene.

Wide-open countryside stretched away from the landing strip, affording no place for a task force to be hiding. Of course, there were those two little planes....

Speculatively, he eyed the Cessna and the home-built, tied down on the far side of the strip. Agents might be hiding in them, although there wouldn't be room for more than a few.

But the last thing he had to worry about was the bureau's not having a solid plan. As soon as he'd let his superior know this was where the rendezvous was going to be, his people would have come for a look. And they'd have figured out how to cope with the lack of cover.

Even so, he could feel himself beginning to

sweat—despite the fact that Billy had left the engine running and had the air conditioner set on arctic.

Then, above its hum, he heard the drone of a small but powerful engine. He spotted a plane making its descent just as Billy cried, "That's it! That's a Lear! There it is!"

There it was all right. But where was the bureau's team?

HAYLEY SAT IN THE CAR beside Marshall, watching the sleek little jet set down, her heart in her throat and every nerve ending in her body raw.

She wished she'd asked Sloan more about how takedowns like this worked, because she couldn't for the life of her figure out how there was going to be one here. Not a successful one, at least.

Unless she was missing something, the Pelican would be able to see trouble coming long before it got near him. And as soon as he spotted anything suspicious he'd take off—whether Billy and the others had already boarded or not. Then…

Looking over into the Jeep at Max and Sloan once more, she couldn't help thinking that if Billy saw that plane start taxiing down the runway without him, he'd go berserk. And the first thing he'd do was shoot Max. She just knew it.

She tried to tell herself Sloan wouldn't let that happen. But to prevent it he'd have to kill Billy. And that would result in a bloodbath, because Marshall, Dunne and McIver would turn their guns on the Jeep.

"Nice little plane," Marshall said. "Looks like a six-seater."

When she focused on it again, it had reached their end of the runway and was turning around.

Beside her, Billy opened the front door of the Jeep.

Marshall opened his door as well, saying, "You, too. Move it."

By the time she got out, Sloan and Max had already climbed from the Jeep. Nobody said a word when Max rushed over to her. She hugged him, then furtively looked around, hoping to see something that would reassure her.

When she didn't, she glanced at Sloan. That only made her heart sink and her terror intensify. He seemed awfully worried.

"Okay, let's get our stuff onto the plane," Billy yelled as the aircraft completed its turn and came to a stop.

McIver and Dunne already had the luggage out on the ground. They each grabbed two of the suitcases and started toward the runway.

"After they all get on, then we're going home, right, Mom?" Max said.

"Yes." Taking his hand in hers, she looked around once more.

Still nothing. There was no task force. They were on their own. And if Marshall had convinced Billy he shouldn't leave any loose ends, they'd probably be dead within the minute. Sloan might be able to handle one of them, but she doubted he could take them both.

"Well, this is it," Billy said above the noise of the plane.

"Enjoy South America." Sloan managed to smile, but just barely. Something had gone terribly wrong.

Then he saw what he'd been watching for but hoping not to see. Marshall shot Billy a glance and Billy nodded. Almost imperceptibly, but it was a signal.

Marshall turned toward Hayley, reaching for his gun.

Sloan beat him to the draw. His Glock roared. Marshall screamed. He grabbed at his shattered shoulder, his gun bouncing onto the Jeep's hood.

Yelling "Get that!" to Hayley, Sloan whirled on Billy and leveled the Glock at his chest just as Billy pulled his gun from his belt.

Sloan quickly stepped forward, shoved the muzzle of the Glock beneath Billy's chin, took his gun from him, then stepped back again, training the Glock on Billy's chest once more as he stuck Billy's gun into his belt.

His expression livid, Billy opened his mouth to speak, but his words were lost as a huge yellow chopper came churning through the air, its thunderous rumble drowning out the Lear's engine. The chopper flew low across the field, raising a huge cloud of dust as it zoomed toward the runway at top speed.

The Lear began to move, but in mere seconds the chopper was hovering above it, creating a turbulence that made it difficult for the jet's pilot to steer, let alone pick up enough speed to take off.

McIver and Dunne, who'd almost reached the Lear, had dropped the suitcases on the landing strip and were running back toward the cars. They stopped dead when a voice, so amplified it sounded like a sonic boom, yelled, "FBI! Throw down your weapons or we'll shoot!"

Sloan glanced at Hayley. She'd retrieved Marshall's gun and was crouched on the ground, her arms wrapped tightly around Max.

"Cover Billy," Sloan told her.

She aimed the gun—a bit shakily but steadily enough that he could risk taking his eyes off the man for longer than a second.

He looked toward the Cessna and the homebuilt and saw he'd guessed right. There'd been half a dozen agents concealed inside. They were on the ground now, sticking to the shelter of the small planes and sizing things up.

Then two armored trucks roared off the side road and onto the airfield, and he realized the agents had just been waiting for the cavalry to arrive. The lead truck drove onto the landing strip and stopped nose to nose with the Pelican's plane. The other headed toward the parked cars.

As the chopper began to set down, the amplified

voice boomed, "You in the Lear jet! There's enough firepower in that truck to blow your plane to smithereens. Come out with your hands behind your neck."

The second truck pulled up near the cars, and agents wearing full body armor and toting machine guns began pouring out of it.

Sloan's heart, already thudding against his ribs, started beating harder yet. If even one of those men opened fire, this could still turn into a disaster.

He aimed his Glock at Billy again and glanced at Hayley. "Toss that gun under the Jeep. Then you and Max start walking toward the truck with your hands in the air."

She shook her head, looking petrified.

"Go!" he ordered.

She hesitated for only another second before scrambling to her feet. Tossing the gun, she raised one hand high in the air and grabbed Max with the other. Then they started forward.

Sloan didn't breathe until they reached the truck and a couple of agents hustled them behind it.

By that point, several other agents had closed in on the cars, one of them screaming at Sloan to put down his gun.

He raised both hands above his head, then carefully set the Glock on the roof of the Jeep.

"And the other one!" the man ordered, close enough now to see Billy's gun stuck in his belt.

As he slowly pulled it out, one of the agents said

to Billy, "Well, Mr. Fitzgerald, you've had quite the adventure, haven't you?"

When another of the agents gave Sloan a covert nod, he exhaled slowly. They knew he was one of theirs, but they weren't going to let Billy know.

That was rule number one for protecting a cover in a takedown—treat the undercover agent the same way you're treating the bad guys.

"Looks like you'll be joining me at Poquette," Billy said, giving him a nasty look.

Ignoring it, Sloan glanced toward the airstrip. The Pelican was just emerging from the Lear, hands locked behind his neck as he surrendered without firing a shot. But what choice did he have? Other than being blown to smithereens.

"HEY," ONE OF THE agents said to Max. "Do you know how to play I Spy?"

Max nodded.

"Good. Then how about if we stay here in the back of the truck and play for a few minutes while your mom goes outside? Someone wants to talk to her before you two head home."

When Max looked at Hayley, she nodded, her heart racing. The someone just had to be Sloan.

"Go on," the agent told her.

She climbed down from the truck, rushed into Sloan's arms and clung to him for dear life, her emotions all over the map. They'd made it through alive, but where did things go from here?

He gave her a long, passionate kiss that she

wished would never end. When it finally did, he stepped back just a little and draped his arms over her shoulders.

"We've only got a few minutes," he said quietly, "but I couldn't disappear without seeing you again."

Disappear. From her life. The thought sent a shiver through her. "Where are you going?"

"I don't know yet. But the story will be that I had a concealed gun and managed to escape during questioning. That way, my cover doesn't get blown. Billy will have his suspicions, because if I'd actually escaped it would have been quite a feat. But he'll never know for sure that I betrayed him."

"He'll know you pulled a gun on him, though, so won't he tell his people to—"

"I only pulled it because they were going to kill you. Not that he'll be happy I did it for *any* reason, but that's not as bad as his knowing I'm an agent. I doubt his boys will try too hard to track me down."

"They *will* try, though?"

"I honestly don't know," he said, shaking his head. "But I'll certainly never risk showing my face in New Orleans again."

She simply nodded, her throat so tight she knew she couldn't speak.

He leaned closer and kissed her forehead, then said, "The bureau will keep watch on you and Max for the next while. They'll be invisible, but they'll ensure you both stay safe."

"I'll feel a lot better knowing that," she managed to say.

"Me, too. But...look, you'll probably get a visit from someone in Billy's 'family.' The agents won't interfere unless it turns into a problem, because we figure you'll handle it okay. If someone does show up, though, just say you don't know a thing about me except that I worked for Billy. And that you saw nothing of my escape, that it happened while the feds were questioning you."

"All right."

She waited for him to continue; when he didn't, a grim sense of foreboding filled her. Wasn't he going to say he'd contact her just as soon as he could? What if...?

Sure that if she never saw him again it would break her heart, she searched for the right words to ask what was going to happen to the two of them. Before she had time to find any words at all, an agent approached.

"Dr. Morgan," he said.

She looked at him.

"I'll drive you home. We should get your son and go now."

When she turned back toward Sloan, he said, "I can't say goodbye to Max. Can't let him see I'm here with you when the media will be saying I escaped. But you'll tell him you know I wish I could have seen him again? And give him a hug for me?"

"Oh, Sloan," she whispered.

"I'll be in touch," he said softly. Then he strode away. Without a backward glance.

HAYLEY WALKED MAX and his pint-size two-wheeler down the block to Anne Kelly's house, managed a smile and a few words for Anne, then began listlessly retracing her steps.

Her parents had pretty well recovered from the trauma of having their only child and grandchild kidnapped, the event was no longer the main topic of conversation with her friends and she was gradually getting back to normal, going to work each morning and making it through the days. But she felt more like a robot than a woman—except for the pain. A robot wouldn't be on the verge of tears every waking minute the way she was.

Well over a month had passed since the takedown, and she hadn't heard a word from Sloan. With each passing day she grew more convinced she never would. And her pain grew stronger.

If not for that, she suspected she might be wondering if she hadn't dreamed the entire misadventure.

For the first few days after the bureau recaptured Billy and nailed the elusive Pelican, the media had paid attention to little else. Sloan's name had been mentioned frequently—usually in relation to criticism of the FBI. As far as the public knew, the bureau had slipped up and let him escape during questioning.

But once the feds identified the Pelican as the

son of a notorious Colombian drug lord, the media had focused on that part of the story and forgotten about Sloan.

Eventually, everything about the takedown had become old news. There were no longer daily reminders of what had happened. And no nightly reminders, either. Max, thank heavens, had stopped having nightmares and was back to sleeping through till morning.

So, if not for the constant ache in her heart—

"Dr. Morgan?"

She glanced toward the man who'd spoken, then nervously watched him get out of his car.

Just as Sloan had predicted, she'd had a visit, weeks ago, from a member of Billy's "family." She'd thought she'd convinced the man she knew nothing, but maybe she hadn't and this man was—

"Dr. Morgan, I'm Special Agent Gary Brown, Federal Bureau of Investigation." He flashed his I.D. "I wonder if you'd mind coming with me. We have a few more things we need to ask you about."

She shook her head. "I'm sorry. I was just leaving for work. It'll have to be another time."

"I'm afraid it can't be. We need to go over some details at the motel where you were held hostage, and the owner's making a lot of noise about our intruding, so we'd like to wrap things up there today."

"But—"

"You can use my cellular to call your office. If

any problems arise from your absence, the bureau will take care of them.''

''All right, fine.'' She never wanted to see that motel again, but Special Agent Brown was clearly telling, not asking.

He proved to be talkative, and as he drove he told her about his family—his sons who played in Little League and his daughter who wanted to be an astronaut. His family life sounded perfectly normal, and the more he talked the more he made her think about Sloan—about how impossible it had to be for undercover agents like him to have even seminormal family lives.

She'd thought about that before, of course. In fact, by now she must have told herself a thousand times that it explained why she hadn't heard from him. Told herself he really *had* fallen in love with her, but he'd decided there was no possible way they could be together, and it would make things easier on both of them if he simply didn't get in touch with her again.

But her rationalization hadn't made even a little of the pain go away.

About half an hour out of New Orleans, Brown turned off the highway into a little roadside park. ''Just have to use the facilities,'' he told her. ''I'll only be a minute.''

As she absently watched him walk away from the car, her peripheral vision caught a movement. When she turned her head, she saw Sloan standing beside a tree, gazing at her.

Her heart skipped ten beats, even though she knew it wasn't really him. Over the past weeks she'd seen a hundred different men who, for a few seconds, she'd thought were him. They'd all turned out to be strangers, though, and each time a rush of disappointment had replaced her momentary excitement.

Yet, as this man walked toward her now, the nearer he got the more he looked...

Hastily, she opened her door and climbed out of the car, not taking her eyes off him, certain he was a figment of her imagination and would vanish any instant.

"Hi," he said quietly.

For a moment she stood frozen. Then her feet sprouted wings and she flew into his open arms—his solid, very *real* arms—and kissed him half to death.

Finally, he took a backward step and smiled at her. "I gather you're glad to see me?"

"Oh, Sloan, glad comes nowhere close."

"Good, because I...let's sit down for a minute." He led her over to the lone picnic table and sat beside her on the bench, holding both her hands in his.

"Hayley, first off, I'm really, really sorry this took so long. But I had to find out what my options were and do a lot of hard thinking. Had to be sure what I wanted before I could ask what you wanted."

"And what do you want?" she whispered.

He hesitated, then said, "I want to marry you."

Inside her head, an imaginary choir began singing hallelujahs.

"I want to marry you. And be a father to Max. And I'd like to have other kids. But I can't do any of that if I take on another undercover assignment. That's just not the sort of thing a married man… So I thought, if you were interested…"

"I'm interested," she said, knowing she was grinning like an idiot but unable to stop.

He squeezed her hands, grinning right along with her. "I wasn't sure."

"Oh, Sloan, I love you, and Max thinks you're absolutely wonderful. How could you not have been sure?"

"I guess…I just kept thinking there'll always be the risk that, no matter where I am, one of Billy's people might someday see me."

"Is it *much* of a risk?"

"Probably not, but—"

"Sloan, people take risks every time they get into their cars."

That earned her a smile.

"Right, I know. But then I started thinking about all the things you'd have to give up to be with me. Your job and—"

"The job that almost got Max and me killed? You know, when I walk into Poquette these days I can hardly force one foot in front of the other. I was going to look for something else, anyway."

"And you wouldn't have a problem with moving to another state?"

"Which one?" she asked, even though she'd move to the ends of the earth if that was what it took to be with him.

"It could be pretty well any one—although the farther from Louisiana, the better."

"Wouldn't the bureau have a lot to say about where you go?"

He shook his head. "I'd leave the bureau. Start actually practicing law."

"Practicing law. But—"

"That's what I always intended to do, until the bureau recruited me. The feds could easily arrange to have my credentials altered. I'd have a different name, be a new face in some town where you could get a job you liked."

"But…you'd be okay with leaving the bureau?"

"Well, I can't stay in undercover work and have you. It's just not a viable option. And taking on any other sort of assignment with the feds would be risky in another way. Sooner or later Billy would learn—"

"But you'd be changing your entire life. What if you did that then came to regret it?"

She gazed into the blue depths of his eyes, not knowing what she'd do if he said that was even a possibility. She'd never want him to think he'd sacrificed too much for her.

"How could I regret changing anything in the world," he said softly, "if it let me spend the rest of my life with you?"

"Oh, Sloan," she murmured. "Do you have any idea how happy you're making me?"

"Why don't you show me," he whispered as his lips met hers.

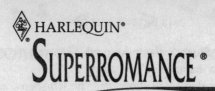

**Two women—who are going to be mothers.
Two men—who want to be fathers.**

EXPECTING THE BEST by Lynnette Kent
Shelly Hightower falls for Denver cop Zach Harmon—but she
figures he's done with raising kids. He has to convince her that
he *wants* to be a father to their baby....
AVAILABLE IN OCTOBER 1999.

THE FAMILY WAY by Rebecca Winters
Wendy Sloan is pregnant by her husband—and mourning his
death. She doesn't understand why she's so attracted to the
mysterious stranger who's come into her family's life—the man
who wants to be a father to her kids. Including this new baby...
AVAILABLE IN NOVEMBER 1999.

**Two deeply emotional stories.
Read them both.**

Available at your favorite retail outlet.

"Don't miss this, it's a keeper!"
—**Muriel Jensen**

"Entertaining, exciting and
utterly enticing!"
—**Susan Mallery**

"Engaging, sexy…a fun-filled romp."
—**Vicki Lewis Thompson**

See what all your favorite authors
are talking about.

Coming October 1999 to a retail store near you.

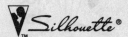

HARLEQUIN®
Makes any time special ™

WIN A DREAM

In celebration of Harlequin®'s golden anniversary

Enter to win a *dream!* You could win:

- A luxurious trip for two to **The Renaissance Cottonwoods Resort** in Scottsdale, Arizona, or

- A bouquet of flowers once a week for a year from **FTD**, or

- A $500 shopping spree, or

- A fabulous bath & body gift basket, including **K-tel's** *Candlelight and Romance* 5-CD set.

Look for **WIN A DREAM** flash on specially marked Harlequin® titles by Penny Jordan, Dallas Schulze, Anne Stuart and Kristine Rolofson in October 1999*.

FTD

RENAISSANCE.
COTTONWOODS RESORT
SCOTTSDALE, ARIZONA

K-TEL

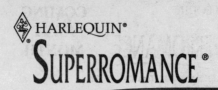
HARLEQUIN®
SUPERROMANCE®

Three childhood friends dreamed of becoming
firefighters. Now they're members of the same team
and every day they put their lives on the line.

They are

AMERICA'S BRAVEST

An exciting new trilogy by

Kathryn Shay

#871 FEEL THE HEAT
(November 1999)
#877 THE MAN WHO LOVED CHRISTMAS
(December 1999)
#882 CODE OF HONOR
(January 2000)

Available wherever Harlequin books are sold.

HARLEQUIN®
Makes any time special ™

#864 MY BABIES AND ME • Tara Taylor Quinn
By the Year 2000: Baby

She's a goal-setting, plan-making kind of person, and one of Susan Kennedy's goals is to have a baby by the age of forty. That's coming up fast. A couple of problems, though. There's only one man she can imagine as the father of her child. And that's her ex-husband, Michael. She gets pregnant on schedule, but then there's another problem—well, not really a problem. She's expecting twins!

#865 FAMILY REUNION • Peg Sutherland
The Lyon Legacy

Family means everything. Scott Lyon's heard his great-aunt's words forever. But now Margaret's disappeared, and the closer Scott comes to finding her, the more family secrets, betrayals and deceptions he uncovers. And then he meets Nicki Bechet, whose grandmother knows more about the Lyons than she's telling.

Join Scott and Nicki in this thrilling conclusion to the Lyon Legacy as they search for the truth and learn that family—and love—really do mean everything.

#866 A MESSAGE FOR ABBY • Janice Kay Johnson
Patton's Daughters

Abby's the third Patton sister. The baby. The one everyone said was privileged, spoiled. But childhood with a harsh, unapproachable father and only a vague memory of her mother wasn't easy, even if she did make it look that way. So now Abby's determined to live up to her image and have fun. Then she meets Detective Ben Shea—and he has news for her. *Sometimes it pays to get serious.*

#867 A RANGER'S WIFE • Lyn Ellis
Count on a Cop

Lawmen know that everything can change in an instant. The smart ones don't take their lives or their promises for granted. At least, that's what Texas Ranger Ty Richardson believes. Before his best friend, Jimmy Taylor, died in the line of duty, Ty promised to take care of Jimmy's wife and young son. And Ty intends to honor that promise—to help them, protect them, be there for them. But he'll never forget that they're Jimmy's family, not his—no matter how much he loves them both.

#868 EXPECTING THE BEST • Lynnette Kent
9 Months Later

Denver cop Zach Harmon's finished with raising kids. As the oldest of eleven, he spent too much time helping out with his siblings. But then, he never expected to fall so hard for Shelley Hightower—who understands his feelings all too well. *Now* he has to convince her that raising their child together is exactly what he wants to do.

#869 THE RESCUER • Ellen James

Dr. Alexandra Robbins may be a successful psychologist in Chicago, but her own marriage wasn't a success. She's in the middle of a messy divorce. So it's a relief for her to escape to Sobriety, Idaho, and complete her research on type R men—rescuers, compelled to risk their lives to save others. Colin McIntyre, the object of her study, fascinates her big-time, but the more he attracts her, the more frightened of him she becomes. And she doesn't understand why....